I hope you feel
the love in
every page!

HELLO TEASE

KELSIE HOSS

kh

Editing by Tricia Harden of Emerald Eyes Editing.

Proofreading by Jordan Truex.

Cover design by Najla Qamber of Najla Qamber Designs.

Have questions? Email kelsie@kelsiehoss.com.

Readers can visit kelsiehoss.com/pages/sensitive-content to learn about potentially triggering content.

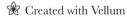 Created with Vellum

For my friend and photographer, Michelle Betz, who's so talented at capturing the beauty around her!

CONTENTS

1.	Larkin	1
2.	Larkin	7
3.	Knox	14
4.	Larkin	20
5.	Knox	27
6.	Larkin	32
7.	Knox	37
8.	Larkin	43
9.	Knox	50
10.	Larkin	57
11.	Knox	66
12.	Larkin	71
13.	Knox	82
14.	Larkin	88
15.	Knox	94
16.	Larkin	101
17.	Knox	108
18.	Larkin	113
19.	Knox	120
20.	Larkin	124
21.	Knox	128
22.	Larkin	134
23.	Knox	137
24.	Larkin	140
25.	Knox	146
26.	Larkin	150
27.	Knox	160
28.	Larkin	163
29.	Knox	169
30.	Larkin	174
31.	Knox	180

32. Larkin   187
33. Larkin   190
34. Knox   199
35. Larkin   203
36. Knox   212
37. Larkin   216
38. Knox   220
39. Larkin   226
40. Knox   232
41. Larkin   237
42. Knox   245
43. Larkin   250
44. Knox   257
45. Larkin   264
46. Larkin   269
47. Knox   273
48. Larkin   278
49. Knox   282
50. Larkin   286
51. Knox   291
52. Larkin   296
53. Larkin   300
54. Knox   303
Epilogue   306

Bonus Content QR codes   309
Author's Note   311
Acknowledgments   315
Join the Party   317
Also by Kelsie Hoss   319
About the Author   321

1

LARKIN

"I'VE BEEN online dating all of one day, and I already have three dick pics in my inbox," I said to my sister, Taylee, who was stifling laughter on the side of my tablet screen. I adjusted the device in its protective case shaped like a dinosaur, feeling so opposite from my sister.

Even though all I could see behind her were gauzy curtains and white textured walls, I easily pictured her view of the Seine from her apartment balcony. Meanwhile, I was surrounded by boxes in the world's smallest two-bedroom house in an equally small Texas town.

Even though she was in her late thirties and I was five years behind her, I'd always looked up to her, from her string of French suitors to her beautiful Parisian apartment and her job as a professor at a university there. I could live vicariously through her.

"It's all a numbers game," she said, ever the math professor. "If you meet enough men, there is sure to be a diamond in there somewhere."

I gave her a look and held up my phone with one of

the offending pictures. "I'm deleting this app. Dating in my condition isn't a good idea anyway."

"You're a single mom, Larkin, not dying of syphilis," she retorted.

I laughed. "I don't think you can die of syphilis."

She shrugged. "Maybe Seth can test that theory."

"You're bad," I said with a laugh. "I'm trying to be nice about him, for the kids' sake. He's taking this move pretty hard."

"He's a piece of shit who doesn't deserve the benefit of the doubt," my sister replied. "Leaving you and those precious babies for another woman."

My lips pressed together, and I tried not to be bitter about the small, shabby house we were renting in the small town where I'd never planned to settle down. But I needed support, even more so now as a single mom, and I didn't have enough of it in Dallas or make enough money on my own to hire help there. For all Seth's flaws, his parents loved our two children to death and offered to babysit them for free. "I will admit, it was the most awkward month of my life, living in the house with him after the divorce while I waited for this place to open up."

Tay pointed at her mouth like she was going to be sick. I couldn't blame her. The whole situation was not one I would have chosen for myself, but here I was.

"I gotta go pick up the kids," I said. "I told the grandparents I'd be there at five so they could go to their church dinner."

"I should probably grade these papers," she replied. "You'll get through this and land on your feet, Lark. I know you will."

I lifted a corner of my lips, thankful for her faith in

me but not feeling quite as confident in myself. "Love you," I replied, clicking out of the call, and then taking a couple deep breaths before standing up.

I'd spent the day unpacking, but it felt like I'd hardly made a dent in the place, other than setting up the room Emily and Jackson would share for the time being. But it was important to me that my children felt at home here, especially Emily. Jackson was only one, but at four years old, Emily had taken the split so hard, crying more nights than not over the last month. She used to be such a lively and playful four-year-old, but she'd changed into a reserved, quiet little girl, and it broke my heart. Hopefully having all her things set up would help her feel more at home here.

With a sigh, I grabbed a cookie from the plate one of our new neighbors, Mrs. Halstead, had brought over earlier with a smile that made the wrinkles deepen all around her lips and eyes. The gesture was so kind I'd almost cried. Probably shouldn't mention that on the dating app.

Not that signing up for it had been my idea—my sister encouraged it, saying that a rebound was exactly what I needed to get Seth off my mind. With the onslaught of dick pics, I wasn't sure a good rebound was in my future. I'd have to heal the old-fashioned way— with time.

I crossed the small living room to the front door, grabbed my keys from the Command hook on the wood paneled wall, and went outside. There were two steps down to the cracked sidewalk that stretched to the street. The lawn had been mowed but consisted mostly of weeds. I stepped slightly off the sidewalk and into the "grass," sending small grasshoppers and other insects fluttering up before falling back down to the ground. Ugh. I hated bugs. Luckily there was a small park just a couple blocks away I could take the kids to.

Reaching my minivan, I opened the door and got in. I hated the car now—it had been a "push present" from Seth after having Jackson, a reminder that we wanted to have a big family together with at least four kids just months before I found out he'd been cheating on me while I was still pregnant and on bedrest.

Maybe it was because I was mad, but I lost track of my speed, and suddenly, I saw red flashing lights behind me as I drove out of town toward their grandparents' house. And when I looked down, I realized I was driving ten miles over the speed limit.

"*Shit. Shit. Shit,*" I muttered. A speeding ticket was the *last* thing I needed right now with money so tight. I was half tempted to turn onto the next dirt road and see if I could ditch him. But who was I kidding? I wasn't some hot-rodding teen. I was a thirty-four-year-old mom in a minivan.

I sighed and pulled off to the side of the highway, putting the car in park and taking out my license, registration, and proof of insurance. I glanced in my rearview mirror, noticing a man getting out of the cop car.

He was tall—had to be over six feet—with a taut body and strong arms with tattoos winding down from his uniform sleeves.

My mouth went dry.

My marriage may have been dead, but my libido was not. In a quick glance, this man was doing more for me than any of the explicit pictures I had received on my phone.

If I hadn't been terrified of getting a ticket, my imagination may have run away with me, thinking up all the things he could do with that pair of handcuffs dangling from his hip. I swallowed, hard, and prepared myself for his approach.

He reached my vehicle and spun his finger for me to roll down my window. My chest heaved with the force of my breath.

"Ma'am, do you know how fast you were going?" he asked, all stern voice, aviator glasses giving nothing away.

"I'm so sorry," I said quickly. "I'm running late to pick up my kids from their babysitter's. I really can't be late. Is there any chance you'd let me go if I promise to drive the speed limit from here on out?" I may not have been as cute as I once was, but I batted my eyes in what I hoped would be an effective display of outright begging.

He lifted his aviators, revealing a set of deep blue eyes and long dark lashes that would have taken my breath away if it weren't for the outright skepticism in his pursed lips and arched eyebrows.

Looking pointedly at my back seat, he said, "If you have kids at daycare, where are their booster seats?"

Did he think I was *lying*? Why would I drive this vehicle if I didn't have children? "I had to leave them for the sitter, in case she wanted to take them somewhere."

"Uh huh," he deadpanned.

"Do you not believe me?" I asked, incredulously.

There was a spark of amusement to his voice. "How about this? If you really are late to get your kids, I'll personally offer you a police escort so you can make it on time."

My jaw dropped, just the expectation of embarrassment coloring my cheeks. I could only imagine what Seth's sharp-tongued mother would say if she saw me pulling up with a police officer flashing his lights. "No, I—"

"Or you could take a ticket." He shrugged, reaching for a pocket notebook. "Up to you, darlin'."

Something about the way he said darlin' made my shoulders snap straight with defiance. "Fine," I huffed. "After you."

"What's the address?" he asked.

I rattled off the street name and number, and he nodded. "Follow me. With that lead foot, you should have no problem keeping up."

My jaw dropped open in indignation, but he didn't notice, already turning back to his car.

2

LARKIN

I MUTTERED MORE than a few choice words as I followed the annoying officer in his police car with its flashing lights driving far faster than the speed limit. At least I wouldn't be late. Even if it felt like every single person was staring at us and memorizing my car so I would be even more of an outcast in this tiny, one-stoplight town.

We reached my former in-laws' house, and I parked behind him in the driveway. I got out of the car, indignant. "Happy?" I asked him as he stepped out, coming my way. When he got closer, I realized he was a good eight inches taller than me. I hated that I had to lift my chin to meet his eyes. Or how hard I had to work to pull my gaze away from his tatted biceps.

"Thank you for the escort," I said. "You're free to go now."

He chuckled silently. "How am I supposed to know you're not just going to a friend's house to get me off your case?"

I narrowed my gaze. "Fine, wait here."

But he didn't need to wait because the front door opened, and Emily came running out, followed by her grandma, Nancy, holding Jackson in her arms.

"Mommy!" Emily said, jogging a few steps forward. But she stopped a couple feet short of me, still on her grandparents' wraparound porch, eyeing Knox.

"This is—" I began.

He stepped forward and got on his knee in front of her and stuck out his hand. "I'm Knox Madigan, and I wanted to welcome you all to town! What's your name?"

Emily answered softly, "Emily Cappes."

"Nice to meet you. Would you like a badge, Emily Cappes?"

She gave a tentative smile and shook his hand, nodding.

He let go of her small hand and then reached into his pocket, still kneeling on the ground in front of the porch so he could be at eye level with her. I could feel Nancy giving me a quizzical look, but I couldn't take my eyes away from the interaction.

Knox reached his large hand into his pocket and pulled out a shiny golden badge. "It's got a little poke on the end. You might want to have your mama help you put it on, okay?"

She nodded dutifully, taking the badge from him.

"What do you say?" I asked her, not wanting to get on this guy's bad side my first day in town.

"Thank you," Emily said.

He grinned back at her. "You're welcome."

He stood back up and smiled at my mother-in-law.

"Nancy. Nice to see you. Didn't know you were watching your grandkids nowadays."

She smiled back at him. "Just started today," she said with a smile that belied her upset at the divorce. "What brings you to our neck of the woods?"

Knox tilted his head toward me, and I internally cringed. Nancy would not like the sound of me speeding. But he told her, "Ran into Larkin here, and she said the kids might enjoy seeing police lights."

A sense of relief swept through me. Nancy might have been supportive of the kids, but I was on thin ice.

"What's your name?" he asked, giving Jackson a little wave.

"Jackson," Nancy and I answered at the same time.

He grinned at my son, who was eyeing him curiously.

Emily said, "Can I ride in the car?"

"Oh, honey," I said, "I'm sure Officer Madigan has important things to do." *Like pulling over other moms on their way to pick up their kids.*

"Nope." He popped the p. "If your mom tells me where to go, you can ride with me."

Emily jumped up and down in front of me. "Can I, Mommy? Please?"

I hesitated, but Nancy said, "He's a local hero, Larkin."

I had to hold back a roll of my eyes. But because Emily looked so happy and hopeful, I couldn't say no.

"*Fine*," I said. "But we need to put your car seat in his car first."

Nancy took Jackson to the shade of the front porch and sat in her rocking chair while I went to get the car seats. Jackson giggled happily as he held on to his grandma's hands, pushing himself up to stand in her lap. He still had yet to walk, but at least he was using his legs.

With those two occupied and Emily asking Knox all sorts of questions, I took Emily's car seat from Nancy's Oldsmobile first, carrying it to the cop car, hoping this was the first and last time my daughter would be riding in the back of one. When I reached the car, where Knox was showing her all the equipment inside, I said, "Can you unlock the back door so I can put this in?"

"No need," Knox said, turning away from the car and giving me a smile. His teeth were perfectly straight and white like he was secretly a model instead of a small-town police officer.

But even his charm couldn't distract me from car safety. "Yes, there is a need. She's safest in a harness, and I will not have her riding without one, even with a 'local hero.'"

He tipped his chin down so I could see his eyes narrow playfully behind his glasses, like he was amused by me instead of annoyed like I was with him. "I took a training on installing car seats. I can put this one in. Trust me, I wouldn't risk a hair on your daughter's head."

The fiercely protective way he said it caught me off guard. I was used to Seth being annoyed that Emily wasn't at least in a booster seat.

I handed the seat to him, watching as he properly anchored it into the vehicle. I had to admit, he'd done it perfectly.

When he noticed me watching, he explained, "I have some nieces who like to ride along from time to time, so I became a certified car seat safety technician."

Damn my ovaries for getting too excited.

It was just all this talk about rebounds with my sister. After all the garbage I'd seen on the dating app already, the thought of a man who was interested in caring for children and actually knew how seemed like a fairy tale.

"Why don't you get buckled in, Emily?" Knox said, oblivious to my inner dialogue. "We'll wait for your mama to get the little guy loaded up before we go."

Emily got situated in her car seat and started talking his ear off. "That's my baby brother, Jackson. He's a year old. He doesn't talk yet. Mostly eats and sleeps. He does crawl now..."

I listened for a moment, gauging how Knox engaged with her. He didn't act bored like most guys my age did with little kids. Or like he was just placating her. He actually appeared interested in hearing what she had to say.

I couldn't hear them while I walked over the concrete driveway to Nancy's car and took out the other car seat for Jackson. We kept the base in Nancy's car since she was getting older and it was easier for her to use, and I set it in the back of my car before going to get him.

Nancy kissed the top of Jackson's head, leaving a ring of red lipstick before passing him to me. "That Knox really grew up well. It was touch and go there for a moment."

I glanced over at the car where he was standing, talking with my daughter, who had buckled in. "What do you mean?"

Shaking her head, Nancy replied, "Always pulling pranks around town. Saran Wrap over the pool, sombreros on the Sinclair dinosaur, you name it, he did it. About got in serious trouble."

"And now he's the one in charge of town safety?" I observed.

She shrugged. "Someone's gotta do it."

I shifted Jackson to my hip, holding him tight and looking him over, from his short soft brown hair to his dark blue eyes, pale skin, and rosy cheeks. "I'm so happy to see you, sweet pea." I pressed a kiss to one of his full cheeks then blew a raspberry, and he giggled happily.

Nancy said, "Getting settled in at the new place?" There was a tinge of sadness to her voice. She was way more disappointed in the divorce than her son.

"Trying to, at least," I said. "Thanks for watching the kids today."

A frown tugged at her lips. "Too bad you and Seth couldn't make things work like some couples do after a slip. I know a marriage is hard but—"

"I know it is," I said, trying to hold back my frustration. He was the one who cheated, not me. It *was* too bad. But this was reality. I wasn't going to stay with a man who could sleep around on me while I carried his child. "You'll watch them for my first day at work on Monday?" I asked.

She nodded, pushing up from her rocking chair. Then she called over to Emily, saying, "See you soon, Em!"

Emily waved back before Knox shut the door.

Then I carried Jackson to the minivan and put him in his seat. He instantly started fussing and fighting. I swore no one was stronger than a toddler who didn't want to be put in a car seat or have a diaper changed.

When I was done, I pushed the button to slide the door shut and looked over at Knox, who stood at the open door of his cruiser, forearms resting on the doorframe.

"Where are we going?" he asked.

I told him the address, and a look I didn't quite understand spread on his face. "I know that place."

"How's that?" I asked.

His grin turned into a smirk. "I'm your new neighbor."

3

KNOX

HER FULL PINK lips parted as annoyance and shock warred in her pretty green eyes. Her nose, dusted with freckles, scrunched, and she said... "Neighbors?"

I nodded. "You rented from Dustin Jenkins, right?"

A frown was all the confirmation I needed.

"Trust me, I don't bite." I had to wink.

She groaned and walked to her minivan with me chuckling silently behind her. Before opening her driver's side door, she said, "Drive my daughter safely, okay?"

I held up two fingers. "Scout's honor."

"And stay away from Sinclair dinosaurs," she retorted.

That was the first time a woman had surprised me in quite a while. I was about to ask her where she'd heard about my high school escapades, but she got in the van and slammed the door.

When I glanced at Nancy, she wore a pinched look on her face under a head of salt and pepper hair. "Have a great day, Mrs. Cappes," I said.

"You too, dear," she replied with a wave.

I got into my seat and buckled up. I knew Emily's dad, Seth, in high school and heard from the grapevine about his divorce—I just hadn't known his ex was moving to town. Maybe the rumors had been wrong. Glancing to the back seat, I asked Emily, who had her mom's wavy brown hair and freckles and her dad's brown eyes, "All buckled in?"

She nodded seriously. Apparently, she'd gotten that from her mom.

"Wanna use the police radio?" I asked her.

Her brown eyes lit up, and she nodded quickly.

"Okay, tell your mama we're getting ready to go." I opened the window between the front and back seat and then passed her the mic. When she held it in her hand, I pushed the button that activated the speakers outside the car. "Push the button and let her know."

"Mommy, we're getting ready to go!"

I smiled at the excitement in her voice and kept smiling when I saw Larkin's expression soften through the passenger window. "Now tell your grandma goodbye."

"Bye, Grammy!"

Nancy waved from the front porch.

"Should I turn the lights on?" I asked.

"Oh, yes!" Emily said.

I smiled, pushing the button to make the lights go, and then began driving away from the Cappeses' house. Then, I switched the radio to talk with our daytime dispatcher, Whitney. "Officer Madigan to dispatch," I said.

"Copy," she replied.

"I have a little kid in the car, Officer Emily Cappes,

and will be busy for the next half hour. Let me know if anyone needs backup."

"Sounds good. Have fun, Officer Cappes!" Whitney replied.

I glanced in the rearview mirror, seeing Emily shimmy happily.

With the speaker back on its rack, I said, "Tell me, Miss Emily, what brought your family back to Cottonwood Falls?"

Despite being so happy just moments before, her features sagged. It was like seeing a light dim. My heart squeezed before she even spoke in a small, sad voice. "My daddy and my mommy divorced."

"Oh no. I'm so sorry," I said.

She looked up and then back down again, brown hair falling across her face. "My daddy's with his new girlfriend in Dallas, and Mommy and Jackson and me moved here."

My lips parted as I tried to wrap my mind around it. Seth was in Dallas with his new girlfriend while his family moved here without him? Larkin wasn't from around here, but I guess it made sense if Seth's parents were babysitting.

And I hated to say it, but Seth was always a blowhard growing up. He loved to show off when he got the chance and oftentimes flirted with girls from multiple towns in the area at the same time. Sucked he hadn't changed much, especially with two babies.

Finally, I said, "I'm sorry, Emily. If you and your family ever need help, I'm right next door, okay?"

She nodded and then looked out the window.

"What's your favorite thing to do for fun?" I asked her, trying to perk her back up.

Her expression lifted slightly. "I love to go swimming and do crafts. With glitter."

I chuckled. "I have a niece I think you'd love."

"I wanna meet her!"

"Let me ask your mama." We pulled up in front of the house, and I noticed it in a way I never had before. Chipping paint, weedy yard. That was no place for a child to kick their shoes off and play. But I schooled my expression as I got out of the car and went to open the door for Miss Emily.

"Can you unbuckle me?" she asked.

"Sure thing, chicken wing," I said.

She giggled. "My name's not chicken wing."

"Ohhh. I gotcha." I unclipped the belt and she slid out of the car, running over to her mom, who was bent over the back seat, pulling out her baby. I had to look away to keep from ogling her curvy backside. And then a fresh wave of frustration rolled over me. What kind of guy cheated on a woman? Especially one who carried his children?

From what I could see, she was good-looking and had enough spark to burn down half the prairies in Texas. Was there something under the surface I hadn't noticed?

"Can we, can we?" Emily begged.

Larkin approached with Jackson on her hip, wearing a confused expression. "What is she asking about, 'local hero'?"

Oh, she was a feisty one. If only that didn't intrigue me more. I held my hands out, trying to make her more at ease. "I'm having some family over for dinner tomorrow night, and I think Emily would love to meet my niece. Well, nieces, but one of them's just a toddler, so they might not have much to talk about."

Larkin chuckled, as if despite herself, while Emily tugged at her shirt, revealing more of Larkin's ample cleavage.

Good God, I need to keep my eyes above her damn shoulders.

Pulling back up at her shirt, Larkin said, "That's awfully nice of you, but don't feel like you have to invite us."

"No trouble at all," I said. "I'm sure my sister-in-law would like to meet you too."

She shifted Jackson to her other hip, and he looked up at me with wide brown eyes just like his sister's.

"You're welcome to come too, Jackson," I said with a smile. "He's a cutie."

Larkin's smile seemed unrestricted now as she grinned down at her son. "We're fond of him."

Emily tilted her head. "Well, I wasn't so sure at first, but he's okay."

I chuckled.

"High praise from this one," Larkin said, running her hand over her daughter's wavy brown hair. "It would be great to meet some new people. What can I bring for food? Or do you and your girlfriend have that covered?"

Most people might not have noticed the hint of color that tinged her cheeks or the way her eyes quickly glanced down before meeting mine again. But I was trained in reading people, and Larkin was curious about me.

What I didn't understand is why that thought had a light feeling bubbling up in my stomach. She was freshly divorced with two children. Dating me was probably the last thing on her mind. "No girlfriend, and no need to bring anything. I'm actually a pretty decent cook."

"Is that so?" She raised her eyebrows like she didn't quite believe me.

"When you lose your mom young, everyone has to learn to pitch in," I said. The wave of sadness that came along with that fact was a regular part of my life, but Larkin's features fell since it was news to her.

"I'm so sorry, I—" she began.

"No need to apologize," I said quickly. "Just bring your appetite and your kiddos. We'll have a grand old time." I gave a little wave to Jackson, saying, "See you tomorrow, buddy. See you later, Officer Cappes."

Emily grinned and waved, and I swore, I saw a small smile on her mother's face as well.

I walked away and got in my car. As soon as I was out of sight, I pulled over along the curb and got out my phone, sending a text to my family's group chat.

Knox: You're all coming to my place for supper tomorrow night. Bring something good to eat.

4

LARKIN

I SET my curling iron down and checked my phone again, hoping for a response from Seth.

Larkin: Emily misses you. Can you please make time to video call her today?

Three hours had passed since I sent the message and still nothing, and it was getting to be time to go to our neighbor's house. I knew it would be harder for him to stay connected to the kids when I moved two hours away, but I didn't know he would act like the kids were his last priority.

We'd been in this house for three days now, and nothing. No phone call, no texts. Emily cried for him every night before bed, and I had to make up excuses for him, saying he was busy working, that they would talk soon. It broke my heart for her every time and made me feel guilty that I chose him to be her father. I thought he was better than that.

Taking a breath to calm myself down, I left the bathroom to check on the kids. Jackson was hopping in his bouncer while Emily watched an episode of *PAW Patrol*. They both seemed content, so I went back to the bathroom to put the finishing touches on my look, my hands shaking with nerves.

I normally kept my makeup simple and opted for a ponytail, but I wanted to make a good impression in this town. It may have been too late for Knox, but it wasn't for his family. I was alone here, unless you counted Seth's parents. But I always got the feeling from them that I was just the wife, the parent of their grandchildren, not a true part of their family. I wanted to have a real community for my children and me. Especially if Seth wasn't going to be a constant for them.

I texted him again.

Larkin: We're going to be busy for the next couple hours. Any chance you could talk with her now?

I looked at the screen, a read receipt coming up.

Hope fluttered in my chest. Not for me, but for Emily. She loved her daddy. But as the minutes passed, that hope fell away.

I might not be willing to talk shit about Seth out loud, but a million and one insults went through my mind. I didn't understand how he could act like we were just out of sight, out of mind.

With a sigh, I set my phone down and looked at myself in the mirror, checking my appearance one last time. I'd gained so much weight during my pregnancy with Jackson. Hardly any of my pre-pregnancy clothes fit me, and I hadn't bought a ton of nicer, newer clothes in the last year, hoping I could lose the weight. But it had been a year, and it didn't look like the weight was going anywhere. And with my new job as a nurse, I'd spent most of my clothing budget on scrubs.

Today, I wore one of my nicer tops, olive green with short sleeves and buttons up the front to show a slight amount of cleavage. I stepped back to see my full outfit in the mirror. The shirt went well with some distressed jeans and leather sandals.

I was determined to be confident in myself for my daughter's sake. I didn't want her to grow up stressing about the insane physical judgment I had felt from my ex and from society.

I grabbed my phone from the vanity, tucked it in my back pocket, and went out to the living room to get the kids.

"Ready?" I asked Emily as I went to pick up Jackson. He fussed a bit as I pulled him out of his bouncer.

"I know, you could do that forever," I said to him. Then I looked to Emily, who was still glued to the TV. I went and used the remote to turn it off, and she groaned at me.

"I asked if you were ready," I said. "You didn't say anything."

"Can I talk to Daddy?" she asked, her eyes lighting up.

I hid my own disappointment and said, "No, we're going to Knox's house."

She whined, "But I wanted to talk to Daddy."

"I know you did, but he can't right now," I said. "Let's focus on meeting our neighbors. Maybe you'll make a new friend tonight."

She nodded, pushing herself up from the chair. "Can I bring a toy?"

"Of course you can," I replied.

She ran off to her room and came back carrying her Dallas Diamonds football.

"Are you sure you want to bring that ball?" I asked. "What if they're not Diamonds fans?"

She held it tightly to her chest. "Who doesn't like the Diamonds? Ford is the best quarterback in the league." For being a little girl, she knew more about football than me. She and Seth watched the games every Sunday before the divorce, and he explained the ins and outs to her in a fun way that kept her invested.

This was one battle I did not think was worth the fight.

So I grabbed the diaper bag, and the three of us trekked around the sidewalk to the house next door. Unlike mine, this home had fresh paint, a lawn full of actual grass, and even a small bed of petunias up front. This man had to be some kind of special specimen to be a bachelor with such a nice-looking house.

I reached for the doorbell, but Emily screeched, "I want to ring it!"

"Try again," I told her, glancing around to see if anyone else's ears were ringing. There were already several cars parked along the street and in the driveway, and I had to wonder: How big was his family?

Emily looked up at me. "Can I *please* ring the doorbell?"

"Sure," I said, taking a deep breath to ease my nerves.

She reached out, pressing the button, and we heard the bell muffled from inside the house. She jumped up and down as if she could possibly reach the decorative window at the top of the door. I smiled at her excitement.

The front door opened, and Knox stood there, grinning at us. Instead of his police uniform, he had on a heather-blue T-shirt that hugged his muscular arms and drew out the blue in his eyes. I almost didn't notice the jeans he wore, which fit him just right—not too tight or loose.

"It's great to see y'all," he said with a smile. "Come on in."

We followed him into the house, all of us looking around curiously. And again, I was pleasantly surprised. The home opened up to a dining room and kitchen. The counters and table were loaded with pans of food. Then we walked through the house, seeing nice leather couches in the living room, a basket full of throw blankets, and a TV mounted above a gas fireplace.

"Everyone's out back," Knox explained. "You can follow me."

We did, my eyes inadvertently glancing to his backside. Damn. I needed to stop checking out my neighbor. That could get messy real fast.

But then again, my mom always used to say the phrase "look don't touch" applied to more than store items.

There was a hallway to what I assumed were bedrooms and then a utility room with a washer and dryer, a rack of coats, sporting equipment of all kinds, and a table.

Knox tapped on a door in the corner of the utility room. "This is a bathroom you can use." Then we followed him through the screened back door. The smell of the grill filled my nostrils as we stepped onto the shaded cement patio.

I could see all the people in his backyard that came with the vehicles parked out front. All fifteen or so of them looked at us as we stepped outside. I wondered what Knox had told them about us—if he'd said much of anything at all.

Knox put his hand on Emily's shoulder, saying, "I want you to meet my nieces." He led her to a small sandbox shaped like a turtle off to the side, and I followed along, feeling eyes on me as I went.

A girl who seemed around ten with long, caramel-colored hair played with a younger girl around two. Next to them, a fluffy dog that looked to be part Australian Shepherd watched dutifully.

"This is my niece, Maya." Knox gestured to the older girl. "And this is Leah." He tickled the stomach of the little girl with dark brown pigtails. "And this is their dog, Graham. Girls, this is Emily. I'm sure you'll be great friends."

Maya smiled and said, "Wanna play with us? We're building sandcastles."

Emily gave me a questioning look, and when I nodded, she set the football down and got into the sandbox with the other two.

"Do you like the Diamonds?" Emily asked Maya.

"Yeah. My uncle's the quarterback." She said it so matter of factly, I almost believed her.

"No way," Emily said.

"Yeah," Maya replied. "He's right over there."

All of us spun our heads in absolute shock where Ford Madigan was standing, drinking beer with a couple people I didn't recognize. Emily jumped out of the sandbox, sprinting over to him and yelling, "HI, FORD!"

"Oh my gosh," I muttered, following her, Jackson fussing in my arms at the change in pace. "Sorry," I said over my shoulder to Knox.

If he replied, I didn't hear him. No, I heard the star quarterback for Texas's pro football team, saying, "Nice to meet you, Emily."

5

KNOX

SO I MIGHT HAVE the hots for my neighbor.

And I *may* have made up an entire event to get to know her better.

Inviting over my pro-football-playing brother was just the cherry on top. But now that he was here, I realized it could have been an amazing or a horrible idea, depending on how this went. Either she was impressed by my cool family, or he fell in love with her instantly and swept her away to his mansion in Dallas. And with how beautiful Larkin was, there was a good chance he'd be enamored with her too.

But her eyes were mostly on her four-year-old daughter, who was chatting up the best quarterback in the league like he was just another kid on the playground.

"Will you throw less interceptions this season?" she chided him.

Everyone around her chuckled, and Ford's cheeks tinted pink as he drew his hand through short brown hair. "That's the goal."

"And I think you should run more on the fourth down instead of kicking it away."

He folded his arms over his chest. "You think so?"

She nodded. "You gotta take a risk sometimes. And I—"

Larkin put her hand on her daughter's shoulder. "I'm sorry. She's a big fan."

"I guess there's a fine line between fan and critic," Ford teased with a chuckle.

Larkin blushed hard. "Yes. We watch a lot of football in our house. And of course we cheer for our local team."

Emily piped up. "Do you know Alex Hill?"

"He's my best friend," Ford replied.

Emily grinned like she'd died and gone to heaven. "I have some things to say to him too."

Larkin shook her head at her daughter. "Let the man enjoy his party. You go play with Maya."

"But, *Mom*," Emily whined.

"Three... two..."

"Fine," Emily piped off, spinning on her heel and marching across the grass to the sandbox.

"Sorry about that," Larkin said to Ford. "She'd probably act the same way with Blippi if she ever met him."

Ford tilted his head. "Which team does he play for? I thought I knew all the quarterbacks in the league."

Everyone else cracked up, including me.

My sister-in-law, Liv, stepped closer, explaining, "He's the star of a kids' TV show."

"Right," Ford said, shaking his head. "I'm getting a drink. You want a drink?" he asked Larkin.

She nodded. "A beer would be great." Her eyes lingered on my brother for a moment as he walked away, then she looked back at me, hitting my shoulder with her free hand. Baby Jackson copied her, and she held his hand. "How could you not tell me someone famous would be here?"

I chuckled, shying away, and said, "Guess he's just 'little brother' to me."

Liv rolled her eyes at me and then extended her free hand to Larkin. "I'm Liv, married to Fletcher." She gestured toward my oldest brother standing next to her.

"It's nice to meet you, Larkin," he said, shaking her hand. "And you too, Jackson." He gave a little wave to Jackson, who waved back.

I breathed a sigh of relief that Liv didn't mention all of this had been thrown together last second or that I had to promise Ford I'd cook according to his dietary plan to get him to come.

Liv asked Larkin to go sit with her at the folding table and started asking her all sorts of questions. I went with them, listening intently while trying not to act too invested.

Larkin had grown up in Houston, moved to Dallas with her mom and sister when her dad passed in her teenage years. She worked as a nurse and had been hired to work at the local retirement home but was thinking about working in a school setting when her kids got older so they could be on the same schedule. Her sister lived in Paris, her ex was in Dallas, but her former in-laws were so supportive of the kids she decided to move here for free babysitting.

When Ford brought her beer out and Larkin was thanking him, I whispered to Liv, "You should be a detective."

Liv laughed, tossing dark brown hair over her shoulder. "I already have my dream job, being a stay-at-home mom."

"Wait a couple years for Maya to be a teenager and being a detective will sound a lot more attractive."

"True," she replied, then she focused her attention on Larkin, who was trying to keep her beer away from her grabby baby.

"Mind if I hold him?" Liv asked. "I love a squishy little babe!"

"Are you sure?" Larkin asked. "He's a handful."

"Of course." Liv reached for Jackson, and even though he fussed for a second, she soon had him laughing by making silly sounds and faces.

Larkin rolled her shoulders before sitting back in her folding chair and taking a sip of beer. Her eyes trailed over to the sandbox where Emily, Maya, and Leah were balancing sand toys on their heads. Her eyes formed a soft smile to match the curve of her lips.

When she looked at me, her smile turned a little shy, like she knew I'd been watching her. She took a quick sip of her beer and asked, "So there are three of you Madigan boys?"

I smiled at the phrase. I'd spent my whole life in Cottonwood Falls being one of those "Madigan Boys." I explained, "There are five of us. My youngest brother's in college. Fletch, Hayes, and I live here—Fletcher's the doctor in town and Hayes owns the body shop—and Ford lives in Dallas."

"Hayes?" she asked, looking around.

"Late," I said, "As usual."

She arched a brow. "Does that bother a... rule-abiding citizen such as yourself?"

I couldn't help my smirk. "You'll get it when you see him. He makes his own rules."

"Ah," she replied with a smile. "Sounds like my sister. She never did what was expected of her." There was something more to her tone that had me curious.

"Do you wish you hadn't done what was expected of you?" I asked. The shock in her eyes was apparent, and I added, "It's my job to read people."

"Get out of my brain," she said with a nervous laugh. "And no. I love my kids. But I wouldn't mind a view of the Eiffel Tower right now either."

"I don't know," I replied. "I think this view's pretty great."

I wasn't sure what I expected from her, but it was definitely not the laugh that fell off her lips.

"Are you flirting with me, Officer Madigan?"

I hadn't realized we still had an audience until Liv laughed heartily, and Fletcher stifled a chuckle of his own.

"She got you," he mumbled.

"I hate you." I replied.

Then I heard a loud engine approach. "Thank God," I said, pushing up from the table. "Hayes is here."

6

LARKIN

I WATCHED for a second longer than I should have as Knox retreated into his house. His physique in those jeans and T-shirt from behind? Just as good as the front.

Even more of a reason to stay away.

Fletcher, Knox's brother with dark brown eyes and hair to match, pressed up from the table, saying, "I'm going to see if he needs any help with the food."

After he got up to leave, Ford looked nervously between us and said, "Yeah, me too."

With all the guys gone, Liv looked at me over Jackson's nearly bald head. "You sure know how to clear a room." My cheeks heated, until she added, "Teach me your ways."

I let out a laugh. I liked her already.

She was curvy like me, had brown hair that fell past her shoulders in waves, and big blue eyes that practically sparkled with her smile. She also had quick wit and a way of cutting to the point, which I really appreciated.

She bounced Jackson on her lap, making him giggle.

"You're so good with him," I commented. "And your daughter plays so well with Emily. Usually kids Maya's age are trying so hard to be cool that they're annoyed by younger kids."

Liv cast a smile my way, crinkling her blue eyes at the corners. "We love kids. I was actually a nanny before being a stay-at-home mom."

"They were lucky to have you. A good nanny is hard to find."

There was a sparkle in her eye I didn't quite understand, but then she said, "Look at them, heading inside to cause some trouble." I followed the nod of her head to see Maya and Emily creeping toward the back door while Leah toddled our way.

"Should I stop Em?" I asked.

Liv shook her head. "Maya loves playing pranks on her uncles. Looks like she's bringing Emily in on the tradition."

And by the way Emily was smiling, I couldn't begrudge her the moment. Leah drew near the table, taking us in with her brown pigtails and big brown eyes, and I smiled at her. "Hi, sweetie," I said.

"Hi," she replied in a sweet, raspy voice.

"Want to sit with me?"

Her answer was to grab my knees and climb into my lap.

"Impressive," Liv said.

I raised my eyebrows.

"She hates everyone except Mom and Dad. Oh, and Knox."

I chuckled, bouncing her in my lap. "I remember Emily wouldn't sit still for anyone but me until she was two years old, when we took her to Paris to see my sister. Luckily Jackson's a little more easygoing." He was still happy in Liv's lap, playing with a spoon from the table.

Liv tilted her head thoughtfully. "You know, some friends and I are doing a girls' night next weekend. Want to come?"

"I haven't had a girls' night in... years," I said honestly.

"Years?"

I nodded. "My ex-husband worked evenings and weekends a lot, and when he was off, I wanted to spend time with him." Now, I realized how much I'd been missing out. Because I didn't have a husband, and I didn't really have friends who weren't "our" friends. Now I just wanted to leave all of that behind.

Liv reached over, squeezing my arm. "Well, that's changing next Saturday."

I smiled. "I can't wait." My mind was already turning with ideas. Hopefully my in-laws would be okay with an overnight with the kids.

There was a loud commotion inside, and I snapped my gaze in that direction.

With a chuckle, Liv said, "And that's the prank."

The girls bolted outside, giggling, ponytails flying behind them with their speed, and behind them followed... Knox Madigan, his face covered in whipped cream.

"I'm going to get you back for that!" he yelled playfully, making both the girls let out peals of laughter. He caught up to Maya first and picked her up, hugging her close so her cheek got whipped cream on it too.

Emily put her thumbs by her ears and wiggled her

fingers. "Can't catch me!" She darted behind a tree, hiding.

"Oh yes I can!" Knox said, putting Maya on the ground. Maya grabbed onto his shirt, tugging him back. The fabric pulled taut, showing every line of muscle. Knox pretended like the little preteen was slowing him down while Emily giggled loudly behind the tree, and then she snorted.

Liv broke out laughing, and my eyes felt hot with tears for my daughter. This was the happiest I'd seen her since the split.

Leah squirmed out of my lap, moving as fast as she could toward Knox. She tugged on his shirt too, laughing. And Knox said, "Emily, you win this round, but I'll get you back!"

Laughing, Emily ran up to me, wisps of hair loose from her ponytail and light shining in her eyes. "Did you hear that? I won!"

I smoothed back her hair and kissed the top of her head. "You sure did."

She ran off to play with Maya, and then I heard Liv say, "That's Hayes."

I glanced toward the back door, and my lips parted.

Holy hell, what did they put in the water in this town? Hayes looked like the kind of guy who would give you the night of your life and leave your bed empty the next morning.

He had on a white shirt, tattoos swirling down his muscled arms and up his neck. A ring glinted on his lip, and a dangerous spark glinted in his steel-colored eyes. His lips lifted in a smirk as he pinned me under his gaze and said, "So you're the new neighbor?"

I had to swallow to find my voice, not sure who caught me off guard more—his professional-football-playing brother or him. Here I thought I'd moved to a sleepy small town where nothing ever happened, but looking at the crowd around me, I had a feeling this place was anything but boring.

"I'm Larkin," I managed.

He walked up to me, leaning on the table, and said, "Welcome to Cottonwood Falls."

7

KNOX

I USED TO WORK NIGHTS, but when the dayshift officer retired, I took his place. Waking up early was still an adjustment, and it was hard for me to remember that I woke up the same time as most people nowadays. So when I heard the doorbell and saw it was seven in the morning, I let out a groan and wondered who it could be.

I smoothed my ruffled dark blonde hair, threw on a T-shirt to go with my sweats, and walked to the front door. When I opened it wide, I had to smile. Larkin was dressed in green scrubs, standing with Emily beside her and Jackson on her hip. She also had two plastic bottles of water in her other hand.

"Didn't scare you away with the party?" I teased.

She chuckled and said, "Actually the opposite. Do you mind if Emily uses your bathroom?"

I gave her a confused look, but she winked at me in explanation.

That adorable wink. I would have done anything. "Okay. You remember where it is? In the laundry room?"

Emily giggled evilly and nodded, then zipped past me.

As I let them all inside, I asked Larkin, "What's that about?"

She chuckled, shaking her head. "We lay in bed for half an hour yesterday coming up with ways to prank you again. She had so much fun with Maya on Saturday, and it's the happiest I've seen her since... the divorce." Larkin looked down at the ground, clearing her sad expression, and then handed me a bottle of water. "I would have brought you coffee, but my machine busted in the move and it's going to take two days for my new one to get here."

"We can't have that," I replied, gesturing toward the empty chairs at my table. "Let me make you some."

"Are you sure?" she asked over a peal of laughter from Emily. She cringed, and I had to laugh.

"Of course," I said. "Any hints on what's going on back there?"

Larkin laughed, sitting at the table with Jackson. "Nothing destructive." She let him stand on his feet and held his hands to keep him up.

"That's a relief." I went to the coffee pot in the corner of the kitchen and took out a few bags of ground coffee. "Do you have a preference? Dark roast, blond? I have some vanilla or hazelnut flavored blends as well."

When I glanced over my shoulder, I saw Larkin sitting at the table, haloed by the light coming through the window. Jackson stood on shaky, pudgy legs dressed in denim shorts while hanging on to her hands. The scene belonged in a painting.

Larkin looked over at me, her smile just as bright as the morning light. "Are you a coffee connoisseur?"

"That's two things cops are experts on, right? Coffee and donuts?"

A laugh fell past her lips, and I fell for the sound. A full, throaty, all-consuming sound that brought a smile to my face. "I guess that's so," she said. "Honestly, I'm not picky. Anything hot with caffeine will do."

"Low standards. Just what I like in a woman."

She laughed again, and I smiled to myself as I turned, deciding to go with my favorite vanilla blend, roasted at a small coffeeshop in Dallas called Barry's. While the pot gurgled, Emily came running out of the bathroom, breathless with wisps of brown hair askew.

"Did you fall in?" I teased her.

"No!" she said too fast.

I held back a laugh, half eager, half nervous to see what she'd done in there. Then I noticed the square box stuck into her leggings. Oh boy.

Larkin said to her daughter, "What do you tell Officer Madigan for letting you use his bathroom?"

"Nothing," I answered, leaning back on my counter. "But you can tell Knox anything you want. I'm off duty."

Larkin's cheeks tinged with color while Emily said, "Thank you, Knox."

The coffee pot sputtered like it had brewed all the water, and I turned to find it full. "How do you take your coffee?" I asked her.

"Sweet," she replied. "I like a little coffee with my sugar and cream, if you know what I mean."

Chuckling, I said, "Can do." I got the milk from my fridge and frothed it, then dropped a spoonful of sugar into a travel mug. After adding the coffee, I poured in the milk, making a heart shape. I handed it without the lid to Larkin so she could see.

Her eyes softened with a smile. "I love this." She showed her daughter. "Look, Emily, a heart."

Emily smiled. "Can I have one?"

Larkin said, "I'm sorry hon, I don't think we have time for him to make a whole new drink."

"I can do it with hot cocoa next time you're over," I supplied.

Larkin adjusted her hands so she could have a free one and still keep Jackson upright.

"I can hold him," I offered.

"You sure?" she asked.

"Of course." I walked over to them and scooped him up, making an airplane sound. He giggled happily, sounding so much like his mom. It made me like his laugh even more.

"Higher!" Emily told me.

And I lifted Jackson, flying him through the kitchen while Larkin got situated and took the first sip of her drink. I didn't miss the way her eyelids fluttered closed or how her throat moved with her swallow.

I brought Jackson down to my chest, his bottom resting on my forearm. "You're going to be a pilot one day, aren't you, little flier?"

He just blinked his big eyes up at me and made a sweet babbling sound.

"No words yet," Larkin said sadly. "Emily could already say nine or ten words at this age."

I looked down at Jackson, seeing more than a cute little baby. I saw someone who'd lost his dad and his voice along the way. My youngest brother had done the same after our mom passed. He was two at the time and stopped talking completely for months. "You'll figure it out in your own time, won't you, buddy?"

Larkin took him from my arms, resting him on her hip. "I hope so."

Then I said, "Will you all wait while I use the bathroom? I want to say goodbye before you leave."

Emily said, "Do you poop forever like my daddy does?"

Both Larkin and I burst out laughing, and Larkin coughed a little on her drink.

"It will be a quick one," I said with a chuckle.

Larkin gave me an amused look while Emily bounced up and down. "Can we wait for him, Mom? Please?"

"Okay," she said.

I turned and went toward the bathroom, then walked inside looking for Emily's prank. That was until I lifted the toilet lid and found it wrapped in Saran Wrap.

"Classic," I chuckled. Then I let out a louder, "OH NO!"

Even from here I could hear Emily's hysterical laughter.

I carried on while I turned on the sink and splashed water on my shirt and sweats.

Then I went out to the kitchen, where Emily was doubled over from laughing so hard.

"I made a mess of myself, Emily!" I said, gesturing at my wet clothes.

She laughed harder, her face turning red. Even Larkin and Jackson were laughing along now.

I bent over, putting my hands on my knees. "I'm going to get you back, Emily! Better watch out!"

She went to her mom, clinging to her leg, and stuck her tongue out at me before laughing again. When I looked up at Larkin, there was something I couldn't quite place in her eyes as she mouthed, *Thank you.*

8

LARKIN

AS I SIPPED my coffee on the drive to work, I was still thinking about all Knox had done, first thing in the morning, to make my kids smile. The kids were already at their grandparents, and Emily had told Nancy all about the prank as soon as we arrived.

Nancy gave me a judgey look that I tried not to think about. It said *shame on you for having a moment with a man so soon after the divorce.*

And to be fair, she wasn't wrong about us having a moment. There was so much to like about Knox, I knew I'd get burned if I let myself get too close.

For one, the way he looked bent over his coffee maker, giving me this gourmet drink, muscles visible through his shirt and gray sweatpants. The outline of his package, showing me he had more than enough to work with. His slightly messy hair. The way he played up the prank to make Emily happy. I sipped my drink slowly, not wanting it all to be gone. But once I hit the last sip, I promised myself that I would be practical when it came to Knox Madigan, both in my thoughts and in my actions.

I could just hear my sister chastising me for thinking of any man as more than a potential rebound. And I knew Knox was more than that. He was the first man to make my children smile that way since their father left, and I could never risk that for them by involving my heart.

The retirement community came into view through my windshield, and I slowed, easily finding a parking spot up front. This was definitely an upside from living in the big city—parking everywhere! And completely free, no meters or anything.

I took it as a good sign as I got out of my car and walked up to the front door. I had to ring the bell, but soon the community director, Bernice Williams, came up to the front, smiling at me through the windows. I recognized her from our video interviews.

"I'm so glad you're here!" she said as she swung the door open to let me in. "Our last nurse was amazing, but she's staying home with her children, and we've really needed an extra hand. It's not so easy to convince talented nurses to move to a small town."

"I'm glad to be here," I said honestly. I missed having a job outside the house when Seth and I decided I should stay home to raise our children. Work was the one place I had to myself, where I really felt like I knew what I was doing. Often, it felt like more of a vacation than real trips did because I didn't have to worry about taking care of my kids or my spouse. I could just be me.

"Let me give you the grand tour," Bernice replied, linking her arm through mine.

We walked the halls of the building, meeting residents along the way, and she showed me the bedrooms, community center, and then brought me to meet the CNAs who were busy with their shifts and some of the residents in various stages of their day.

It made me miss all the residents from my last job, before I had Emily. I'd loved being a nurse in a retirement home, hearing so many life stories and becoming family with all the people there. It felt like a part of me was coming back to life, just walking down these halls.

Bernice lowered her voice as we approached an older man wheeling himself down the hall. "I know we're not supposed to have favorites, but this is mine." Then, louder, she said, "Grandpa Griffen, this is our new nurse, Larkin Cappes."

"Cappes," he said. "Like Nancy and Jerald."

"I used to be married to their son," I confirmed.

With a twinkle in his eye, he said, "He let a beaut like you walk away? What a dumbass. I have to say, youth is wasted on the young."

I grinned, extending my hand to shake his. "Nice to meet you."

He nodded. "Now if you'll excuse me, I'm going to beat the shit out of Clifford in a game of Sequence."

"I'm pulling for you," Bernice replied, giving him a wink.

As he continued on his way, I leaned closer to Bernice and said, "Now I know why he's your favorite."

Just a couple hours into my job, I already knew I was going to like it. Bernice seemed really friendly and the residents were welcoming to me, although I knew they missed the last nurse.

I spent the rest of the day getting familiar with the computer system used to track medications and other medical information. Then I made a point to meet with everyone I could and get a feel for the culture here. Still, the highlight of my day was meeting Grandpa Griffen. Between the tobacco tucked into his lower lip and the sparkle in his misty eyes, I knew he'd keep me on my toes.

When it was time for me to go home, I said goodbye to Bernice and went to pick up the kids. As I walked up to Nancy and Jerald's sage-green farmhouse in the Texas countryside, I couldn't help remembering the first time I came here to visit.

I'd been in my early twenties and completely enamored with their son. Seth was in sales and liked to show me how special I was with each of his commissions. Some online therapy I'd done since discovering the cheating told me what he'd been doing was love-bombing. But back then, I didn't know it. I just thought I was in heaven.

Nancy and Jerald were so warm and welcoming to me. Treating me to a home-cooked meal like I hadn't had since my mom passed away when I was still in college. They insisted Seth and I sleep in separate bedrooms even though we were basically living together in Dallas. He snuck into my room at night and cuddled with me until the early hours of the morning when he snuck back to his room like we were both teenagers in high school.

Things were so different now as I walked up the steps, past the potted flowers, and knocked on the front door. It swung open, and Emily said a quick, "Hi, Mom," before walking back to the living room.

"Gee thanks, missed you too," I muttered, stepping inside and looking around.

The house was dated, with wood-paneled walls like in my rental and thick brown carpet, but there were sweet touches, like a wall covered with framed pictures of the kids, another with all sorts of crosses.

Passing by the living room where Emily was watching her favorite show, I found Nancy in the kitchen, cooking while Jackson toddled in his little walker with sensory toys sticking up on the front. When he saw me, his feet danced over the floor, and he screeched.

Nancy jumped, fumbling the spatula, while I laughed at my son's excitement. I hoped he wouldn't grow out of this. "Hello to you too, baby."

Nancy gave me an exasperated look and blew her bangs out of her face. "When is that kid going to start talking?"

"Soon." *I hoped.* I bent over, picking up the squealing Jackson and holding him close. "I'm so happy to see you, sweet boy!"

He gave me a slobbery open-mouth kiss, and I chuckled, happiness tugging against all the achy parts of my heart. It was amazing how being a single mom starting over again could be both the biggest pain in my life but also bring me more fulfillment than I ever knew I could have.

But that ache was hard to ignore as I stood in the kitchen with my ex's mom. "Have you heard from Seth recently? Emily's been wanting to talk to him, and I haven't been able to get in touch with him since the move."

Nancy didn't look up at me from the beef she was browning on the stovetop, but I noticed the lines deepen at the corners of her mouth and eyes. "I haven't. I'm sure he's just worried what will be said if he calls. I know tensions were high between you two that last month you lived together."

My eyebrows rose. "What do you mean?" We hadn't been in Cottonwood Falls long, but I was already really bothered by the comments Nancy made about the split. I knew I shouldn't look a gift horse in the mouth, considering she was babysitting for free, but Seth made his choices.

Nancy looked up at me. "He feels guilty enough without anyone adding on to it."

I opened my mouth to say he *should* feel guilty. He cheated on his wife and broke up a family. But I clamped my jaw back together. This was his mom, not mine. She would always want to see the best in her own child. It made me miss my own mother that much more. And reminded me that the only person I had truly in my corner lived in Paris. And not the one in Texas.

"Will you be staying for supper?" Nancy asked, sounding like she was trying to put a pleasant tone back in her voice.

I shook my head. "I picked something up after work. Thank you for the offer though. I really appreciate you and Jerald watching the kids."

"Of course," she said. "At least part of our family is living closer now. Too bad it couldn't happen sooner, but you know Seth's job."

"I get it," I said. "But I'm really tired from my first day. I'd like to head home and get ready for bed." I went to the living room, calling for Emily. "Give your grandma a hug goodbye and then let's get going."

"But I want to watch this."

My nerves were beyond frayed, but I kept a patient tone. "Honey, we need to get going."

"I WANT TO WATCH *PAW PATROL!*" she wailed. "I WANT TO WATCH *PAW PATROL.*"

Nancy said, "You can stay."

My eyes were already stinging, more from frustration than anything. I just wanted to get out of here. And now Jackson was fussing, squirming in my arms. I tightened my grip on him, then went to take Emily's hand. "We're leaving," I said, and we walked to the door. "Bye, Grandma, see you in the morning!"

No matter how many suggestions I offered on the way home, from letting her pick the radio station to watching an episode of a show at home, Emily did not calm down until I said, "I wonder how we can prank Knox next time?"

9

KNOX

ONE DAY A MONTH, my entire family went to Dallas for dinner and reserved the biggest table at our favorite steak restaurant, Rare. (Which, if you're asking my opinion, is the best and only way to eat a steak.) Located on the north side of the city, it was the most convenient place for all of us now that one brother played for a professional football team in Dallas and my youngest brother, Bryce, went to college in Oklahoma.

We used to pile into Dad's truck to go there, but now with Fletcher having a growing family, we took two separate cars. Fletcher, Liv, and their two in one vehicle. Hayes, Dad, and me in another.

We all got there around the same time for our reservation, and once we walked inside, the regular hostess, Rhonda, gave us a big grin. "There're those motley Madigans!"

Liv went up with Leah on her hip and gave Rhonda a hug. Rhonda returned it with a kiss on the cheek for Liv and Leah both. "Great to see you again."

I leaned closer to Bryce, saying, "If you're not getting any action at college, Rhonda'll give you a big ol' sloppy kiss on the cheek."

Bryce shoved my shoulder, an annoyed smile touching his lips. "Don't you worry about me."

I roughed his shaggy brown hair. "Killing it with the ladies?"

He rolled his brown eyes at me. "Not bribing my famous brother to help me get a girl, if that's what you mean."

My cheeks got hot. Okay, he might have had me there. Shaking my head, I followed everyone back to the big round table we always used and slid in the middle between Bryce and Leah. The table fit all of us, but barely.

Rhonda smiled as she handed out menus to all of us sitting there, her bright red lipstick still intact despite all the cheek-kissing. "Soon you'll have to rent out the whole place to fit your family."

Bryce snorted. "Not for Knox." He ribbed my side, and I got him back.

On Bryce's other side, Dad said, "You take your time, Bryce. The others..." He tapped his wrist where he never wore a wristwatch. "I'm waiting."

Rhonda smiled while Ford, Hayes, and I did our best to look distracted. "You know, I have a niece who would be just—"

Hayes cleared his tattooed throat. "Rhonda. You don't want me anywhere near your niece."

She gave him a look, all his tattoos and lip ring on display, and swatted her hand at him. "I see through you,

Mister Tough Guy. You have a secret heart of gold under all that ink."

I swore Hayes was blushing before he hid his face behind a laminated menu.

Rhonda and Dad exchanged a friendly look, and she said, "I'll be back with your drinks shortly." She winked at my niece, Maya. "Extra cherries in your Shirley Temple, right, dear?"

Maya nodded happily.

As Rhonda left, we began catching up. Ford told us about the weight training he was doing. Fletcher shared about owning the medical office in town. Hayes had plenty to say about a hot girl who came into the shop. And Bryce caught us up on how his studies were going in computer science.

But then I swore I felt everyone staring at me.

Hayes gave me a shit-eating grin before breaking the silence. "How's your new neighbor?"

"Oh shut up," I muttered.

Of course little Leah immediately copied me. "Oh shut up. Oh shut up."

Fletcher glared at me while Liv just laughed. "She's heard worse from my brother Rhett."

I felt relieved at that. "Larkin's daughter pranked me the other morning. Put Saran Wrap on my toilet. Classic."

Chuckles echoed around the table, and Ford said, "So when are you taking *Larkin* out?"

Liv spared me an answer, saying, "I'm taking her out first... if she can find a sitter."

Dad's thick gray eyebrows drew together. "Thought the grandparents were helping out?"

"Apparently they're busy Friday night."

"I'm not," I said before I could think of what a terrible idea it would be to babysitter-zone myself before I could even ask her on a date. "I could watch the kids."

Liv's eyes sparked. "That sounds so fun. I'll text her and let her know."

"Wait, wait—"

But then Fletcher said, "The girls and I could come over too. Make it a little less creepy than a strange single man watching her kids."

Thank you, I mouthed to Fletcher.

Hayes said, "I'll be anywhere else."

Everyone laughed at that, and then Rhonda came back with our drinks. Thankfully, that was enough conversation to move us on to another topic. Like how everyone in town thought Dad was dating Agatha, the waitress at Woody's Diner.

FRIDAY NIGHT CAME SOONER than I expected. Luckily, I'd had enough time to get the house ready so when the doorbell rang, I was ready for Larkin and her kids. I knew it wasn't Fletcher because he and Maya knew they could always walk right in.

When I swung the door open, Larkin held two large bags on one shoulder and had Jackson in the stroller in front of her. "Are you sure you're up for this?" she asked nervously. "Because if you aren't, I can always reschedule with the girls."

"What, you don't trust me?" I asked with a laugh that quickly faded at the look she gave me.

"Of course I am," I replied seriously, reaching for the bag on her shoulder. Something inside made a robotic squeaking sound, and I nearly dropped it. "Is that possessed?"

"Oh gosh, you aren't ready for this," Larkin said worriedly.

"It's okay. Here, let me show you all the setup so you can feel more comfortable." I shouldered the bag, stepping back to let them through the entryway. Emily came running past me while her mom parked the stroller and took Jackson out.

Larkin gave me a grateful look. "That would be amazing."

So I walked them through the rest of the house more thoroughly than I had at the dinner party. They had already seen the kitchen and living room, but I pointed out discreetly to Larkin how I kept the knives and cleaning supplies up higher and out of reach of children.

Then I led them to the living room. "Look at this," I said, walking to a chest in the corner by the bin of blankets. "You can open it, Emily."

Emily looked up at her mom, and when Larkin nodded, the little girl pulled the lid open and gasped. "Are these all for us?"

I smiled big at her delight. "I wanted to make sure everyone had toys they liked. What do you think?"

She pulled out a *PAW Patrol* stuffie of a little brown dog and hugged it tight to her chest. "I love it!"

I smiled. "I even have a playroom set up. Let me show you." We went to the other bedroom on the same level, and I pulled the door open, showing them inside.

"A BUNK BED!" Emily cried. "I'VE ALWAYS WANTED ONE OF THESE!"

I had to chuckle and smile over at Larkin, who looked happy tinged with a little bit of grief. Like she felt bad that Emily didn't have a bunk bed of her own.

"You're always welcome to it," I said to Emily, "any time your mama needs a break. I also put up this sensory swing, and there's a bookshelf with all sorts of books and a reading tent in the corner. I have a pack and play I'll set up later for Jackson if he gets tired."

Emily took a book off the shelf and climbed inside the purple tent. With the flaps closed, she yelled, "I love it!"

Larkin let a wiggling Jackson on the carpeted floor, and he crawled toward the tent with Emily. "Let your brother in," Larkin said, and Emily opened the flap just long enough for him to crawl inside. Within moments, Emily started reading *Brown Bear* to her little brother and making all the animal sounds I was sure her mama had made a hundred times.

My heart swelled in my chest at the sight, and then Larkin placed a hand on my arm, warming me in a way I wasn't used to.

"Thank you for this," she said, looking up at me with big blue eyes that were hard not to get lost in. "I'm sure you had this set up for your nieces, but Emily feels like a little princess already."

I had to clear my throat to speak. "I meant what I said. You're all welcome over any time."

The front door banged open, and Maya sang, "We're heeeeeere."

Larkin quickly dropped her hand from my arm, and the absence of her warmth felt just as palpable as her touch had been.

10

LARKIN

TOUCHING KNOX'S arm had been a mistake. It was firm, warm, and far too apparent just how much I enjoyed it. When his family arrived, I quickly pulled away like a kid caught with my hand in the cookie jar. Which meant he was far too tempting, and I had to get better at controlling myself. Even when I was overcome by the kind way he treated me and my children.

How sad was it that the simplest gesture of kindness brought on such strong emotions? I think I got so used to Seth and how he slowly withdrew affection that I didn't fully realize how much I'd missed the love and attention he used to shower me with.

Knox's gaze slid over me before he stepped away, giving no hint that we'd been even remotely close to touching. When Maya burst into the room, followed by a cute brown, black, and white dog, she had a gallon of ice cream hooked over one arm. "We're doing an ice cream bar tonight!"

Emily crawled out of the tent, clinging Marshall to her chest. "Can I have some, Mommy?"

I brushed back her soft brown hair. "Sure, baby."

She went over to Maya like she was approaching an old friend. "Did you hear about the prank I did?"

"With the plastic wrap? Classic. Tell me more." Maya took Emily under her free arm, walking with her toward the living room.

I went to pick up Jackson, but he'd crawled out of the tent to Knox's leg. Like it was the most natural thing in the world, Knox scooped him up, holding him in tanned arms decorated in swirling black tattoos. I noticed a turtle amongst the designs and had to wonder what it meant, if it had any meaning at all.

When I glanced back up his way, he hadn't even noticed me staring. He was looking into my baby's eyes, a warm smile on his lips as he spoke softly. "Hey, little guy. You are just the cutest thing. I can't wait for you to start talking so I can hear what's going on behind those big brown eyes."

I blinked quickly, ducking my head to follow the girls out of the room where I could hear them playing some kind of game in the living room. When I got there, I saw Maya and Emily on the couch, sitting cross-legged and facing each other, doing some activity where they slapped their hands in a pattern while little Leah sat in front of them in awe. Liv and Fletcher came in from the kitchen, Liv wearing an adorable floral romper with cowboy boots, and suddenly, I felt insecure about the denim shorts, plain blue T-shirt I thought brought out my eyes, and a pair of sandals.

Not wanting Emily to see me get down on myself for

my appearance, I pasted a smile on my lips and said, "Wow, Liv, you look amazing."

She grinned and tugged at the flowy shorts of her romper. "Thank you! It's new, and I wasn't sure how I felt about it."

"Maybe you can help me pick something too?" I replied. "I'm not used to the going-out part."

"Of course." She walked to me, putting her arm around my shoulders. "Let's get going," Liv said, brushing dark brown curls back over her shoulder. "Let me tell the girls goodbye."

A sudden worried ache formed in my chest. Leaving my children with their grandparents every day was hard, but I could justify it, saying I needed to earn a living to keep a roof over our heads. But saying goodbye to them now, when I was doing something purely for my enjoyment? It was totally foreign.

But I thought of Emily being a mom someday, and I didn't want her to have to sacrifice the way I had for the sake of a man who couldn't even be bothered to call his own children.

I drew in a steadying breath and went to kiss the top of Emily's head. Then I went to Jackson, still in Knox's arms. I reached out to hold him, but he squirmed, clinging to Knox. I tried to hide my hurt as I kissed the top of his head. "Bye, Jacks," I said.

"We'll take great care of them," Knox said. "And I'll send you pictures every hour."

I tilted my head in gratitude. Why did it feel like this man could read my every thought? "Every other hour will do," I only half-teased.

He chuckled. "Sounds great. Have fun."

"She will," Liv promised, looping her arm through mine and walking with me out of the house. As we walked down the steps, she told me, "He and Fletcher are really amazing with kids. You don't need to worry about a thing."

"It's good he's had practice with his nieces," I commented.

"He always comes over to our house when we need help with the girls," Liv said. "They have a great time together."

And as we walked around the sidewalk toward my house, I noticed something I hadn't before...

The stack of cardboard boxes beside his trash can. Brand new from a bunk bed and several of the toys I'd seen inside.

I glanced back toward his house, seeing them silhouetted through his living room curtains.

Knox hadn't had all of those items on hand... Had he gotten them... for us?

The question ran through my mind as Liv and I went to my house, going through my closet until we found a summery cotton dress I could wear with a pair of cute cowgirl boots. "You'll want your toes covered up when we go dancing," Liv said with a wink.

"Dancing?" I asked.

"It's a girls' night staple," she said, and then we walked out of my house and to her truck, which she introduced as Bernice.

"That's my boss's name." I laughed.

"Oh my gosh, it is." She laughed along with me. "Maybe don't tell your boss I've been riding her all over town."

I giggled, feeling like a dorky teenager with an indent in my hair from wearing my braces headgear at night. Liv seemed so cool and confident, effortless in a way that I never possessed. "I feel out of my league," I admitted. "I think the last time I went dancing I was still in college."

"When did you meet Seth?" Liv asked.

My lips twisted to the side, my mind immediately taken back to that day eight years prior. "I'd just graduated from nursing school and passed my exams, so a group of friends took me out to celebrate. He was schmoozing potential clients at the bar that night, and before they left, he pulled me aside and convinced me to call him."

Sometimes I wondered what my life might look like if I'd gone to a different bar that night. If I'd missed one too many questions on the exam or hadn't called the number on the business card he slipped me. But I couldn't go down that path.

"He was so charming," I said. "At least he started out that way."

"That's the Seth I knew," Liv agreed.

"Sometimes I forget everyone knows everyone here." I said. "Give me the dirt."

She cast a look my way, illuminated by the dash lights of her truck. "You sure?"

I nodded.

"I'm the messenger, you know," she said.

"I'm the only Texan who doesn't own a gun, so you're safe," I teased.

She laughed, then sobered. "He was a couple grades behind me, and he moved to Dallas after he graduated, so this is just what I know about him. He was always dating a different girl from a different town, sometimes more than one at a time. But even knowing that, the girls here loved him. He had this charm about him that was hard to resist."

"That tracks," I muttered, and I had to wonder if the time I found out about was really his first indiscretion with me or if there had been others before. But I knew I'd never have the truth—I couldn't trust Seth. Not anymore.

Liv gave me a sad look. "He was popular, all the guys liked him, and he was so persuasive. He could sell a red popsicle to a woman in a white pantsuit."

That made me laugh. "I can see that."

"But we don't need to talk about him. I want to know you."

What was there to know? I thought about what I enjoyed that was just for me. "Outside of being a mom... I have a lot of fun with my Cricut. I like making shirts, sweaters, things like that for special occasions."

"So fun," Liv said.

I nodded. "I love yoga, but don't ask me to do Zumba. Ever. It's horrifying."

She giggled. "Noted. I haven't done yoga before, but I'd love to try it sometime. There's a yoga and mimosa class in town the first Saturday of the month," Liv said. "We should totally do it together."

"That sounds so fun," I said, meaning every word.

She stopped in front of a house, the front porch light illuminating a pretty wreath with a *D* in the middle. Liv leaned on the horn, an ornery grin on her lips. Then a pale redhead came out the door, wild curls bouncing at her bare shoulders. She wore a soft yellow camisole, a denim skirt, and boots, along with a leather purse. When she climbed in the car, Liv said, "Larkin, this is my bestie for the restie, Della. Della, this is Knox's hot new neighbor, Larkin."

My cheeks were already heating, and that was before Della let out a low whistle. "You weren't exaggerating, Liv. Knox is in deep shit with this one next door." She shut the truck door behind her, and Liv took off. "You're a total babe, Larkin."

With heat radiating from my cheeks, ears, and neck, I said, "No need to worry about Knox. It would probably be a bad idea to date him."

Liv glanced in the mirror at Della, and I felt a silent conversation taking place between the two of them.

"What?" I asked.

"You know what they say about bad ideas," Liv said.

Della smirked. "They're the best kind."

I laughed. I could already tell tonight was going to be fun. Liv pulled up in front of a big brick building with a sign that said The Hen House illuminated out front. She didn't honk this time, instead getting out her phone and texting.

"This is my brother and sister-in-law's place," Liv explained. "They own boutique assisted-living apartments all over Texas, but they live in this one."

The front door opened, and a curvy woman with glowing bronze skin came out dressed in a sleeveless blue dress. A gold necklace shined on her neck and a gold headband pulled back short, curly hair.

"She's gorgeous," I said.

"Agreed," Della said. "Total bombshell."

She came to the other side of the truck, getting in the back seat. Liv introduced us, and Henrietta said, "So you're the famous Larkin. Everyone in town has been talking about fresh meat."

I laughed. "Not sure I'll get used to that."

"You don't," Henrietta agreed. "I moved here from California. Years later, and I'm still surprised how much I learn about myself when I go to the grocery store."

Smiling, I realized I already felt at ease around her. Liv started driving, saying, "We're meeting my other sister-in-law, Maggie, and her friend Camryn at the bar. It's not too far from here."

"Sounds good," I said.

My phone vibrated, and I glanced down at it to see a new text message from Knox. Inside was a photo of Emily and Maya on the couch with Jackson bundled up in a blanket between them. Emily had her open mouth on Jackson's forehead while he grinned, all the teeth he had showing. The message said...

I told the girls they could have ice cream, but they made a burrito instead.

I smiled down at my phone, and from the driver's seat, Liv said, "I recognize that smile. Who's the guy you're texting?"

My cheeks instantly heated. "Knox sent me a pic of the kids."

"Let me see!" Henrietta said.

I showed her the phone, and her lips spread in a smile. "They are so cute, Lark!"

"Thank you." I knew I liked her. Then I showed Della, and she smiled. "Gosh, I hope I get to have a family someday. They are so adorable."

"Is it hard to date in a small town?" I asked. Maybe a little bit for personal reasons.

They all exchanged looks, and Liv answered, "I married my brother's best friend and Henrietta met my brother while he was working in California."

"So yes," Della finished. "There aren't a ton of men to choose from."

"Just the Madigan family?" I asked. "What about Hayes? He's got that whole bad-boy-begging-to-be-tamed thing going on."

Della laughed. "Remember the part where I said I wanted babies one day?"

With her eyebrows waggling, Henrietta said, "You'd have a good time with him though."

"Worth it," Liv teased. "So you'll have spicy memories for when you're a married old broad like me." She parked diagonally on Main Street in front of a flickering neon sign reading Twisters. "Ladies, time to make some wild memories."

11

KNOX

NINE O'CLOCK, and all of the younger kids were asleep. My house looked like a tornado had gone through it, but it was more than worth it for all the fun we'd had. After eating pizza for supper, we did an ice cream sundae bar and then had the world's biggest prank battle for an hour and a half.

I sank into the couch across from Fletcher and Maya, who were curled under a blanket watching "Is It Cake?" I don't think I'd ever been this tired in my life, and I'd survived the police training academy and ran a marathon a few years back.

Fletcher pressed pause on the TV and said, "Holding up okay?"

I let out a chuckle. "The Icy Hot on the toilet seat was a bit of a surprise." Maya cackled next to him, and I got up, going to tickle her. As she squealed and giggled, I said, "I *knew* you were the mastermind behind that one." Her dog, Graham, gave me a warning yip, and I backed up just so he wouldn't wake the kids.

"Ha ha," Maya said and stuck out her tongue. "I'll sic my guard dog on you."

I rolled my eyes at her and began picking up the living room. "Think the girls are having fun?"

Fletcher gave me a look and pressed himself up to help me. "If Liv's involved, you know they're having too much fun."

"What does that mean?" Maya asked.

"Nothing," Fletcher and I replied at the same time.

She let out a grunt.

"Let's clean up now," Fletcher said, "so you won't have to deal with the mess in the morning. Princess Maya can keep watching her show."

She stuck her tongue out at him, and we got to work.

For the next half hour or so, my brother and I worked our way through the house, picking up toys, cleaning dishes, and throwing out trash. When we were done, I went to the guest bedroom to check on the kids. Emily was on the top bunk, the guardrail holding her in, Leah lay in the bottom bunk that was at floor level, and Jackson slept on his back in the pack and play, arms splayed above his head, hands forming little loose fists. I snapped another picture of the kids sleeping and texted it to Larkin.

Knox: We wore them out for you. :)

Then I tucked my phone back into my pocket and walked back to the living room, where another episode of the show started playing. We had fun making guesses out loud, seeing who was right. But it came to an end, and Fletcher told Maya it was bedtime.

He kissed her cheek and hugged her, then she gave

me a quick hug before heading back to my guest bedroom.

"Want to keep watching this?" Fletcher asked me.

"Sure," I said. "I actually kind of like it."

My phone vibrated in my pocket, and I shifted my hips to see what Larkin had texted me back, my heart picking up speed like it had when she touched my arm earlier.

I told myself it was because I wanted her to trust me as her neighbor, but I wasn't much for lying, especially to myself.

But when I glanced at the screen, it wasn't Larkin. Instead, it was a group chat with some guys who graduated the same year as me and still lived in town.

Garth: FRESH MEAT *peach emoji*

My eyebrows drew together.

A video came through, and I recognized the place immediately. There were purple, blue, and white lights illuminating the dance floor at Twisters, where Larkin was dancing along with Henrietta, Liv, Della, Maggie, and Camryn.

Usually Garth was harmless, making dumb comments here and there, but an uncomfortable tension tightened my jaw.

Especially when some of the other guys replied...

Ron: DIBS!

Mike: We're grown men. You can't call dibs.

Garth: Should have come out with Dennis and me if you wanted dibs. I'm moving in on this one. *grapefruit emoji* *water drops emoji*

My hand clenched on the phone. *Fuck.*

I could feel eyes on me and glanced over to see Fletcher watching me.

"You okay?" he asked.

I let out a heavy breath as I passed him my phone. He swiped through, his eyebrows raising. Then he cringed.

"What?" I asked.

He flipped the phone my way to show me a lewd GIF Garth sent.

"That fucker," I muttered.

Fletcher looked at the screen again. "Why didn't you call dibs?"

I rolled my eyes at my brother.

"We all know you're interested. Plus, you look like you want to punch someone over some locker room talk."

"Of course I'm interested. Have you seen her?" I shook my head. "But she's fresh out of a divorce. I wanted to give her space, a chance to settle into town."

Fletcher handed me my phone back. "Garth's not giving her space. He's getting as close as he possibly can."

I nearly broke my phone in half.

He laughed.

"Fuck you too."

He reached beside the couch, getting a throw blanket and settling it over his lap. "Why don't you just text Garth and tell him to fuck off? Or heck, go to Twisters and stake your claim. Make a move."

"I can't leave the kids here when I'm supposed to be babysitting."

Fletcher coughed and mumbled something that sounded a heck of a lot like "friend zoned."

"Oh no." I stood up, pacing my living room floor. "I am *not* getting friend zoned."

"Uh huh," Fletcher replied. He sat back like he wished he had some popcorn. Ignoring him, I continued my trajectory back and forth in front of the coffee table.

"I just have to ask her out tonight, right?"

"After Garth's put his greasy mitts all over her and given her enough free drinks to ease her inhibitions, right?" Fletcher asked.

"We might be grown, but I'm not above roughing you up," I replied, only half joking.

Fletcher laughed. "Look, you just..."

But I didn't hear the rest because another text came through my phone.

Garth: Fuck. She's got kids. Not worth the trouble.

Garth: But then again if she's got a sitter we can have a fun night.

I saw fucking red.

"Take this before I say something I'll regret," I said, handing Fletcher my phone.

He read the message as I ground my teeth together and clenched my hands into fists. Fletcher let out a low hiss.

Silence passed between us for a beat before my vision cleared a bit and Fletcher said, "What are you gonna tell him?"

I shook my head. "I'll handle him in person."

"And Larkin?" Fletcher asked.

"I'm not wasting any more time. I'm going to ask her out. Tonight."

12

LARKIN›

IT HAD BEEN years since I'd gone out dancing with girlfriends, and I felt every one of those years after doing the Wobble. My knees definitely didn't feel like this last time. And Twisters wasn't like any dance hall I used to frequent in Dallas.

This building had an unassuming brick façade matching the rest of the buildings on Main Street, and when you walked in the door, there was music going, loud enough to dance to but not so loud you had to shout to carry on a conversation.

The dance floor was made of black and white tile and surrounded by tables made of plywood and two-by-fours. Each table was covered in writing, and while Liv got us drinks, I sat with Hen, Della, Maggie, and Camryn, looking at everything written on its surface.

There were couples' initials, cusswords, and in between, I noticed the same turtle design that had been tattooed on Knox's arm. My eyebrows drew together as I traced my fingers over the design. Had Knox drawn this?

"Here's your drink, lady." Liv set my favorite drink in front of me—grapefruit vodka and Sprite—then sat beside me.

Della made a face at Liv. "We saw you talking to Garth."

"Ugh." Liv groaned. "I couldn't dodge him. He is seriously the worst."

I looked over Liv's shoulder, wondering which of the several guys standing by the bar she was talking about. I was so absorbed in the table drawings that I hadn't noticed. When I glanced back at the girls, I said, "Which one is he? So I can stay away."

Liv set down her beer and said, "Big dumbass with the black hat and red face."

I thought that wasn't the most helpful description, but then I turned and he stuck out like a sore thumb. "What did he do?" I asked.

With a frown, Liv leaned forward. "Let me give you a heads-up. You're new in a town with a very limited dating pool. Which means guys are going to treat you like you're a shiny new toy."

Della nodded, wryly adding, "Like a bunch of kids who never grew up and left the sandbox."

My heart sank. Maybe some part of me had hoped to find someone truly good, when I was ready. But now that was seeming like a very distant possibility. Especially when the one "good guy" I knew was off-limits.

Hen patted my hand. As if reading my mind, she said, "There are lots of nice people here."

My heart warmed at the kindness in her eyes. "You said you used to live in California. When did you meet your husband?"

Her smile seemed bright amongst the dimly lit bar. "I worked for an apartment company that was building a new complex, and Tyler was the head contractor on the job. Sometimes it seems crazy that out of all the people we could have hired and out of all the projects he could have worked on, we were in the same place at the same time."

Della grinned. "Three years in, and they're still one of the happiest couples I know."

Hen responded with a bashful smile. "When you get married, I'll give you the advice my dad gave me. Changed everything."

Someone tapped on my shoulder, and I turned, looking to see who it was. A tall, stocky guy with wide-set brown eyes and brown curly hair grinned down at me. "Can I trouble you for a dance?"

Thankfully, it wasn't Garth, but Liv's warning went off in my mind. Was I really just a shiny new toy to this guy? Was he staking his claim or something? But surely a dance couldn't hurt.

"Um, okay," I said. As he took my hand and turned to lead me away, I sent a quick, questioning look at the girls.

Liv gave me an encouraging smile, and Della did a double thumbs-up.

Pleasantly surprised, my heart relaxed a little bit as he stopped midfloor and easily guided my hand to his shoulder. He took my other hand in his and settled a large hand at my waist. He led me in a slow dance to the warbling country song.

Seeming so at ease, he gave me a smile and said, "Nice to meet you. I'm Bennett."

Relaxing a bit more, I said. "Larkin. Nice to meet you too."

Up close, I thought he wasn't my usual type, but there were things I liked about him. He had a nice smile. Kind eyes...

"I haven't seen you around town," he said.

"I just moved here not too long ago. I'm the new nurse at the retirement home."

"Oh nice. My grandma lives there. Maybe I'll see you around."

"Who's your grandma?" I asked.

"Mary Ellis Smith," he replied.

"I love her!" I said. "I mean, I've only been there a week, but she's already mopped the floor with me in Rummikub."

He tossed his head back, laughing. "That's Granny. She didn't even let me win when I was a kid."

I laughed. "I could see that."

Despite chatting, he led us both, not missing a beat of the music. "What else should I know about you?"

My lips pressed together for a moment. I'd thought about how to handle having children and dating, but this was my first time other than my failed tryst on the dating app. "Well, the most important thing is that I have two children."

I could feel his hands tense. "I'm not about to get beat up, am I?" he half-joked.

Which was actually funny because he was a big enough guy anyone would be an idiot to start a fight with him. "No," I said. "I'm divorced."

"Sorry to hear that," he said.

I shrugged, because, really, what else could you say?

"If it's not too forward, I'd love to take you out to dinner sometime. There's not much fancy here in town, but there's a steak restaurant in a town not far from here we could go to."

The closing chords of the song played, and I stepped back, feeling... so much. Excited, nervous, breathless. Was I really getting asked on my first date in eight years? A tight sensation filled my chest. Nerves maybe. Because I had thought plenty about a rebound, but now that the opportunity was here, it didn't feel right.

My sister's words echoed in my mind, reminding me that I needed to get back out there and do something for myself. So I nodded. "Dinner sounds nice." It didn't have to go further than that if I didn't want it to.

"Can I have your number?" he asked.

"Sure." We walked to the side of the dance floor to get out of the way of the other people dancing, and once his phone was out and ready, I recited the numbers to him.

He saved them in and said, "How's next Friday?"

"Seven o'clock?" I suggested. That would give me time to get ready after work.

"Sounds like a deal," he replied.

I gave him a smile and said I was going to hang out with my friends. He promised to call.

It was all very... practical. Decent. No drama. No games. No awkward flirtation. Maybe my sister was wrong—in-person dating was still the way to go.

I walked back to my friends, and I could see them all trying not to stare yet waiting to grill me.

When I got to the table, Della leaned forward, red curls falling over her shoulders. "Tell us everything!"

My cheeks heated, and I felt young again. "He asked me out to dinner."

Henrietta grinned. "What did you say?"

"I told him I would."

I looked at Liv to see what she thought, but I noticed a slight frown before she tugged her lips into a smile. "That's great, Lark."

My eyebrows drew together. "Oh no. Is he not a good guy? I thought y'all gave me the go-ahead earlier."

"No, he's great." Liv rubbed her neck. "I guess I got my hopes up that you and Knox would have a thing. I got ahead of myself."

The mention of Knox had my cheeks heating. Especially since they had all noticed me looking forward to each of his text messages all night. "Knox is my neighbor," I reminded all of us.

"And? Easy access," Liv replied.

Della nearly spit out her drink, and Henrietta chuckled.

I shook my head. "The kids love him. I'm not going to mess that up."

Liv replied in a sing-song voice, "Been there before."

"What?" I asked.

She told me that she was Fletcher's full-time, live-in nanny for all of a summer before they decided they couldn't deny their feelings anymore. They'd been married for two years now.

"So Maya..." I asked.

"Is my stepdaughter," Liv said.

"You two seem so close," I replied.

There was a soft smile on Liv's lips as she said, "As far as I'm concerned, she is my daughter. She just has two moms. But I'm excited for you. Bennett's a great guy. You two will have a good time."

I gave a tentative smile. "I hope so."

The four of us didn't stay out too late, which I appreciated because no matter what time the kids went to bed, they always woke up at the same time every morning.

When we pulled up along the street in front of mine and Knox's homes, I noticed just the porch and kitchen lights on at Knox's place.

"So what did you think?" Liv asked. "Was girls' night a success?"

I took my gaze off Knox's place and smiled over at her. "Honestly, I think it's just what I needed. Thank you so much for including me. You're great, and your friends are so fun. I hope we can do it again sometime."

"Heck yes," Liv said. "You fit right in, too. We'll plan something soon!"

I hoped she meant it because as we got out of the truck, I realized there was so much I'd been missing during my marriage to Seth. Romance. Friends. Fun. A true partnership. And even though I moved to Cottonwood Falls to pick up the pieces of my life, it felt like I was finding pieces of myself too.

We reached the front door, and Liv let us in. The place was quiet, save for the two men sitting at the kitchen table with a stack of cards between them.

Fletcher and Knox both smiled at us, and something in my chest clenched. I hadn't realized how much I missed someone smiling at me when I got home. They got up from the table, and Fletcher immediately took Liv in his arms, kissing her lips.

"How was it?" he asked.

Liv sent me a wink. "We had a great time. Got up to all sorts of trouble."

"Oh really?" Knox asked.

"Nothing we can say in front of a police officer," I teased.

He chuckled, the sound warming my chest. "I'm off duty."

Glancing at the table, I asked, "What are you two playing?"

Fletcher cleared his throat but still spoke too softly for us to hear.

"What was that?" Liv asked.

"Go Fish," Fletcher said louder. "We couldn't agree on what to play, so this was it."

I had to chuckle at the thought of two grown men playing Go Fish after all the kids had gone to bed.

"Don't make fun," Knox said, tattooed arms folded over his chest. "There was a lot riding on this game."

"Like what?" Liv asked.

Fletcher said, "He was about to mow our lawn in his underwear."

I had to laugh at that mental image.

Knox shook his head. "His neighbors would love it."

Liv shook her head at the pair. "I'm going to use the bathroom. Fletcher, can you grab the girls?"

"Sure," he said.

"I'll go get my kids," I said. "Thanks so much for watching them."

"I'll help you. I don't mind carrying them next door," Knox quickly offered.

It was so nice of him to help me. Or maybe that was the vodka Sprite making me feel so warm. "Thank you."

We went back to the bedroom where he'd shown Emily the toys, and in the nightlight, I could see Jackson, cozy in his pajamas, booty in the air, as he lay in his pack and play. Then Emily was cuddled up on the top bunk, the blanket tugged up to her chin.

"I'll get Emily," Knox offered.

I nodded, going to pick up Jackson. He let out a small sigh, smacking his lips and then settling into my arms. It was so sweet. I held him close as we walked out of Knox's house and across the way to my place.

I fumbled with my keys, finally hitting the lock, and then we went inside. I guided him through the house, showing him the room Emily and Jackson shared. I set Jackson in his crib soon enough to stand and see Knox carefully spreading the blanket over my daughter.

It was so tender, just another reminder that I was making the right choice by dating elsewhere. Knox was a great neighbor, I adored his sister-in-law, his brother was the town doctor, and Emily loved pranking him and spending time with his nieces. It was all too much for the first relationship after a divorce.

Once the kids were settled, I walked to the front door with Knox and we stood in my small living room. It seemed even smaller with his six-foot-two body standing there too.

"Thank you so much for watching the kids," I said again. "Were they okay for you?"

"They were great," he said. "Minus the Icy Hot burns on my butt."

My jaw dropped. "Emily?"

"And Maya." He cringed.

I covered my mouth to hide my giggle.

"Hey now," he replied, his smile so bright, even in the dim room. I swore there was something else in his eyes. "If you ever need a sitter again…"

"How about next Friday?" I suggested, half joking. Hopefully their grandparents would be available… and not ask me too many questions.

"Another girls' night?" Knox asked.

"Actually… a date." I couldn't quite meet his gaze right away, but when I did, he was wearing an encouraging smile that told me I'd been in my head for nothing.

"Good for you," he said. "Who is the date with?"

"Bennett Smith," I replied.

"Clean record. I approve," Knox teased. "Let me know if the grandparents fall through. No dates for me— next weekend at least."

My pride took yet another hit. He wasn't bothered in the slightest that I was going out with another man. I'd been tying myself in knots over someone who only saw me as a neighbor. A mom.

Time to go lick my wounds. "Well, goodnight. And thanks again for watching the kids. It was really nice of you."

"If you need anything, I'm right next door." Did he smile at everyone like that? Because the way his eyes held mine made me want to melt, even though I knew there was nothing between us. Knox Madigan was a tease. Did he know he was doing it?

He gave me a wave and turned to walk outside. I watched through the screen door as he walked down the sidewalk, treating my weedy lawn just as well as anyone would treat the finest grass.

Before he could see me staring, I shut the door and hoped the heaviness in my chest would eventually fade.

13

KNOX

I WAITED in my cruiser outside of Woody's Diner, where Garth ate breakfast every morning. He was a farmer on his family's operation, but I was pretty sure he did more bullshitting around town than he ever got work done.

A glance at my dashboard had me letting out a string of swears. I had ten minutes until my shift started, and I wanted to handle this off the clock.

Looking back at the diner, I saw the front door swing open, and I got out of my car, walking up to Garth and catching him on the sidewalk.

"Knox, they don't serve donuts he—"

"Shut up," I said. "And walk with me."

He seemed confused, so I grabbed his arm, guiding him around to the back side of the diner.

He shook his arm out of my hand. Maybe I had been squeezing a little too tight. "What the fuck?" he said, anger flaring his nostrils.

"What you said about Larkin was uncalled for." I kept my voice firm but even.

"Larkin?"

"The single mom you didn't want to 'waste your time on,'" I snapped, anger flooding at the memory of those texts.

Garth raised his eyebrows, lines forming on his ruddy red forehead. "We say stupid shit in the chat all the time. It's what we do."

I shook my head, wondering why I still put up with guys from high school. We clearly had grown in different directions. But could he really not see what was wrong with what he said? "It's one thing to have some locker-room talk and another to make fun of a single mom just trying to get by."

He smirked. "Looked like she was getting by just fine on that dance floor."

My hands clenched, and if I were seventeen, I would have decked him. Instead, I was a grown man representing Cottonwood Falls. I leaned in, getting right in his face, and made my voice deadly. "Single moms have the whole fucking world sitting on their shoulders, and they don't need to take any shit or deal with any judgment from the likes of you."

He held up his hands. "Sorry, I was just fucking around in the group chat. I didn't know it was that big of a deal."

I shook my head. "Having integrity is a big fucking deal. Do better."

Once he nodded, I stepped away and walked off. But then he called after me, "You're with her, aren't you?"

My jaw ticked as I turned to face him. He had a dumb smirk on his face like he'd gotten me good with that remark. But I curled my lip in disdain. Not just because

Larkin had thoroughly friend zoned me last night and was going out with another man, but because I hated it when people made comments like that. "You're not one of those guys, are you?"

He jutted out his chin. "What do you mean?"

"One of *those guys* who only gives a shit about a woman if she means something to you. Not because it's the right thing to do."

He drew his eyebrows together. "What's it to you? It was a dumb text in a group."

And maybe he did have me there. Because if I made a habit of getting onto every person who said something stupid, I'd never have time for anything else. But I settled for the truth. "I don't want to be a part of a group that's okay with talking about women like that. We're too old for that shit, Garth."

He nodded then scratched the back of his neck. "What do you want me to do?"

I barely kept from rolling my eyes. You could lead a horse to water, but... "You post in the chat and say you messed up last night and won't do it again, then we're square."

He tugged his lip up like he'd smelled something bad.

"You have ten minutes. And I have to get to work." I turned and walked back to my car.

In seven minutes, a text came through my phone.

Garth: Sorry guys. I drank too much last night and didn't mean that stuff about that mom. Gotta be gentlemen around here, right?

He sent a cowboy emoji.

Trent: You? A gentleman? Why are my feet feeling cold? Hell freeze over?

Dennis: Hell yeah, Garth. Cowboy up.

A couple other guys chimed in, but I didn't reply. I had half a mind to tell those guys to never talk to me again. But at least we were moving forward without any more of that nonsense coming through my phone.

$$\mathcal{L}$$

AFTER WORK, I went over to Hayes's garage to blow off some steam. Every so often, we got some guys together to play beer pong or poker, depending on what kind of mood we were in.

Today, when I walked into his garage, freshly changed and showered from work, I found a mix of Madigans and Griffens gathered around a big round table. Our two families had grown up on neighboring ranches and remained close friends throughout the years. Tonight it was Hayes, Fletcher, Rhett, Tyler, and me around the table.

They each acknowledged me, and I went to the fridge to get myself a beer. "Anyone need another?" I asked.

Hayes said, "Always." So I grabbed one for him too and went to sit at the white plastic table in an empty folding chair between Tyler and Hayes.

Glancing my way, Tyler said, "Been a while."

I nodded in agreement. "You've been too busy for us, opening up the new locations for your apartments."

He smiled at the mention of his thriving business. He and his wife had gotten an investor to help them expand and convert several more out-of-commission buildings around Texas into boutique senior apartments. "Good problem to have, I guess," he said.

A strange feeling filled my chest, and... fuck, I had to admit I was jealous of him. He had it all—a job he loved and a wife to come home to. Someone to build a life with him. I was tired of doing it all on my own. I wanted a partner, in every sense of the word.

But with everyone I dated lately, it seemed like something was missing and it ended shortly after it began. I couldn't, in good faith, keep dating someone when I didn't see a future with them.

Fletcher shuffled the deck of cards in his hands and said, "If we don't start playing soon, I'm going to fall asleep."

Rhett covered his ears. "I don't need to hear about your sex life keeping you up at night when it includes my sister."

Shoving him, Fletcher said, "I wish. Leah's in a sleep regression, and Liv's with her all day, so I've been taking the night shift."

Rhett made a face, and Hayes said, "If you keep talking about kids' sleep schedules, *I'm* going to fall asleep. This is why I'll never have kids. You pop one out and get *boring*."

Fletcher rolled his eyes at our brother, and Rhett laughed, saying, "Never say never or fate will bend you over and fu—"

"Just deal," Tyler chided with a mix of humor and exasperation in his eyes.

Fletcher started passing out the cards.

They slid over the plastic table, and for the next couple hours, we played and ribbed each other.

It was exactly what I needed to get my mind off Larkin.

Until I pulled up to my house and found her sitting on my front porch.

14

LARKIN

I LOOKED AWAY from my baby monitor positioned in the kids' room so I could see them sleeping as headlights flooded the street ahead of me. Knox was home, thankfully, because I'd been waiting about ten minutes, hoping I might catch him after his shift, and was about to give up.

He got out of his cruiser and sent me a smile that shined even this late in the evening, barely a hint of light left in the sky. He wore a loose white shirt and jeans with cowboy boots. I found I liked those on him just as much as his other clothes. Made him seem more down to earth somehow.

"I didn't order any of you," he teased.

I smiled at him, standing up with the monitor in one hand and a pan of brownies in the other. "Going to return me to the store?"

"I could never." He stepped under the glowing porch light, and the way it caught the blond strands of his hair had me so distracted.

Trying to tame the butterflies in my stomach zooming around like the June bugs outside, I said, "These are for you." I passed him the brownies. "For babysitting the other night. I'm still getting on my feet, so I can't afford to pay you yet, but—"

He waved his hand at me. "Don't worry about it." He lifted the glass pan to see underneath the foil. "Are these brownies?" He looked at them like they were the best gift he'd ever gotten.

"My mom's recipe," I said. "Which may or may not have come in a box."

His low chuckle warmed my heart. "Want to share one with me? Brownies are always best with ice cream and—"

"I hope you're going to say iced tea," I finished. That was my mom's magic combination.

His dark brows pulled together. "How did you know?"

"Lucky guess." I shrugged. I knew I should go back to my place—it was safer for me to keep my distance when he seemed so wonderful. Seth had seemed great at first too and look where that ended up.

"Don't make me eat these alone. I have a physique to maintain." He ran his hand over his hard stomach, and the hem of his shirt lifted to reveal a strip of skin.

Damn. That was definitely my kryptonite. "If the monitor reaches inside, I can come."

"Great." He brushed past me, the smell of his cologne subtle but still knee-weakening, as he bent to unlock his door.

"You might be the only person in town besides me who locks their door," I noted. I couldn't believe people felt safe enough here to leave their vehicles running outside of stores or their homes unlocked all day.

He glanced over his shoulder at me just as the key found purchase. "Not everyone's experienced Cottonwood Falls the way I have."

I waited for him to explain, but he just stepped inside and turned on the light, holding the door open for me. As I walked by him, my shoulder brushed his chest, and my stomach tensed.

If my sister only knew how strongly my body was reacting to simply grazing against a man's chest. She would have a field day and sign me up for another dating app immediately. This was making an even stronger case for me to go out with Bennett and get my hot neighbor off my mind.

"Does the monitor reach?" he asked, startling me from my thoughts.

I checked the screen, still seeing my children sleeping, and showed him the image. His lips curled into a soft smile. "They're precious."

"Even more so when they're asleep," I joked.

He chuckled. "Less pranking that way." He nodded toward the table. "Take a seat. I'll get you a bowl."

I went and sat down, propping the monitor in front of me while he went about preparing the brownies. My feet were so tired from standing all day at work and then taking care of kids and cleaning up around the house, I welcomed the relaxation.

He heated up the brownies in the microwave, topped them with a scoop of ice cream, and drizzled chocolate sauce over the top. When he brought my bowl to me, looking like it had come out of a professional kitchen, my mouth was already watering.

"How did you make these look so good?" I asked.

He slid into the chair across from me. "You like?"

I nodded and dug my fork in. The taste of home instantly flooded my mouth. I closed my eyes, and it was almost like I could picture being younger, my mom pulling a batch straight from the oven.

When I opened my eyes, I saw Knox watching me.

My cheeks burned as I asked, "They remind me of my mom. Do you like them as much as I do?"

His eyes crinkled with his smile. "I sure do." He took another bite, and as he moved his arm, I noticed the turtle again. It wasn't a sea turtle, more like a land turtle you might find alongside the road.

"Can I ask about your tattoo?" I asked.

"Which one?"

I tapped my finger on the turtle, his skin so hot against mine, my reaction to it so strong, it took all I had not to jerk my hand away. When I met his eyes, they were dark, stormy blue. He reached for a napkin from the holder in the middle of his table and wiped his lips.

I couldn't look away from those lips.

"You can ask," he said, his voice low.

Despite the white noise crackling from the monitor, it felt like all the air had been sucked out of the room, leaving space only for Knox and me. "What does it mean?" I nearly whispered, my fingertips still on his tattoo.

He covered my hand on his arm, holding us still for a moment before taking a breath. "I got it for my mom."

My heart clenched, and even though we were so close, too close, I couldn't pull my hand away.

His lips turned at the corners, like he was smiling at a memory. "Every summer out in the country, you see turtles crossing the road. And it's safest to just keep driving because if you overcorrect on a dirt road, you're at risk of rolling the car."

I nodded, remembering my mom and Tay taking me on back country roads to practice driving when I was fourteen.

"Most people don't even bother slowing down. But whenever my mom was driving and we saw a turtle, she'd slow down and stop. Then she'd put the car in park, turn on her hazards, get out of the vehicle and move that turtle across the road, at least a good ten yards away, even if the weeds in the ditch were waist high, so the turtle wouldn't get a death wish and cross back over again."

I found my own lips curving at his statement. "She seems so tenderhearted."

He nodded. "One day, I was running late to baseball practice, and she still slowed down and stopped. I was worried about my coach making me run extra laps, kind of annoyed with her, so I asked her why she always did that, even when we had places to be. And she told me something that's always stuck with me. 'Someday, if I'm stuck in a bad place, even if I got myself there, I hope there will be people around to help get me out of it, even if it's a little inconvenient for them.'" He turned those dark blue eyes on me, like he had shifted out of his memory and back to the present. "It's funny, all the things your parents tell you. Be good. Do your homework. Hold the door. Say thank you. But it's their actions that teach you the most."

He glanced down, breaking the spell, and let go of my hand.

I brought it back to my own lap, coming back down to earth. He was right about actions speaking louder than words. I was a mom first, and I wanted my kids to know, to *see*, that I always prioritized them, even if it meant setting aside my feelings for Knox so he could be their friend without my heart getting in the way.

15

KNOX

THOSE BROWNIES WERE the best I'd ever had. But the company was even better. I lay in bed that night thinking about Larkin and how different she was from anyone I'd met.

Women had commented on my tattoos before.

Told me they were hot.

But never had someone taken the time to ask me questions like that and then truly listened for my answer when I spoke, not asking for anything in return, not expecting anything of me, just... sitting with me and understanding me.

As a kid who grew up feeling misunderstood most of the time, I appreciated that more than Larkin would even know. Unfortunately, she was going out with Bennett on Friday, and I needed to respect that. But how could I when I liked her so much?

Just a few days after eating brownies with her, my evenings were feeling emptier than they had before. I missed eating brownies with her before bed, and we weren't even together. I kept glancing over to her house, wondering what she and her kids were up to. Seeing them play in the backyard or haul a wagon across the street to the closest park.

So I was glad when my dad called me on Thursday and asked if I would go and check cattle with him. It had been a little while since we hung out, so it would be nice to catch up with him and see how he was doing. When you lose a parent, you never forget how important the remaining one is to you.

I drove my truck out to the country, going past the Griffen Farms sign until I saw the sign for Madigan Ranch. There were so many memories attached to this place, good and hard. For a long time, it was difficult to see my childhood home and not think of how my mom passed away in her bedroom when I was still a boy.

But time had given me the gift of perspective. Of new memories and the ability to remember the good times with Mom like I wasn't able to do when the pain was still so fresh. I didn't see Dad's pickup by the house, so I drove on past to the dark red barn farther down the trail. As the corral came into view, I could see him adjusting the saddles on two horses.

My eyebrows rose as I pulled up. I got out of the truck and called over to him, "I thought we were *driving* to check cattle!"

Dad gave a wry smile that deepened the wrinkles on his face. "The horses needed some attention. Figured a young guy like you wouldn't mind."

"Which is why you included that tidbit of information when you called?" I quipped. I reached the metal fence panels and climbed over. "At least it's nice out." This time of year in Texas, it could easily hit the hundreds, but it was supposed to rain overnight, so the temp was in the eighties with a cool breeze.

Dad nodded, handing me the reins to his younger horse, Acres. I walked the four-year-old out of the corral, holding the gate open for Dad, who rode by on his roan quarter horse, Blister. Gross name, I know. He'd gotten the thing as a colt ten years prior and said he got the worst blister riding in a new saddle to train him, so that was the name he settled on.

Once he was out of the corral, I latched the gate shut, gripped the saddle horn, put my foot in the stirrup, and hauled myself on to Acres's back. He stood still, waiting patiently for me to nudge his side, and once I did, he started walking after Dad and Blister.

I rubbed his neck, ran my fingers through his rough chestnut mane. "Good boy," I hummed. Then I sat back in the saddle and took in my surroundings.

Even though I lived in town now, I loved being back on the ranch. There was so much space, it just felt easier to breathe. And I felt closer to Mom here too. She and Dad had made a true home here, a family, a life.

Maybe someday, when I had a family of my own, we'd settle down in our own little country home.

Dad and I rode in silence, side by side on the ruts of a trail cutting through the pasture, until Dad said, "How're things with the neighbor girl?"

When he phrased it like that, I felt like I was fifteen years old again, crushing on Liv Griffen even though I could tell my brother had the hots for her and just wouldn't make a move. "What things?" I finally asked.

Dad snorted. "Still a terrible liar."

I grimaced. "I wasn't lying."

"Just evading," he teased.

I shook my head at him and scanned the grassy hillside dotted with black Angus cattle and Yucca plants. The herd seemed healthy so far. "What about you and Miss Agatha? Huh?"

Dad's cheeks instantly went red. "Not going there."

I had to laugh. "You know, we're okay with you dating again, Dad."

His hands rested on his denim-clad thighs, leather reins gripped loosely in his fingers. "I know that. I'm just not sure I'm okay with it."

My lips pressed together. "You know Mom wouldn't hold it against you."

"I know."

"Then why hold back?" I asked.

He huffed out a laugh. "If I told you, it'd sound stupid."

"Stupider than me calling everyone in my family for a last-minute supper so I could hang out with my hot new neighbor, who just so happens to be going on a date with Bennett Gardner tomorrow night?"

Dad winced.

"Uh huh."

After a beat or two, Dad said, "You know, one of the things that got me through losing your mom was knowing I'd see her again in heaven. But how does that work when you fall in love with another woman? The three of us gonna be standing around awkwardly in heaven with Jesus mediating the whole thing? Your mother would have my head before she shared custody of me."

I let out a laugh, more out of surprise than anything.

"Maybe Mom's a freak now. Could have some fun."

Dad's face went redder than I've ever seen it. He nudged his horse into a trot.

"What are you doing?" I called after him, getting my horse to speed up.

"Getting away from you before your mom gets God to strike you with lightning."

Now I was really laughing. Coming out to the ranch had been a great idea.

WHEN I GOT HOME, well past ten since Dad and I had decided to have dinner and drink a couple beers, I glanced out the window at the house across the way. I couldn't see inside, but I noticed the bedroom window light was on. I wondered what Larkin was doing up so late. Had Jackson woken and needed care? Was she up talking on the phone to her sister in Paris? Texting someone?

The thought of her texting with Bennett nearly made my blood boil.

I went to the bathroom and took a shower, trying to clear my head, trying to see sense and reason. But there was another visceral part of me that hated how I'd missed my chance this early on.

What if this date with Bennett went so well that I never got another opportunity?

What if he moved in with her? Had to see his truck parked out front throughout the night?

Had to see him playing with her children. Making her smile. Putting his hand on her waist.

The thoughts kept spiraling, making me so angry and jealous that I was just as worked up when I got out of the shower as I was when I got in it.

I threw on a pair of boxers and paced my bedroom. I had to do something... but what?

I couldn't storm over there and knock on her door. I'd wake up the kids if they weren't already. Not to mention I'd look like a complete fool.

But then I got an idea. I pulled my phone from the top of my dresser. I could send her a text message. Make sure I was the one on her mind tonight. But I stood in my bedroom, thumbs poised over the digital keyboard, completely lost at what to say.

Hi, don't date Bennett? Date me instead?

I was just thinking about you in the shower?

I rolled my eyes at myself. I was a grown man, but I felt all the jitters of being young and dumb and in love for the first time all over again. I needed to remind myself who I was. I'd faced down criminals knowing men just like me didn't always finish their shift alive. I could send a text message to a woman. Especially one as kindhearted as Larkin.

Knox: Couldn't sleep and noticed your light was on. What are you doing up so late?

I stared at my phone as I went to my bed, pulled back the covers, and climbed in. The cream linen sheets were cool against my heated skin.

A bubble with three dots appeared on the screen, and I held my breath, waiting for her reply.

A photo of her with Jackson in her arms, his eyes half closed, came through the phone, and I smiled at the image. Then another text.

Larkin: Little boy doesn't know you're supposed to sleep when it's dark outside.

Larkin: What's keeping you up?

I can't stop thinking about you.

I ran my thumb over my bottom lip, knowing I couldn't tell her that without coming on too strong.

Knox: Was over at my dad's, guess I'm having a hard time winding down.

I sent the text and waited for her reply. Wondered if she would.

I hadn't asked her a question, and my fingers itched to fire off another message with one just to feel like I had some connection to her. But then a new message came through.

Larkin: What did you and your dad do together?

Knox: We rode horses to check cattle and then went back to the house. He made me dinner and we had some beers. Just hung out. It was nice.

Larkin: Wait. Did you say horses?

Knox: I mean, technically I typed it.

Larkin: *Eyeroll emoji* Do you think there's any chance Emily could ride a horse one day? She's OBSESSED.

Knox: I think I can pull a few strings. ;) So she likes horses and the Dallas Diamonds. What do you like?

The text bubble appeared for a long moment then disappeared and came back again.

Larkin: It's been a long time since someone asked me that.

My heart clenched in a way I wasn't used to feeling.

Knox: I'm here when you have an answer.

I hoped maybe I could be a part of it.

16

LARKIN

I WAS EATING lunch alone in the employee break room, watching a video about yoga for seniors, when the call from Nancy came through. Worry immediately hit me because she usually didn't call throughout the day, only sent a text or two to let me know if something happened out of the usual or if I needed to restock diapers or something like that.

"Hello?" I answered. "Is everything okay?"

I could hear the choppy, robotic sound of music from a child's toy in the background as she replied, "We're fine here, but I just realized I can't keep the kids overnight for your date tonight."

I waited for her to explain further, but then it hit me. She said *date*. And I hadn't told her the reason for the sleepover was a date—I'd just said I needed some time to myself.

What they said about small towns was true. Everyone knew everything about everyone here. There was no such thing as a secret.

My heart sank, because even though I'd been nervous to go out with Bennett, I'd been looking forward to going on my first date since the divorce. And getting some distance from Knox, since our text conversation the night before had my heart even more involved than it should have been. Everything about him screamed tenderness and care, two things I desperately desired and yet had no business dreaming about getting from him.

"That's too bad," I said, my voice coming out a whisper.

"It's really too soon for you to be dating anyway," Nancy said. "Especially with two small children at home. You know some men target single moms because of their children?"

My lips parted in shock, and the familiar sting of anger hit my veins. Was she really questioning my judgement as a mother, telling me it was too soon to date? I wanted to tell her that her son hadn't thought it was too soon when we were still married, but I bit my tongue. She and Jerald were doing me a huge favor by watching the kids for free while I worked. So I simply said, "Thanks for letting me know. I'll pick them up after work."

Hot, angry tears stung my eyes as I hung up the phone. I set it down on the table and got up, irately pacing the break room.

It wasn't fair. Seth was off doing whatever he wanted with whomever he wanted. He didn't have to do anything more than write a check. Meanwhile, I was watching the children, making a new home, working full-time, staying up with Jackson at night, comforting Emily when he wouldn't call. It was all so much.

I needed a break. And a lot more coffee.

I shoved my meal aside and decided to walk to the diner to get some space and a fresh coffee. As soon as I was out of the building and on the sidewalk, the hot midday sun beat down on me. I wished my sister was here to talk with me, but I did the next best thing, taking out my phone and calling her. I put my earbuds in and listened to the phone ring. At least I knew she would be there for me no matter what.

After a few rings, she answered, "Hello, gorgeous."

"Hey." My voice broke.

"What's going on?" Her concern nearly broke me, but I held my head high, walking along the wide sidewalks.

"My in-laws found out about my date on Friday, so they won't babysit anymore. I think I'll have to cancel the date." I wiped at my eyes, the tears mingling with fresh beads of perspiration.

"Damn it," she muttered. I could hear her turn off the TV in the background. "There has to be another person in town who will babysit. What about—"

"Don't say it," I muttered.

"Your sexy, tatted neighbor?" I could hear the Cheshire grin in her voice.

That definitely distracted me from the tears. Because he *had* said I could ask him anytime. But this last minute? For a date? Would that be awkward?

Only if he actually had feelings for me, I thought.

But judging by how happy he acted about my date, he didn't have feelings for me like I did for him. And then I remembered the text Bennett sent me earlier today.

Bennett: Can't wait for our date tonight. *rose emoji*

Taylee said, "The worst Knox can say is no. The best he can say is, 'Let's skip your date and do it on the kitchen floor.'"

I snorted so hard I nearly choked on my spit. "You're terrible."

She smiled. "I'm here for you always. And I'm buying those tickets for you to come visit over Thanksgiving, okay? I want to see you and hug you and squish Em and Jack's little cheeks."

"You mean it? I know they're not cheap."

"Bitch, I'm a single professor. I can afford it."

I smiled, shaking my head. "We'll be there." It hit me how great it felt to be able to make Thanksgiving plans all on my own. In the past, Seth always insisted we go to his parents' for every holiday, but he hadn't called me or the kids since we moved here. As far as I was concerned, this was my decision, one I was happy to make.

I got closer to the diner, seeing Knox's cop car out front. "I've gotta go."

"*Au revoir*," she replied in her flawless French accent.

"*Au revoir*."

I took a deep breath and walked up the cement ramp into the building. Through the heavy glass door up front, I saw quite a few people inside, enjoying meals together. It made me miss lunches with my sister when she was getting her doctorate in Dallas. Maybe I could invite my new girlfriends out for a meal sometime.

When I walked inside, a wave of air-conditioning coming over me, I immediately scanned the place for Knox. It was like some masochistic part of me had to know where he was, had to see his smile, especially when I was feeling low.

I found him sitting a few booths away from the entrance, across from an older man I assumed was his dad. His eyes glanced up and landed on me. And then he gave me one of those smiles. The kind that made everything feel better.

I walked toward him, a moth drawn to a flame.

They both smiled up at me, so much alike, but different at the same time. Knox was like an echo of his father. Same blue eyes, blond hair instead of gray, similar broad shoulders and easy smile.

"Nice to see you again, Larkin," his dad said, seeming to mean it.

Knox nodded, something behind his expression that I couldn't quite read. "Care to sit with us?"

"I'd love to, but I'm just ordering coffee before I get back to work."

Knox moved over. "You can order here as good as anywhere else."

My heart beat quickly as I realized Knox was inviting me to sit by him in this diner booth. And even if I wanted to, it would have been rude to turn him down. So I sat next to him, our arms brushing. My body instantly reacted, like simply touching his arm was the thrill of my lifetime. When would I stop reacting like this to him?

Gray took a sip of his tea, then said, "Knox told me your daughter's interested in horseback riding?"

I nodded, thankful to him for starting the conversation. But I was also hyperaware of Knox next to me, of the view he had of me. What did I look like to him wearing scrubs, my brown hair up in a ponytail, only foundation and mascara for makeup? I tried to bury those self-conscious thoughts as I said, "Every girl I know

Emily's age is obsessed. I think it's something about that age."

Gray nodded. "Any time you want to come out, we'll saddle up the horses and take her for a ride."

"You mean it?" I asked. I was used to people making "someday" promises that they never planned to follow through on.

"Of course. I can't this weekend, but what about next Saturday? Hell, I can have Fletcher and Liv bring over the girls too. I'm sure they'd have tons of fun riding together. We could get some steaks on the grill and make it a day."

My heart warmed. It was exactly what I imagined life would be like if I had a big family all in the same place. "I'd love that. Thank you."

Gray dipped his head in a nod. "Knox here could give you directions to the home place."

"Of course." Knox's low voice hummed through my body.

I gave him a grateful smile, trying not to show how every bit of him captured my attention. Just his voice made butterfly wings tickle my stomach.

But then I remembered my predicament, what brought me to the diner in the first place, and my stomach dropped. "Actually, there was one more favor I've been meaning to ask."

"Anything," Knox replied. I felt the movement of boots under the table, probably Gray adjusting his legs.

I bit my lip, glancing at Gray before turning back to Knox. "Can you watch the kids tonight?"

A thousand emotions flickered over his face before he

settled on a smile and dipped his head in a nod. "I'd love to."

17

KNOX

AS SOON AS Larkin walked her sweet self out of Woody's Diner with a Styrofoam cup of coffee in hand, my dad gave me a look.

"What?" I asked in a hushed voice so no one sitting around us would overhear.

Agatha brought us heaping plates of food, giving Dad a smile that lasted a little longer than the one she gave me.

"Thank you," he said, his voice rough.

She nodded then stepped back, smoothing her shirt. "You two enjoy."

"Sure will," Dad returned.

When she walked away from our table, I gave him a look. "I'm not hearing anything from you, sitting over there and giving Agatha moony eyes."

"Okay, Mary Poppins," he retorted.

I grunted and began eating my burger.

I had to prepare myself mentally to babysit for the

woman I was crushing on while she went on a date with another man.

JUST A FEW HOURS LATER, I heard a knock on my front door and opened it. I wasn't sure what I was expecting when Larkin and her children arrived, but it was not what I saw.

Her brown hair was curled, framing her face, and her beautiful blue eyes stood out with a little more makeup than she usually wore. She'd painted her lips red, the shape perfectly pouty and kissable. But her dress. Fuck, her dress.

It was dark blue, hugging her curves and showing her cleavage, and I wanted nothing more than to take her in my arms, lock the door to my home, and tell Bennett to fuck off for forever and a day.

I was so caught up in admiring her that I almost didn't notice Emily on one side and Jackson chewing on his stroller strap on the other.

I opened my mouth to say something, anything, but no words came out until Emily worked her way between her mom and the doorway, saying, "KNOX!"

I smiled at her. "Hello, Officer Cappes. Jackson." I looked back up at their mom, my throat going dry. "Larkin," I rasped. "You look nice."

"Oh." She seemed half surprised by the comment, looking down at her dress like she'd forgotten the tantalizing outfit she had on. "Thank you." She tipped her head, long hair brushing across her shoulders. "And thank you so much for watching the kids. I would have had to cancel without you."

I fought to keep from kicking myself. To be fair, it was a fight to have a coherent thought at all with her full lips moving around her words.

But I nodded and squared my shoulders. I was a man of my word. So I stepped back to let them through, Larkin's perfume teasing me along the way.

"What are we doing tonight?" Emily asked.

"I actually had a few things I thought we could play with," I said, picking up a cotton tote bag from my table.

"Presents?" she asked, hurrying toward the table.

I sent her a wicked smile. "Pranks."

While Emily clapped, Larkin let out an exasperated chuckle. "You two need to have your own prank show."

I scratched my chin. "What would we call it?"

Emily copied me, tapping her chin, then shrugged. "Probably 'Awesome Pranks'."

"Solid idea," I replied, reaching out my fist.

She bumped it with her own. "I'm gonna go look at your toys!" She zipped off, and I turned just in time to see Larkin bending over to pick up Jackson. The sight of her cleavage almost took my breath away. I forced myself to look away for a moment to gather myself.

She stood back up, and Jackson was babbling away, reaching for me with his pudgy little hands.

"Hey, big guy," I said, reaching for him. I held him against my chest, balancing most of his weight on my forearm. "Look at you chitter-chattering away."

Larkin let out an annoyed breath. "Still no words yet. As his grandparents like to remind me."

I shook my head, giving her an apologetic look. "I

wish people wouldn't put so much pressure on babies. Being an adult's hard enough, and I've had years of practice."

She giggled, the sound warming me from the inside out, and then gestured to the stroller. "I have a change of clothes and some snacks for them in the bag. If you need anything at all from my place, I left it unlocked for you."

I raised my eyebrows.

"I'm not worried." She winked at me. "I have an officer next door."

Oh that wink. The flirty way she lifted one shoulder as she did it. The faith she placed in me. It had me all out of sorts. I barely managed to reply, "Texts every hour?"

"I trust you," she said. As if that weren't enough to get me all in my feels, she drew closer, kissing the top of Jackson's head, then lifting on her tiptoes to place a soft kiss on my cheek.

My eyes closed, and I held my breath as her warm, soft lips pressed against my skin.

It was everything I wanted from her, but not nearly enough at the same time.

She pulled away too soon and gave me a long look before glancing down. "I'm going to say goodbye to Emily and head over to my place. Bennett should be here soon."

His name on her lips hit me like a punch to the gut. It was all wrong. All wrong.

But if she noticed just how out of place it was, she didn't show it. She brushed past me, her perfume dusting over me. I closed my eyes for a moment, settling myself, and then watched from the archway as she bent to give Emily a tight hug in my living room. She whispered something in her daughter's ear then kissed the top of her head.

She gave me a final look and said, "If you need anything, you have my number."

I wished I had more than that.

I wished I had a chance.

18

LARKIN

I PACED my front room while waiting for Bennett to arrive.

I could still feel the ghost of Knox's skin under my lips and regretted more than ever kissing his cheek. It had felt right at the time. That was until I couldn't stop thinking about it. About him despite waiting for a date with another man.

The whole situation struck me as *wrong*.

Seth couldn't so much as call his own children, and yet my next-door neighbor with a heart of gold was more than willing to welcome Emily and Jackson into his home and treat them like precious diamonds. And my children loved him. Looked up to him. Had fun with him like they never did with me. Which meant he was irreplicable, too important to risk an attempt at a relationship.

So I needed this date with Bennett to get Knox off my mind. Especially because he never once insinuated he was interested in me. There were only two ways it could go: I told him how I felt, and he told me he didn't feel the same way, and he'd no doubt want space from me and my unrequited feelings. Or... he did like me. We dated. And he left, just like every other man in my life. As an unrequited crush, he was on a pedestal, and I hated the idea of him ever coming down.

My phone went off with a text, and I walked to where it waited in my purse, sitting on the couch. I took it out, seeing the message on the screen.

Liv: Have fun on your date! Can't wait to hear all about it!

I smiled at the message. It had been a long time since I had a girl friend who wasn't my sister.

Larkin: Thank you! Lunch Monday?

Liv: Would love that! See you then. <3

The bell was broken on the front door, but three knocks announced Bennett's arrival. I took a steadying breath as nerves swept over me. This was just a date. No pressure.

I picked up my purse before walking to the door. When I opened it, he stood with a bouquet of white carnations wrapped in plastic from the store.

He was so big and broad he took up most of my entryway door, but he didn't scare me—more like a big teddy bear kind of guy.

He drew the hat from his head, showing a subtle tan line that proved how much time he spent working outside. "You look gorgeous," he said earnestly, his southern accent strong.

I smiled at him and the flowers. "Thank you. Are those for me?"

He nodded.

"It's been a long time since I've gotten flowers," I

admitted as he handed me the bouquet. I held them gingerly and invited him in while I went to the small kitchen to pour water in a tall glass. I didn't have any vases, or much of anything, really. At first, the sting of sadness took over my senses. I'd worked for eight years to build a life, a home with all the fixings, and then I'd left it all behind. Rebuilding would take time, I reminded myself.

I peeled away the paper, opened the flower feeding packet and poured it in the water. Then I clipped the stems and set the flowers in the glass. I made a point of putting them on the table, adjusting them so they had the best view from the living room. It took a lot to keep my eyes from watering.

Seth only got me flowers after he'd been away on business trips, and looking back, I had to wonder if he'd only done so because he felt guilty.

"Thank you," I breathed to Bennett. He didn't know it, but he was already helping me write over the sad story Seth had written in my life. And all it took was a set of grocery store carnations.

"You're welcome," he said with a grin. "Ready to go?"

I nodded, picking up my purse again and following him out the door. Like I promised to Knox, I left the door unlocked.

Bennett walked me to his truck, which looked like it had been freshly washed. He held the door open for me and even took my hand to help me up the step. He was such a gentleman, but I had to wonder why my body didn't react the same way to his touch as it did to Knox's. Was it just because I'd made Knox off-limits?

I put the thought aside as Bennett walked around the front of the truck and got in on his side. "Any preference on the radio station?" he asked as he put on his seatbelt.

"Whatever you like is fine," I replied.

He twisted the dial, making country music play in the cab, loud enough for me to hear the lyrics but soft enough for us to talk.

"Tell me about yourself," I said to him, fiddling with my hands in my lap. Some part of me missed my wedding ring, if only for something to spin around my finger.

Bennett glanced my way as he drove down the highway and told me all about him. He worked as a welder, doing jobs all around the county. His parents used to own the body shop before Hayes Madigan bought it a few years back and they retired. He had a dog named Boogie and set out food for cats in the neighborhood, but I wasn't supposed to tell anyone that part.

And then he asked about me. Simple questions like where I went to nursing school and how I was liking Cottonwood Falls. The conversation was comfortable, not taking much effort to fill the silence. It was... nice.

By the time we got to the restaurant, I was feeling less nervous than I was before. Conversation flowed easily throughout the meal, talking about easy topics, never dipping below the surface to any difficult topics. He was a perfect gentleman, saying please and thank you to the waitress, and I even glanced at the receipt to see he left a decent tip.

My heart was in all sorts of knots because Bennett was a *good* guy, but I wasn't feeling... anything. What was wrong with me?

Did I only like men who would hurt me? Men I wasn't supposed to have?

We drove back to my place, and he offered to walk me to the front door, but I shook my head. "Thank you for a lovely night, Bennett," I said, putting a hand on his arm.

He nodded like he understood. "Had to shoot my shot," he said with a crooked grin. "Let me open your door at least? It's a ways down."

I smiled, nodded, and waited for him to walk around the truck.

A deep ache, a longing, settled over me as I watched him through the windshield.

He was so nice.

But I had to believe I would feel something when the time was right.

He held the door open for me and took my hand in his, helping me down. I reached up on my tiptoes and kissed his scratchy cheek. "Goodnight, Bennett."

He took off his hat and put it over his chest. "'Night, Ms. Larkin."

I smiled and walked down my sidewalk. I still had half an hour until I was meant to pick up the kids from Knox's, which would give me time to change into more comfortable clothes and sort out my feelings before I came face-to-face with the man who made me feel like my heart was an open book for him to read.

Once inside the house, I looked around to see if Knox and the kids had been over. A glance in the kids' room showed Emily had ransacked almost all her stuffed animals to bring to his place.

I leaned against the door frame, a soft smile on my face. Maybe my kids were the happily ever after I was meant to have. Maybe it wasn't about finding a man to share my life with. Maybe it was about making sure Em and Jackson had a childhood worth remembering.

Pressing off the door frame, I walked to my bedroom to change. It was sparse, with wood floors, a queen-size bed on a basic metal frame, a thrifted nightstand and dresser, then a rocking chair that used to be my mother's, where I rocked Jackson and Emily.

I walked to the window, brushing aside the sheer, light blue curtains. From here, I could see Knox's house. Now I knew it faced his bedroom and the living room. Through the open living room curtains, I could see the three of them, cuddled on the couch, the television's glow lighting their faces. Jackson rested on his chest, and Emily cuddled into his side.

And my heart jerked all over again.

This is what I wanted. Except I wanted to be there in his arms too, not watching from across the way.

I wanted a man to love me. To love my children. To show me fun and pleasure and everything in between. But he was there, and I was here.

I shook my head, letting the curtains fall. Dreams like that were dangerous. But when I pulled open my dresser drawer to get a fresh pair of underwear, I noticed my vibrator tucked amongst silk and cotton.

I bit my lip, thinking of the feel of Knox's cheek under my lips. Of his strong arms, covered with tattoos. Of the way his eyes softened when he spoke of his mother or greeted my children.

And I grabbed the vibrator, knowing with all the emotions swirling in me, this wouldn't take long.

I walked toward my bed, slipping out of my dress, and

flicked on the vibrator, the noise making my heart beat faster.

In a hurry, I lay back on the bed and...

A loud, synthetic fart ripped through the room.

My jaw dropped open as I got up, feeling around for the source of the sound.

Yanking back the covers, I found a whoopee cushion underneath the sheets. My jaw dropped open.

Fucking Knox.

19

KNOX

MY FRONT DOOR CRACKED OPEN, and Larkin's voice called, "It's me."

"In here," I said softly. I didn't want to be too loud since Jackson was asleep on my chest and Emily was asleep on my side. Honestly, I'd needed to pee for the last half hour, but I wasn't messing this up.

She came in, a silk robe wrapped tightly around her curvaceous body. Her cheeks were flushed and her curls slightly mussed.

My stomach fucking dropped.

The thought of Bennett having sex with her made me want to punch a wall and evaporate into thin air, because being in my feelings right now would only lead to destruction. I opened my mouth to speak, but my throat was dry and nothing came out.

But then she held something up, a pink eraser-colored whoopee cushion and I let out an awkward, strangled laugh. Had it gone off while she and Bennett were—best not think about it.

"Knox!" she whispered-yelled as to not wake her children while *Bluey* played on the TV.

"Hold on," I said, carefully easing myself out of my spot. I brought Jackson to the crib in the playroom, feeling Larkin's eyes drilling holes into my back. When I returned, I put a soft throw blanket over Emily where she slept on the couch, brown curls askew around her face.

And okay, maybe I was using the kids to stall, but they were damn cute too. How could you not?

When I finished, Larkin jerked her thumb toward my kitchen then turned to walk away, her silk robe swaying tantalizingly around her ass. In the kitchen, she spun to face me, arms folded tightly across her chest, nipples taut against the matching silk fabric of her nightgown.

Holy shit, she wasn't wearing a bra.

Fuck me. This was so messed up. She'd just been in bed with another man and—I could feel my fists tightening at my sides. I needed to stop thinking about that.

"What's up?" I finally asked her.

She held up the whoopee cushion and smacked it down on the table. "Knox Madigan, what were you doing in my bed?"

I swallowed hard.

"I'm very thankful you watched the children tonight," she continued, and then her chin wobbled, a dozen emotions crossing her face.

"What's wrong?" I asked, confused at the change in direction.

She sniffed, clearing her expression. "I'm sorry. It's just my house is a mess, and I hardly get a full night's sleep with Jackson still waking up in the middle of the night. The last thing I need is you messing around in my bed."

I stepped closer, so close her chest, her tight nipples nearly touched me. I looked down at her, my jaw flexing. With tension. With desire. With everything I wanted to do to her and everything I hoped Bennett hadn't gotten to do.

"Larkin," I said, my voice rough. "Would that be so bad?"

Her eyes flared as she looked up at me, her delectable lips parted. "What are you saying?"

I reached up, cupping her loose and wild mane at the back of her neck. "I'm saying it was fucking torture to watch from this house, seeing him walk down your driveway. I'm saying I died a little inside when I watched him put his hand on your back, helping you into his truck. It was madness to watch you smile through his windshield as you drove away." I gripped the back of her neck tighter, making her darting eyes stay on me. "I'm saying it gutted me to see you come here in your nightgown, face flushed, hair messy, knowing damn well it should have been me making you scream tonight."

"Knox..." she gasped.

But I was a man possessed. Seeing her with him, knowing I could have missed my chance. I was done playing nice. Not when it was Larkin on the line.

I drew my face closer, breathing into her ear. "Tell me you don't feel the same way. Tell me you don't want me to touch you. Taste you. And we'll pretend this never happened. We'll act like you just came over here, got the kids, and went to bed. And we'll never talk of this again."

She shuddered under my breath, her chest arching

until I could feel her hard nipples against my chest, through her nightgown, through the thin cotton of my T-shirt.

Her lips were centimeters from mine when a tired, raspy voice called from the living room.

"Knox?"

20

LARKIN

MY HEART HAMMERED against my rib cage as Knox turned and walked to get my daughter.

What just happened?

I'd been so close to giving in, to feeling what it would be like to have his lips locked with mine. His large hand tangled in my hair still left a tingle at the back of my neck, and my nipples ached against the silken fabric of my pajamas.

I raked my fingers through my hair, trying and failing to dissipate the heat building in my cheeks, in my core. But seeing Knox come into the kitchen with Emily in his arms did just as well as an ice bath would have.

How could I have been so careless to let myself fall into his arms without even a discussion? Shame washed over me. I felt like a terrible mother as Emily curled into his arms, her cheek pressing against his.

"Hey, Mama," she said with sleepy eyes.

"Hey, baby girl," I replied, reaching for her. She easily cuddled into my arms, squeezing me tight. In the back of my mind, I wondered how much longer I would be able to carry her like this. I closed my eyes, breathing in this moment and grounding myself to remember what really mattered.

Knox's voice was soft as he said, "I'll get Jackson and walk you to your place."

I nodded, running my hand over the back of Emily's hair. "Did you have fun with Knox?" I asked.

She moved her head against my cheek. "Did you see the whoopee cushion in your bed?"

I couldn't help but smile to myself. "I sure did."

She giggled maniacally as a sleepy little girl could, and I nuzzled my nose over hers. "Silly girl."

Knox came into the room, Jackson curled against his chest, wrapped in a small blanket. He walked ahead of us, opening the door for Emily and me. On the walk to my place, not a word passed between us as sleeping children rested on our shoulders.

We each went into the kids' bedroom, resting them in their beds. Emily shifted under her covers and said, "Knox, will you sing me a bedtime song?"

I glanced toward Knox, our eyes meeting, holding.

He cleared his throat. "I'd love to, if it's okay with your mom."

I nodded, going to my daughter and kissing her forehead. I didn't know if my heart could take watching. So once she was curled under her blanket, surrounded by her favorite stuffed animals, I stepped outside of the bedroom, standing in the hallway.

Knox's voice was a hum as he asked, "What song do you like?"

"What's your favorite?" she asked.

He was quiet for a long moment, and I had to wonder what was going through his mind as he waited to answer. But then he said, "My mama used to sing me this song when I was your age. Is it okay if I sing it to you?"

"Yes, please," she said with a happy sigh.

I leaned against the wall in the hallway, my eyes already hot with tears. And then he began singing the first lines of an old country song.

From this valley they say you are going, I will miss your bright eyes and sweet smile. For they say you are taking the sunshine, that brightens our pathways awhile.

Come and sit by my side if you love me. Do not hasten to bid me adieu, but remember the Red River Valley, and the cowboy who loved you so true.

A TEAR ROLLED down my cheek as his beautiful voice sang the rest of the song from memory. I imagined little Knox, lying with his mom brushing back his hair, singing this song, not yet knowing she was saying goodbye.

And I listened to it now, knowing what I had to do.

He sang softer toward the end, emotion clear in the tune, and I quietly sniffed, wiping the fresh track of tears from my face.

"Goodnight, sweet girl," Knox said to my daughter. And when she didn't reply, I knew she was sleeping.

He stepped out of the room, and we stood in the hallway. I could sense my bedroom just feet away. Feel the tug of my heart.

I wanted to pull him there. To finish the heated kiss we hadn't yet indulged in, knowing exactly where it would lead. I wanted to believe in love and happily ever afters and that the first man I fell for after the divorce could be the one to never break my heart again.

In the shadows, I saw his throat move with a swallow. His tattoos swirled in dark ink on his arms. And then I looked up into his eyes, pale blue, almost gray in the darkness. It took all the strength I had to say two simple words. "Goodnight, Knox."

He stood still, searching my eyes and finding my answer to his earlier question. His features cleared, removing every hint of emotion. And then he lowered his lips, pressing them against my forehead.

A goodbye kiss.

I held on to his cotton shirt, letting myself feel every moment of warmth, of longing, of passion this man gave me in a simple forehead kiss. And when he pulled back, I released him.

I let him go, knowing he was never meant to be mine.

"Goodnight, Larkin," he uttered. And then he turned, leaving through the front door.

I left it unlocked, some traitorous, selfish part of me hoping, maybe, he would come back.

21

KNOX

DESPITE THE HEAT that stuck around all night in the middle of the Texas summer, a chill swept over me as I walked outside.

I'd taken my chance with Larkin. I'd laid my heart on the line. I'd told her exactly what I hoped we could become. And she'd walked away.

My heart ached from her rejection, from singing my mom's song to Emily, wondering if I would ever be able to sing that song again to her, to my own family, and keep my mom's memory alive.

I knew I couldn't go home. Couldn't see the kitchen where I'd felt her, moments away from giving into me. Couldn't see the couch where I'd sat with the children, dangerously imagining what it would feel like to one day call them my own. To have Larkin sitting on the couch with us. Couldn't walk past the first guest room with the bunk bed Larkin told me Emily would love, where her daughter had read so sweetly to Jackson.

But my dad went to bed early, and Fletcher had a

family of his own to worry about. So I went to see the one guy I knew would be awake. He might not be alone, but damn it, I needed him.

I'd never felt this out of control, not since I was a teenager making every possible mistake. But I was grown now with a job I cared about. I couldn't go down that road again, no matter how tempting it looked with everything I wished for walking away from me.

I got in my truck, firing it up and driving away from our sleepy little street. It took all of a few minutes to get to Hayes's garage. Sometimes he stayed after hours to work on projects when he knew someone really needed their vehicle back quickly.

But the only light on was the security light casting an eerie glow over the large cement parking lot. Heaving a sigh, I continued on my way to his house on the outskirts of town. He lived in a two-bedroom house and kept the guest bedroom filled with extra parts. Not because he didn't have room at the shop but because when you had an extra room, "women got ideas."

Now that I was pulling into his gravel driveway, an extra car parked behind his that I didn't recognize, I wondered why I'd come here at all. Hayes was terrible with women. Or too good, depending on how you looked at it.

But he was here, and judging by the lights on in his front window, he was awake.

So I got out of my truck and walked to the front door, banging on the wooden surface. He didn't reply, so I got out my phone and called him. After a few rings, he picked up, and I heard giggling in the background.

"Is that you outside? I'm kinda busy here."

More giggling.

If I wasn't so upset about Larkin, I might have rolled my eyes. "I need you."

His voice turned serious. "Be right out."

A little of the tension in my chest eased. People could say all they wanted about Hayes, but one thing I knew about him—he'd always be there when I needed him, no matter what.

Within a few minutes, the front door opened, and a woman a few years younger than him stepped outside, wearing a dress and flip-flops. Her hair was messy, and her cheeks flushed as she gave me a sheepish smile. "Officer Madigan."

"Mindy," I replied, tipping my chin.

She walked out to her car, and Hayes, dressed in shorts and nothing else, opened the door the rest of the way. "Come on in, cockblocker."

I gave him a wry smile, following him into the place. His living room was neat as usual, but there was a bottle of wine out on the table and a charcuterie board that had been picked through.

"You must like this one." I gestured toward the table. "Wining and dining her."

He smirked. "I find they have more energy for activities if you feed them first."

Now I did roll my eyes. "You're ridiculous."

With a shrug, he walked to the fridge, showing his back covered in tattoos. "Want a beer?"

I shook my head. The last thing I needed was something clouding my judgement.

He got one out for himself and tossed me a bottle of water. "What's going on?" I caught the bottle, and he walked to his living room, sitting back on the caramel-colored leather couch. He tugged a blanket over his lap and put his feet on the table. "My evening is suddenly free."

My adrenaline was still pounding, emotions already all over the place as I went and sat on his big chair, back straight like I was ready to run, to take off at any time like my body was begging me to do. Run. Escape this pain that was far too strong to be logical.

"I told Larkin how I feel."

Hayes frowned. "It didn't go well? I saw the way she looked at you at the barbecue."

That was enough to surprise me. "What do you mean?"

"For being a human lie detector, you're shit at seeing when someone's into you." He tipped back his beer bottle, taking a drink. The cold of my own water bottle was seeping into my hands. I set it on the floor next to my foot.

"Tell me what you're getting at, Hayes."

He shook his head. "Let's just say if you were a virgin, her eyes would have popped your cherry."

I threw a pillow at him.

He chuckled, setting it behind him and leaning back again. "The point is, she's into you."

"If she was into me, she wouldn't have turned me down," I said. "And I don't know how the fuck I'm going to live next door and see her dating other guys without losing my damn mind." I got up, unable to sit still anymore, and paced his living room in front of his giant TV.

Hayes leaned forward, setting his beer on the coffee

table. "Knox, you see everything as black and white. Just because she's not ready yet for a relationship doesn't mean that she never will be. You gotta give her time. She's fresh out of a divorce, and from what I've heard, it was not pretty. He cheated on her, while she was on bedrest. Lied about it. And then she found out about it when his mistress stopped by the house when she was supposed to meet him at a hotel."

My jaw dropped, and I sat back onto the couch, unable to stand. "How did you know that?"

Hayes shook his head. "How does anyone *not* know something in this damn town. I overheard a couple of my guys talking about it. Sure, it's a rumor, but if it's even halfway true, she's been through it."

I was so stunned I couldn't speak. I just pictured Larkin, the woman I was so quickly falling for, going through that. It made me want to punch her ex and then hold her and make sure nothing bad ever happened to her again.

Hayes said, "People don't take down their walls because someone is nice. Plenty of shitty people look nice at first. If she had a wall a mile high, I wouldn't blame her. The only way to earn the trust of someone who's been burned is to show them who you are, and each action you make will take down that wall, brick by brick."

His words washed over me, and I stared at my brother, shocked. He definitely didn't act like the philosophical one of us. "Where did you come from?" I asked.

He smirked. "Spend enough time with women and you learn a thing or two, whether you want to or not."

I rolled my eyes at him again. "Thanks, Hayes. I needed this."

"Of course. Now get out."

"What?"

He stood up. "Mindy might still be awake for round two."

That was so Hayes. I gave him a half hug, and then went outside, by some miracle, feeling better than I had when I walked in.

I knew what I was going to do.

I was going to prove myself to Larkin, brick by brick.

22

LARKIN

AFTER OVERTHINKING and second-guessing myself for hours, I fell asleep, monitor on my nightstand, blankets pulled tightly around me. But it wasn't Jackson's crying that woke me this morning. It was the sound of water running in the kitchen.

My eyes widened and I jumped out of bed, worried Emily had wandered to the kitchen, trying to cook or make one of her "potions" without me.

But when I rushed in, I found Knox in a spotless kitchen, Jackson on one hip, a dish being rinsed in his other hand.

In fact, every room I could see in this tiny house looked tidier than it had since I'd moved in. Leftover moving boxes were gone, blankets in the living room were carefully thrown over my couch or folded in a basket. Even the floor was clear of crumbs under my bare feet.

I stared in awe at Knox and then caught the time on my microwave. It was past nine, the latest I'd slept in *months*.

"Knox... what... is going on?"

Jackson reached for me, and I took him in my arms, still in shock. Knox handed me a mug full of coffee and said, "I know you said the last thing you needed was more messes to take care of. So I thought I would give you the first thing you needed. A fresh slate."

My eyes felt hot, and I blinked quickly. "But I can't—"

He stepped closer, brushing his calloused hand over my arm. "I don't expect anything in return."

"Then why are you doing this?" I asked. It didn't make sense to me. Seth had taught me that no one did anything unless they wanted something in return.

He looked down, blue eyes on the linoleum kitchen floor, then met my gaze. "I know you're not ready for what I said last night. But I'm not ready to let you go."

That's what he thought? That I simply wasn't ready? The truth was, Seth and I had been over for a long time before the divorce, struggling before I ever knew of his infidelity. "It's not about me," I said. My voice was a whisper as I admitted, "If it was only me, I never could have held back last night."

I was playing with fire, laying my heart on the line in front of him. But I couldn't be the only person holding back here. If he knew my reasons, he could help me maintain the distance my heart was fighting to break down.

"The kids..." he said slowly.

I nodded, looking at Jackson. He was watching us both. "They've lost so much already. They can't lose the one person who's made them happiest since we've moved here." I brushed my hand over Jackson's brown locks and then kissed his forehead.

Jackson opened his mouth, giving me a sloppy kiss on my cheek, and I couldn't help but smile as I held him tight. "I love you too, sweetie. More than anything."

When I met Knox's gaze, there was an understanding there, but something else too that I couldn't quite recognize.

Knox said, "Sit down. I'll make you breakfast."

"But..."

"Just once. Let someone take care of you."

My eyes watered as I nodded and went to the small table off the kitchen.

He'd come back. And he hadn't given me what I thought I wanted. He'd given me exactly what I needed.

Emily woke up soon after, and we were all eating the breakfast Knox made—pancakes with bacon and eggs—when I heard a knock at the door. I was about to get up to answer it, but Knox said, "I'll answer it. You finish your breakfast."

I smiled as I watched him retreat to the door. He had no right to have such a good heart and look so damn good in jeans and a T-shirt. And I had no right to think about him that way when I was fighting to keep my distance. But Knox Madigan was impossible to ignore.

But then he pulled the door back, and I heard a familiar voice say, "Knox, what are you doing here?"

"Seth?" I asked.

Emily screamed, "DADDY!"

23

KNOX

SETH CAPPES KNELT on the front porch, taking his daughter into his arms like he hadn't been ignoring her for the month since Larkin moved to town. And even though he had the most precious child in his embrace, his eyes were on me, like he was trying to send me a message. Like he was staking a claim.

I glanced back to Larkin to see how she was reacting, and her lips were parted in shock, hand holding on to a screeching Jackson. He wanted something but couldn't communicate it. Or maybe he was upset by all the emotions flying around the room.

Readjusting her grip, Larkin walked toward me, standing beside me at the door to see Seth as he stood up, holding Emily on his hip.

"Daddy, where have you been?" she asked, a scolding tone to her voice.

Seth said, "I've been busy with work, Em," his eyes still moving between Larkin and me. "I guess your mommy's been busy too."

My hands curled into fists at my side. This sorry excuse of a man had no business making comments like that about the woman carrying the weight of his poor decisions.

Larkin's voice cut through the red fog of my silent outrage. "Seth, what are you doing here?" There was a shaking tone, like she was somewhere between worried and angry. Her expression pinched uncomfortably, and Jackson continued wailing.

Seth's lips were in a smug smirk. "Are you going to let me in to see my children?"

I waited for Larkin to nod before stepping out of the way. Suddenly, her cozy living room, which I'd spent hours cleaning overnight, felt too small for the three of us. There wasn't enough oxygen to sustain all of us in this small, tense space.

Once Seth was inside, the screen door shut behind him, and he set Emily down. "Give me my big boy," he said, outstretching his arms for Jackson.

Jackson scrambled away from him, clawing up his mom's chest and squeezing his arms around her neck as he wordlessly screeched.

Seth's lips twitched as he shot Larkin an accusatory look. "What have you been telling him about me?"

Larkin stared at him incredulously. "Outside. Now." Her voice was a deadly growl. Her voice softened only slightly as she turned to me. "Knox, hold Jackson please?"

I nodded, and she passed him to me. He barely let go of her before holding on to me for dear life. I could feel his little heart racing against my chest.

"It's okay, buddy," I murmured, my lips against his head.

Seth's pale face was turning redder by the moment, a vein popping in his forehead.

Emily screamed, "Daddy, don't go!"

But Larkin stood firm, her shoulders square against all the chaos. She knelt in front of Emily, calmly saying, "Your daddy and I need to talk." She turned her gaze to him. "Now."

He looked like he didn't want to move, but one glare from me, and he followed her out the front door. It slammed behind him.

Emily ran to the door, yanking on it, but I reached for her, scooping her up so I held both the kids in my arms. She cried against my shoulder. "I want to see him. I want to see him." It was like the real Emily wasn't there anymore, caught in some primal place where she knew the man who made her, the man who should love her and protect her, was outside.

"I know, honey," I soothed, walking them both away from the front door. "Why don't you go to your bedroom and pick some of your favorite toys to show your daddy?" My heart ached as I said it, because I truly didn't know if he would even be back inside with the angry looks he and Larkin had exchanged.

She seemed conflicted, but finally nodded in agreement, running back toward her bedroom. As soon as she was gone, I set Jackson in his playpen and turned on the TV. I wasn't sure how this was going to turn out, but I damn sure wasn't making Larkin go through it alone.

24

LARKIN

I WALKED off the front porch and onto the sidewalk, ready to explode at Seth for showing up without notice after weeks of completely ignoring his children and me. His expression looked just as angry as I felt, red with a vein popping on his forehead.

"Why is Jackson acting like I'm some kind of monster?" he demanded, arms gesticulating his anger.

I must have been acclimating to small town life, because I could only imagine the rumors that would start about us if Mrs. Halstead next door saw him acting this way. But I lifted my chin, unwilling to back down. Let everyone know what a piece of crap he'd been.

"I don't know," I replied. "Maybe because he's barely a year old and hasn't seen you in over a month?! Where the hell have you been, Seth?" I folded my arms across my chest to keep my angry heart from pounding right out of my ribcage.

He raked his fingers roughly through his short brown hair and paced away from me. "I've been trying to come to grips with the fact that we're divorced, Larkin! The woman I married isn't in my house anymore. Our mutual friends are asking where you've been, and I keep making up excuses to explain your absence. My mom's pissed at me that I didn't try harder to make it work after my slip up."

"Slip up?" I asked, genuinely stunned. "Is that what you're calling an affair that went on for God knows how long while I was on bedrest, worried I'd lose our unborn baby while caring for our other child?"

He looked down at the ground, pain in his gaze. "I don't want to go back over the past, Larkin. I came here because I want to get you back. I want our family back."

My mouth gaped open. "You can't be serious. A month of silence, now this? What changed?" My mind raced through the possibilities, and then it hit me. "Oh my gosh," I breathed, shaking my head at him. "You heard about my date with Bennett, didn't you?"

He wouldn't quite meet my eyes.

"You heard I was moving on with my life, and like a crab in a boiling pot of water, you wanted to bring me down with you," I accused.

"No!" he argued, coming closer and taking my hands in his. "The reality of our situation, of what I was about to lose, hit me, and I knew I couldn't live with myself if I didn't at least try to repair us. Think of our children, Larkin. They don't deserve to grow up in a broken home."

I pulled my hands away from him, eyes stinging. How cruel could he be? "No, they don't deserve that. But they don't deserve to see a mom who settles for a husband who sleeps around, doesn't make it a priority to come home at regular times, and who doesn't give their mom a chance to have a life outside of being a wife and mother." I shook my head, tears sliding down my cheeks. "I gave so much of my life to you. I gave up friendships, my career, my body to have children, and you hurt me in the worst way you possibly could."

He gritted his teeth. "And what about you? You refused to touch me, to let me touch you. And even after the pregnancy, you let yourself go. You weren't the woman I married."

His words cut at me, dug at that insecure part of me that wondered if it had been my fault that he needed to go outside of our marriage to get what he wanted. But I lifted my chin and stared him down. I wasn't the meek housewife I'd made myself be throughout our marriage.

I was a grown-ass woman who was already well into the process of rebuilding my life from the ground up. "Seth, you are entitled to see your children three evenings a week and take them for one weekend a month, as stated in our custody agreement. All I ask is that we plan it ahead of time so I can prepare them as to when you will or won't show up."

His jaw twitched. He hated this, when I took all the air out of his angry sails. He wanted to yell and fight and get me to back down so he could win.

He tried a new tactic to get me riled up. "Why am I hearing from someone, other than you, that you're bringing strange men around my children?"

Maybe I didn't care about Seth, but I cared about my reputation as a mother. Why were people running their mouths about me to Seth? I wiped a bead of sweat from my forehead. "There have been no 'strange men' around our children."

He raised his eyebrows and jerked his hairy fucking thumb over his shoulder toward the house. "Oh yeah. You're on a date with fat-ass Bennett last night, and this morning you have Knox in the house with our kids? He was a goddamn criminal in high school. And now he's one with a gun."

I fought to school my expression because I didn't know that about Knox. "Your mother herself said he's a local hero, Seth. And if he's *so* dangerous, why did you leave him alone in my house with our kids? Huh?"

He glared at me, brown eyes almost slits. "Because you wanted to waste my time talking to me."

I shook my head at him. "You know what I think?" I stepped closer, nose to fucking nose. "I think you're jealous. You thought when you cast me aside that you would ride off on your high horse while I lived in squalor wishing I had you back. But you want to know something? Leaving you was the best thing I ever did. It showed me that I poured so much into a relationship with a man who would *never* do the same. It showed our children *exactly* the kind of coward you are. And Knox?" I lifted my chin, knowing I could land the final blow without raising a finger. "He's shown them, and me, what a real man looks like."

"You're a fucking bitch, and you'll never be anything more than a fat waste of fucking space," he growled.

My jaw shook at his words. He'd never dipped so low before, not even in our worst fights. I opened my mouth to reply, but before I could, I heard the door open.

I turned to see Knox shut the door behind him and

stride across the sidewalk, closing the gap. He put me behind him, standing chest to chest with Seth. He was a good four inches taller, and even though Seth hit the gym, Knox had the kind of muscles that matched the deadly look in his eyes.

"What did you say to her?" He glowered down at Seth, daring him to utter those words while keeping me safely behind him.

In Knox's cocoon, I felt safe, protected, precious.

"You clearly heard me," Seth uttered, staring up at Knox, but I could see what little mettle he had fading quickly.

Knox said, "You have two incredible children. You had a woman who's worth the heavens and every ounce of the earth. What you did to deserve them in the first place, I'll never know. But you have two choices. You apologize to Larkin right fucking now, then go inside and treat your babies like they deserve. Or you walk away and don't come back until you can."

Seth's jaw worked, and then he spat, a thick hot glob of saliva landing on the cragged sidewalk just inches away from Knox's shoe.

Knox didn't so much as flinch. He reached back for me, and I took his hand, standing in his strength. In his comfort.

And then Seth turned and stormed away, getting into his car, slamming the door, and peeling away.

My pulse echoed loudly in my ears for three long beats before Knox turned and took me into his arms. I wanted to sob, to fall apart, to give into all the insecure, painful feelings threatening to pull me under. But I had two children I needed to be strong for.

I turned to face the windows, still in the safety of his arms, knowing my babies were inside. "I need to talk to them."

Knox pressed his lips to my head, in a gesture so comforting my eyes burned with unshed tears. "I'm not going anywhere."

I turned and looked up at him. "Thank you," I breathed.

I didn't know what this meant for him, but I knew I didn't want to let him go.

25

KNOX

"SHE'S LOOKING OUT HERE," Larkin said.

I turned my gaze, still holding Larkin in my arms, to find Emily peeking through the window, her eyes wide as the Texas sky.

"I need to go to her," she said.

I nodded. "I'll come with you."

She shook her head. "I need to do this on my own. I'd hate if the kids took their anger out on you. They can take it out on me." She glanced toward the empty spot where Seth's car used to be, and a tear slipped down her cheek. "It's my fault."

"Larkin." I took her face in my hands.

"No," she cut me off, stepping back. "I should have stayed calm, appeased him so the kids could see him. Now I have a heartbroken daughter inside, who doesn't understand why her daddy was here one day and gone the next." She looked so distraught, wrapping her arms around herself like she always did when she was close to falling apart.

My stomach sank, for Larkin, for Emily, for Jackson, who could surely sense the tension but wouldn't know why everyone was so upset. "Listen," I said to her, drawing her close and holding her. Her back was stiff, but in seconds, she melted into my embrace. "You're the best mom I know. You love your kids with all you have. They'll feel that too, even if they're upset."

She looked up at me, her chin resting on my chest. "How do you know?"

"I was raised by a single parent who had to handle all my big feelings. I know."

She blinked, sending more tears down her cheeks, but stepped back and wiped them away. "Can I see you tonight?"

I smiled gently, brushing back a tear with my thumb. "Your porch or mine?"

She let out a tearful laugh. "Let's try mine this time." Then she turned and walked back down the sidewalk toward the house, where Emily watched through the front window. I waved at her, and she lifted her hand, returning a small wave. But as soon as her mom walked back into the house, the curtains closed again.

I stood on the sidewalk, feeling torn. I wanted to be there for them, but this closed door was just a reminder of the wall Larkin had built around her heart. And seeing how Seth treated her, I knew he'd laid every brick.

My phone rang, drawing me out of my thoughts. I pulled it from my pocket, seeing the police station's number.

When I answered, they told me the guy who usually worked on Saturdays had called in sick and wanted to see if I'd cover his shift. With nothing to get my mind off Larkin and nothing to do in my own home, I said okay.

⚘

I THOUGHT about Larkin and her kids all throughout my shift, until I was nearing the end. I was driving along the city streets, making sure everything was safe, when I saw a truck rocking with fogged up windows.

I let out a sigh and shook my head at them as I pulled up behind the vehicle. Probably a pair of teenagers who didn't have the brains—or the patience—to find a private country road. Grabbing my flashlight, I got out of my car, noticing the truck had stopped rocking.

Thank goodness. Hopefully they were decent.

I walked up to the truck, wondering how on earth they got windows to fog in eighty-degree weather, and tapped on the glass. Within a few seconds, the window rolled down, and I stepped back in shock.

These sure as shit weren't teenagers.

"Tyler?" I said. "Henrietta?"

His hair was messed up, shirt crumpled. At least his jeans were on and he was covered up. Next to him, Henrietta's chest moved with rapid breaths, and she looked like she wanted to disappear into the floorboards.

"What the hell are you two doing here?" I asked. "You have a house!"

Tyler gave me a guilty shrug. "Sometimes you have to mix it up. Keeps your marriage fresh."

I held up my hand, trying not to laugh. I felt like a parent who'd caught their toddler doing something bad yet hilarious but didn't want to encourage them. "I'll let you off with a warning this time, but next time I'll ticket you for public indecency."

Tyler and Henrietta exchanged a look.

"Just get out of here," I said, making a shooing motion like they were a couple noisy alley cats going at it.

Tyler started to argue, but from the passenger seat, Henrietta said, "We will! Thank you, Knox."

"I'm on the clock. It's Officer Madigan." I shook my head at them and took a couple steps away. Then I walked back and saw the window was still open.

Tyler said, "Yes, *Officer Madigan?*"

I gave him a stern look. "This is your friend Knox speaking now." I flicked off my flashlight and tucked it in my pocket, keeping a serious expression.

"Yeah?" Tyler swallowed.

I held out my fist. "Good for you."

While Tyler fist-bumped me, Henrietta groaned. Chuckling, I walked back to my car and didn't leave the spot until they drove away.

The looks on their faces had me sporadically bursting into laughter the rest of my shift, but the closer it got to quitting time, the more I thought about Larkin and what I wanted to say to her. I just knew, deep in my soul, there was something more than a crush between us. I was falling for her. And I wanted to do whatever I could to make her smile, to make her laugh.

So on my way home, I made a few calls. And then I walked to her front porch, where she was already sitting under the light's glow.

26

LARKIN

I SAT on my front porch after the kids had gone to bed. It had been a hard morning with them.

Regardless of what society thought or all the reasons I needed to get him out of my head, I couldn't stop thinking about Knox.

Couldn't stop wishing that we could be together.

That it wouldn't break my children's hearts to lose him if things went south.

His headlights panned over the street and then his driveway as he got home from work, and he got out of his cop car, looking sexy as hell in his uniform. The black material hugged his strong biceps, and something about knowing he could protect me, would protect me when the chips were down, made my heart beat faster.

He caught my gaze and started walking my way. "Hey," he said with a gentleness that belied the brute force of his body.

"Hey." My voice was weak. Maybe all of me was weak when it came to him. Or maybe I'd used all my strength standing up to Seth today. Saying the words that were true and holding back even worse things I could have said to him.

He sat beside me on the front steps and glanced to the monitor where my sleeping children lay in black and white. With the volume up, you could hear the soft sounds of their noise machine playing peaceful lullaby music.

"How did they do today?" he asked.

My heart fell for him even more. Because with all the stuff going on between us, he put my babies first.

"It was a rough day for Emily," I said. "All the feelings, all the behaviors. She kept asking to talk to Seth. I called him for her, and of course he didn't answer."

Knox let out a low swear.

"I know. And Jackson feeds off Emily so much that he was a Velcro baby all morning. But after they napped, I took them swimming, and I think that helped take their minds off things. And it tired them out, so they went down pretty quickly tonight."

He reached out, touching my hand where it rested on my knee. It sent warmth flowing from the point of contact. "And how are you?"

How was I? I hadn't even thought to ask myself that question today, knowing I needed to be strong for my children. But here Knox was, looking out for me when I had never asked him to. It took a second for me to feel my feelings and articulate them. "I'm hurt, disappointed. Seth and I didn't have a perfect marriage, but I never envisioned it spinning out like this. I feel guilty, like our problems are keeping my kids from their father. Being a mom is... It's my most important job, and I feel like I'm failing."

"No," Knox said firmly. "You set a boundary that needed to be set. Behave respectfully and he's welcome over. Your kids don't need to hear their dad badmouthing their mom or the other way around."

He saw me through the best possible lens. When all I could find was my dirt, he saw the gold, and it made me feel so much better in a way I couldn't put to words. "I made brownies for you," I told him. "I wanted to thank you for—well, everything. And I wanted to talk to you about…"

"Everything?" he said with a lopsided smile.

"Yeah, that," I replied. "The brownies are inside."

"Let me change, and I'll come over?"

I nodded, taking a breath to steel myself. While he walked back to his place, I stepped inside, propping the front door open to let in a breeze. Utilities were no joke in the summertime.

While I waited for him, I couldn't just sit still. Especially knowing the type of conversation we were about to have. It felt like one of those moments that would change everything. So I made myself busy, getting out plates for the brownies and trying to dish them up special like he had the other day.

I'd paid so much attention to him then, I knew each step, starting with microwaving the brownies. I had to fumble through my cabinets for chocolate syrup but realized that I'd used it all making chocolate milk for Em earlier. Luckily, I kept extra on the top shelf. My fingertips brushed the bottles, and I stretched a bit taller, wondering if I could wiggle it out without getting a chair. I wanted the brownie to be heated and topped with chocolate for Knox when he was done changing and came inside.

But then I felt a warm chest behind me and his arm brush over mine as he easily grabbed the bottle. My heart hammered forcefully as I turned to see him so close to me, heated blue eyes on mine. "Is this what you were reaching for?" he asked, his voice husky.

I swallowed. Nodded. "For the brownies."

He handed it to me, still standing close, and I could feel the heat rolling from him, the fresh cologne. I forced myself to swallow, but my voice was still breathy as I said, "Thank you."

With a nod, he stepped away, reaching for the microwave door to stop the beeping I hadn't even noticed until this moment.

He took the bowls with the brownies out then used the ice cream scoop to dish us both a serving. We worked together silently, a charge humming between us. Once we were at my table, our bowls in front of us, I took a deep breath.

He looked at me, then took a bite. His eyes closed. "So good."

I smiled. My mom would have liked Knox, would have loved knowing that her brownies were bringing us together. I took a small spoonful of my brownie and ice cream and took a bite. Then I set my spoon down, knowing I couldn't eat anymore without knowing where we stood, what was coming next.

"About earlier," I said.

He looked up, searching my expression.

"I..." I glanced down at my lap, fiddling with my nails. "I like you." It was three words. Simple. But powerful enough to change everything.

When I met his gaze again, he didn't look as if he

pitied me or was uncomfortable like I half expected. Instead, a slight smile ghosted along his lips. "I like you too."

Butterflies danced inside my stomach. "But Emily likes you too."

Now his eyebrows drew together. "That's good, right?"

I nodded. "But she can't lose another man in her life because of me." My lips trembled as I held back tears. I hated what my daughter was going through right now. Hated that I had a part in creating this terrible situation.

Knox reached across the table, extending his hand for mine. When I accepted the offer, he covered my hand with his. "Larkin, I don't know what will happen for us. But I want to figure it out with you resting in the fact that I'm not going anywhere when it comes to your kids. I'll be here for them no matter what happens to us."

"You say that now, but..." I had to swallow the stinging lump in my throat. "I've seen how people can change."

He shook his head, resolute. "I lost an adult when I was young, and it wrecked me. I'd never put a kid through that, not if I had a choice."

Every intonation in his voice, every feature on his face confirmed he meant what he was saying. And it made me wonder about what Seth had mentioned earlier. "Seth said..."

"What?" Knox asked, eyes narrowed like he was already poised to defend me.

"He said you got into a lot of trouble. That you were a criminal."

Knox leaned back, taking a long sip of tea. The

movement of his throat was hypnotizing. His large hand on the plastic cup, the chunk of ice against the cup as he set it down. Finally, Knox uttered, "He's not wrong."

I raised my eyebrows. That statement was so at odds with the man I knew. "You? In trouble?" There was only one way I could see this kindhearted man ever doing anything wrong. "A prank went a little too far, right, not anything serious?"

His expression was grim as he shook his head. "It was serious. So serious I got sent to juvenile detention. I was lucky not to be tried as an adult and sent to jail."

Shock parted my lips. "What?"

An invisible heaviness settled over him. "After my mom died, I was *mad*. An angry kid. My dad did his best to be there for us, but he had five kids to care for on top of grief from losing his wife. Fletcher was the perfect one, always getting good grades. Ford threw himself into sports, spending every spare second training or practicing. Hayes just fought all the time, butted heads with Dad, and Bryce was too young to really understand. But me? I wanted *everyone* to feel as badly as I did."

I covered the ache in my chest with my hand. I knew what it felt like to lose a parent, and it was hard as an adult. Inconceivable to go through as a child.

"I fought my dad, fought my brothers, fought my classmates. I tore shit up for the sake of seeing it break. And one day, when I'd had enough, I got behind the wheel of my truck."

I held my breath, already knowing what was coming next.

"There was this teacher who couldn't handle me and my behavior. He said something shitty about my mom getting off lucky and my dad having the short end of the deal for having to stick around and deal with me. So I went to his place, put a brick on the gas pedal, and drove it into his shop."

"Knox..." I breathed, imagining how horrible he must have felt. How bad the fallout must have been for him.

"The engine exploded, and he had gas cans, stain, flammable stuff stored inside. The whole thing went up in flames. No one got hurt; I made sure not to do it when he was home," he said. "But the teacher told the cops I'd threatened to hurt him because I told him he'd regret what he said to me. So they suggested I go to juvenile detention. And my dad couldn't fight it. He didn't know what to do with me anymore. He just let me go. I was there for six months, and I saw two things: I saw the kids on the same path as me. And I saw the cops doing what they could to help us. One of them especially invested in me. Said I reminded him of his younger self, and he told me once I did the work to clear my record, there was a future for me being on the right side of the law. For once, I wasn't angry at the past. I was thinking of the future."

He watched me like he was waiting for me to run away. But I didn't want to. I wanted to hug angry teenage Knox because I knew better than anyone that what he needed most of all back then was for someone to love him and never leave. I promised myself again that I would be there for my kids, no matter what challenges we came across.

I reached out this time and settled my hand on his forearm. "Thank you for telling me."

He nodded.

For a moment, we were silent, all our truths hanging between us.

He broke the silence, saying, "I understand if you don't want someone with my past around your kids. I should have told you sooner. I'm sorry."

I shook my head. "I hope my kids will become as honest and caring as you are when they grow up."

He let out a soft breath, an amazed smile on his lips. "So where does that leave us? I know you're worried and that we've only known each other a little while, but I care about you. I want to give us a shot."

Just the idea of an "us" had nervous, excited bubbles fizzing inside me. But I was scared too. Because dating me wasn't like dating a single, childfree woman my age. "You know, it's not just me. It's my kids too. We're a package deal."

His lips slid into an easy smile. "Which is why I got us four tickets for the Dallas Diamonds game tomorrow. Right in the front row."

I gawked at him, something in my brain not registering. "What?"

He grinned even bigger. "Since you're all such big fans of my brother, I want to take you to a game. If you can take Monday off, Ford offered for us to stay the night at his house. There's plenty of extra bedrooms, and he even has a trampoline room I'd love to show Emily."

Now my eyes were stinging. "Knox Madigan, you're too good to us."

He shook his head, pressing out of the chair, and drew me to his chest. We stood by my table, hugging, and it felt so warm and safe to be cocooned in his arms. But there was a heat too, feeling the strength of his torso, the muscles of his chest against my cheek.

All my emotions I'd been holding back for him came bubbling to the surface, and I tilted my head up to look at him. Our gazes held, and slowly, he lowered his lips to mine. What started slow quickly turned into an unstoppable kiss. I kissed him desperately, wanting to taste all of him, and he met every move of mine with one of his own.

It wasn't fireworks.

It was a flame, consuming every one of my senses. My core burned with heat; my nipples ached with desire. I wanted him to take me to the bedroom and make me forget about this day, make me forget about everything except for him. I broke from the kiss long enough to say, "Knox... I need you."

He stilled, and my heart immediately fell.

A horrified expression took over my face, and I stepped back. "I'm sorry," I whispered, eyes darting about the room. I covered my mouth with my hands. "Oh my gosh. I'm sorry. I know it's too soon. I shouldn't have—"

He stepped closer, silencing me with his hand over my tender lips. "Stop," he said.

I looked up at him, searching for an answer. Had I ruined everything by moving too fast?

He let his hand go from my mouth, bringing his arms around me so my body was flush to his. So I could feel his hard length pressing against me.

"You feel that?" he asked, speaking into my ear, his voice rough.

I felt every inch of his arousal, intensifying every bit of my own. I nodded, lips parted.

"I want you so fucking much." He ground his hips against me like he too was desperate for some form of release. "But not like this."

My eyes fell, but he put the crook of his index finger under my chin, forcing my attention. "When this finally happens, your ex will be the furthest thing from your mind. All you'll be thinking of is me and how good I make you feel."

My throat felt dry as I swallowed, and I stepped back, nodding. Trying to gather my senses. But Knox Madigan was hard to ignore, towering in my kitchen, hard cock pressing against his jeans.

"I should probably take some time to... cool down," he said.

I nodded. "I should get ready for our trip." I swallowed. "Em will be so excited to watch a game in person."

His lips lifted into a gentle smile, and then he gave me another kiss, chaste, like even he, with his steel willpower, couldn't handle fanning the flames. "Goodnight, Larkin."

I breathlessly told him the same and watched as he walked away from my house, imagining what it would be like when he fulfilled his promise.

I FINISHED STRAPPING the car seats into the back seat of my truck and then turned around to see Larkin holding Jackson on her hip and finishing up a game of Simon Says with Emily, who was jumping on one leg. It was one of those beautiful summer mornings where golden sunshine was dripping through the trees and the breeze was just cool enough to cut the heat.

"All done," I said to them.

Emily put her leg down and then pumped her fist. "I winned!"

I chuckled, thinking it was just a minor detail that she was the only one playing the game.

"Ready to go?" I asked them.

Emily tugged at her mom's purple T-shirt and said, "Can we give Knox his shirt?"

The embarrassed smile on Larkin's lips piqued my interest even further. "What shirt?" I asked.

Larkin reached into her diaper bag, taking out a purple shirt with white lettering. On the front, it said GO

#9 with a football instead of an *O* and a diamond inside of the nine.

"That's so cool!" I said, reaching for it. "Did you make this?"

Larkin nodded. "I got out my Cricut last night and played around so I could surprise Em with a shirt. But she insisted I add something to the back of your shirt. For a prank."

My eyebrows drew together, and Emily giggled while I turned the shirt around. On the back, in small white letters, it said, CALL ME STEVE.

"My name's not Steve," I said.

Emily nearly fell over from laughing so hard. Her giggles were so contagious, Larkin and I had to laugh along and Jackson joined in too. I made to put it over the Diamonds T-shirt I was already wearing, but Larkin said, "You don't have to wear it if you don't want to."

"Oh, trust me, I do," I said, pulling it on the rest of the way. Emily laughed so hard she couldn't breathe. "Come on, squirt," I said, hauling her over my shoulder. "Time to get in the truck."

"Okay, *Steve*." She giggled all the while as I put her in the car seat.

Across the truck, Larkin tried to buckle in Jackson, but he wasn't having it. He was stiff as a board and grunting at her. I knew a lot of people might wrestle him in, but instead, she started singing a song to the tune of "Happy" by Pharrell Williams.

BECAUSE I'M BUCKLED,
Buckle in if you feel like a kid who's extra safe.

Buckle in if you feel like you're following the law.
Buckle in if you know that buckling is the best.
Buckle in if you're up for a safe and fun trip.
Because I'm buckled.

JACKSON FOUGHT at first but was captivated by her singing, eventually easing into his seat and giggling as she tickled his little belly. Emily must have caught the smile on my lips because she said, "Mama sings that song *all* the time."

I smiled down at her, adjusting the chest clip so it rested right over her sternum. "Your mama's the best."

Emily nodded like she agreed, and then I snuck a smile at Larkin, who was smiling back at us across the car. "Ready to go?" she asked.

I nodded. "Let's hit the road, Jack."

Emily said, "Her name's Larkin, not Jack."

Laughing, Larkin got in and explained that it was a song. And we played it as we started our way out of town. Something about this trip felt special, like it really was the beginning of a tradition. And maybe even a family.

28

LARKIN

WE WERE SOMEWHERE between Cottonwood Falls and Dallas when Knox reached across the center console and held his hand palm up for me to hold.

Butterflies danced in my stomach at the sight of his hand, at the invitation. At what it meant. And warmth spread through me as I slipped my hand into his, memorizing every bit of our contact, from his calloused skin to the way his hand enveloped mine, the way he wasn't a lazy hand-holder, but actually squeezed my hand like he was grateful for the moment and didn't want to let me go.

I realized I was staring at our intertwined fingers, his tanned, tattooed skin contrasting with my pale and freckled complexion. Then I glanced up to see him looking at the road, a smile on his lips.

Both the kids had fallen asleep, and their soft snores blended with the music playing low on the radio.

I wished I could talk to the old me, in the midst of a divorce, thinking that all men would leave, that men viewed love as a game, and tell her that she'd soon be feeling butterflies in her stomach at simply holding hands with a man.

A good man.

"Tell me about Ford," I said. "We didn't get to talk much at your party. What's he really like?"

Knox let out a quiet chuckle. "He's a shit."

I had to laugh at that too. "Details?"

"He's a terrible liar. Every time he tries, he can't make eye contact, and when you call him on it, he instantly starts smiling. Usually he was just lying about whether or not chores were done, stuff like that. Or when he tried to get Fletcher and me in trouble when we were little kids, you know, usual younger sibling stuff."

I nodded, missing my big sister so much. I couldn't wait to tell her about this trip with Knox.

"He was a really hard worker too," Knox said. "Always stayed late after sports practice to work on a new skill. He could have been the best one on the team and he still stayed after everyone else, trying to get just a little bit better."

"It sounds like you admire him," I commented.

"I do." He glanced my way a moment, gifting me with one of his small smiles. "I guess part of me wishes I could have dealt with things the way he had. I like my life now, but I wish it wasn't as hard to get here, you know?"

I totally understood. "My dad left my mom when I was too young to remember. I know it's not the same as what you went through, but in my teenage years, I was adamant that I wouldn't date until I was old enough to make good decisions with men. In high school, I thought that meant college. But then I told myself I wouldn't date until I graduated nursing school so I'd have time to invest in the *right* guy." I shook my head at my youthful naivete. If only I'd known then what I knew now. "Sometimes I wonder if I'd had more experience dating, would I have noticed Seth's red flags?"

He squeezed my hand comfortingly. "Don't blame yourself for anyone else's bad behavior, okay?"

My chest tightened, fighting against the words. Wasn't it my job to know better?

As if he could hear my thoughts, he reminded me, "Seth is a grown man. He made his choices, not you."

I nodded. But as Knox shifted in his seat, I could tell there was a question on the tip of his tongue.

"Ask me," I said.

He checked the rearview mirror to make sure the kids were still asleep, and then his voice was low, rough. "Was Seth your first?"

I could barely hear my own voice as I said, "He was."

I could see all his suppressed emotions as his eyelids shuddered.

"And Bennett?" he asked.

"Nothing happened," I admitted.

Then he smiled. "Good." His gaze intensified as he pinned it on me, just long enough to make my heart beat faster. "I'm going to show you how a man should treat a woman. In every sense of the word."

My lips parted and my thighs clenched. Every part of me was looking forward to him keeping that promise.

Traffic grew heavier the closer we got to Dallas, and he had to put two hands on the wheel to navigate the zipping and weaving drivers. He followed the directions playing on the truck screen until we reached the parking garage right next to the stadium.

"Knox, it must cost a fortune to park here," I said. I'd only been to a game once before, and even parking a mile away had cost twenty dollars. "I don't mind walking."

He smirked. "Don't worry. I know a guy."

I rolled my eyes at the joke and wondered why I hadn't thought of that. He carefully pulled the truck into a spot, using the palm of his hand to spin the wheel. Something was so damn sexy about that; I had to pry my eyes away so he wouldn't catch me staring.

Once he turned off the truck, we got out to wake the kids, and they were in a good mood, excited to watch the game.

We walked with all the people heading toward the stadium, but Knox took us to a private elevator toward the back where an attendant sat on a small black stool.

"This is fan-cy," Emily said, staring around at the mirrored elevator with elaborate purple and gold tapestry and marble floors.

The attendant chuckled, her dark skin crinkling around her eyes. "Your first game, honey?"

Emily nodded.

The woman reached into a bag behind her and pulled out a small purple football with the Diamonds logo on it and held it out.

"Can I have it?" Emily asked.

"Of course, sugar," the woman said, then she glanced at Knox. "Which suite?"

"Marquise," Knox answered.

And if Emily thought the elevator was fancy, the suite made it look like a dump in comparison.

The room held about twenty people, all famous or relatives of the players. There was a bar with two bartenders on staff, an entire buffet of game day snacks, multiple TV screens showing the game, and then a giant windowed view of the entire field.

"Oh my goodness!" Emily jumped up and down in place as we took in the room, and then she sprinted through the short row of seats up to the window. Knox followed her while I walked in holding Jackson, and the pair of them looked over the field. I could see Knox pointing to show her different parts of the stadium.

After how low she'd been with Seth leaving her in the lurch, my heart warmed seeing Knox treat her like a precious gem... like a diamond.

Jackson squirmed in my arms, so I got him some soft food from the buffet, and we went to sit beside Knox and Emily while Jackson took food in his fists and shoved it into his mouth.

Soon, the game began, and we were swept up in the excitement of the day. Yelling encouragement for the players, groaning at mistakes, and arguing with the refs, who had no chance at hearing us.

But then, during a time-out, the camera panned the audience, showing couples for the kiss cam on the jumbo screen.

And then the cameras landed on us.

And the chanting started. "KISS HER. KISS HER!"

My heart sped up, and my cheeks flushed, and with tens of thousands of people staring at me, I wished I could disappear into the floor. I turned toward Knox. "You really don't have to," I told him. After last night, I wasn't sure he was ready for this again—if it was too soon.

His gaze was on me, all blue eyes and full lips and heat that had no place burning in a public space.

"I'm not ashamed to show fifty thousand people exactly how I feel about you," he said, his voice just low enough for me to hear.

I lifted my chin, entering this special place that existed only for him and me. "And how is that?"

His eyes flicked to my lips, and then he caught my chin in his calloused hand, guiding my mouth to meet his.

The second our mouths touched, it was a shock to my system more intense than any lightning crash. Warmth and tenderness even stronger than the night before, attraction that went beyond anything my brain could think or my heart had felt.

All the yelling, the cheers, the people watching us on the jumbo screen faded away until all I could focus on was this man and the fact that *this* was how he felt about me. And that it just kept getting better.

We broke apart, and my eyes blinked open, stunned at what had just happened and how it made me feel. And when I met Knox's eyes, saw his grin, I couldn't help but smile myself.

Beside Knox, Emily yelled, "ARE YOU GETTING MARRIED?"

Chuckles erupted around the suite.

"What's funny?" Emily asked.

Knox tucked her under his arm. "Maybe I have something funny written on my back?"

She giggled. "Yeah, Steve."

I smiled at Knox, but a part of me was terrified too.

Because it was so easy to fall for him. What happened if he let me hit the ground?

29

KNOX

FORD'S TEAM won the game, and that wasn't even the best part. Afterward, one of the stadium employees brought us out to the field, where the Diamonds had played the Brentwood Badgers. There were still tons of professional players, reporters, and coaches milling around. Emily looked like she was in heaven, stars in her eyes at seeing all these people in real life.

We found Ford doing an interview with a pretty reporter and stood off to the side, Jackson in Larkin's arms and Emily sitting on my shoulders so she had the best view of it all.

Once Ford finished the interview, he walked over to us, holding his helmet by the face mask in one hand, his brown hair slick with sweat. "Brother," he said, coming to give me a hug. He grinned at Larkin and Jackson and then said to Emily, "Is my biggest fan ready for a tour?"

Emily nodded so fast and squirmed down from my shoulders like a little wiggle worm, making all of us laugh. She ran up to Ford and said, "Where do we start?"

For the next half hour, he walked us round the stadium, introducing Emily to everyone from the head coach to the security guards, treating everyone with equal deference just like Dad taught us growing up.

When we finished touring the locker room and meeting some of the players, Emily's eyes were drooping, and I had to carry her. We said our goodbyes to Ford, who said he'd be home later, and then left the stadium.

My brother's house was a good half hour away, longer in traffic, and both the kids had just fallen asleep when we pulled into his expansive driveway. The home cost him seven figures and had more bells and whistles than we ever had growing up. It was set on two acres and had a tall stone fence around the entire property to give him some privacy and security.

The landscaping was simple, but impeccably done with mature trees dotting the grass and casting a generous amount of shade. At the end of the long driveway, his house loomed, an upscale, modern home with a white brick façade and sharp black features, from the double front doors to the grids in the expansive, reflective windows.

"This is gorgeous," Larkin said next to me. "Are you sure they allow the likes of me here?"

I couldn't help the chuckle that passed my lips. "If you're not allowed, I'm sure as hell not."

She giggled. "In all seriousness, I've never been inside a house like this before."

"What should we do?" I asked, coming to a stop in front of the house in the circular drive. Then I put the truck in park and waggled my eyebrows. "Jump in his bed? Streak through the backyard? Skinny-dip?"

Her cheeks tinged pink. "There are a lot of naked activities in that list, Knox Madigan."

I bit my lip, giving her a smoldering look. "Can you blame me, with you looking like that? Those denim shorts have been driving me insane all day."

She ran her hands over her thighs like she was half surprised by my comment. But she seemed to reset her expression and said, "Well, I haven't been able to stop thinking about that kiss."

My stomach muscles tightened because damn, I hadn't either. If we hadn't been surrounded by a stadium of people, including her children, I would have taken her right then and there.

I reached for her thigh, loving the softness of it under my palm. Squeezing lightly, I said, "You are irresistible in the best possible way."

She put her hand atop mine, the heat building between us.

"What do you say we get the kids inside?" I asked her. "Before I get carried away and take you right in this driveway."

Her chest arched distractingly, drawing my gaze to the swell of her breasts, and when I looked back up at her eyes, I saw a look just as hungry as I felt. Her voice was breathy as she said, "That's probably a good idea."

We got out of the truck, me going to Emily's side and her going to Jackson's to get them out. Emily was still sleepy and decided to ride on one wheeling suitcase while I pushed the other in my free hand. Larkin held Jackson on her hip while situating the pack and play in the stroller, and then we paraded to the front door of my brother's mansion.

Something inside me said, *Take note. This moment is special.* And I couldn't second-guess my inner voice. Our first family trip. Emily's first professional football game. The first time Ford saw Larkin as more than my neighbor. The first time Larkin and I would stay overnight in the same house... Regardless of our pasts, we had so many firsts together.

We reached the front door, and I punched the code into the digital display, then the deadbolt clicked. I held the tall door open to let us inside.

Emily stared at the grand entrance with country-style art on the walls and said, "Can I see if it echoes?"

Larkin laughed. "Is it okay, Knox?"

"Heck yeah," I said. "Give it your best, Em."

With a grin, Emily yelled, "ECHO!"

It bounced off the gallery white walls and stone floors, and even the rugs in the living room had no chance of absorbing the echoes that came back. She giggled, and then Jackson let out his own yell, like he was trying to say echo too.

I grinned. "Yeah, buddy. Echo!"

He smiled and squirmed in Larkin's arms.

"Let me show y'all the bedrooms," I said, leading them to the hallway off the living room. "There are six bedrooms in this house, but the five guest rooms are on this side of the house." I stopped at the first bedroom, a massive space with a metal four-poster bed, a sitting area at a window overlooking the grounds, and its own en suite bathroom. After setting Larkin's bags at the door, we went to the room right across the hall, almost identical to the one we saw before. Then I put my bag at the bedroom next to Larkin's. We hadn't talked sleeping arrangements before arriving, and I didn't want her to feel pressured or uncomfortable.

After checking out the rooms, Emily asked, "What are we doing now?"

Larkin looked at me and said, "Would you be okay watching the kids while I take a quick shower?"

"Of course," I replied. "I'll give the kiddos the grand tour." And try not to think about their mom in the shower the entire time.

Easier said than done.

30

LARKIN

WITH THE BEDROOM DOOR CLOSED, I could just faintly hear Knox talking to Emily and Jackson as he gave them a tour of Ford's house. Ford may have been the leading quarterback in the league, but the real star of the day was Knox.

As I undressed and walked to the massive bathroom with a soaker tub and floor-to-ceiling glass shower doors, the day replayed in my mind. Knox had been so kind to my children, so patient with everyone and their dog referring to him as "Steve" throughout the day.

And that kiss.

I turned on the rain shower, half tempted to step into it while the water was still cold just to take the edge off all the steamy thoughts running through my mind. And the way he'd looked over my body? I shuddered, my eyes closing of their own accord. I wanted him to follow through on every lustrous thought I knew had been going through his mind. Because the same thoughts were plaguing mine.

Steam rolled off the downpouring water, and I stepped in, letting it pelt my sensitive body. I longed for Knox in a way I hadn't longed for a man in my entire life. Sure, I'd been horny before, especially with those pregnancy hormones raging through my body, but the desire I felt for him surpassed even that. I wanted to know him, in every sense of the word. Because everything new I discovered about him didn't make me want to turn away—it made me want him more.

With anticipation rolling through me, I took my time in the shower—time I usually didn't get while raising two kids on my own. I shaved, refreshed my scalp and hair, and when I stepped out onto the plush rug, I took time drying myself and applying the expensive, designer-brand lotion resting on the vanity.

My hair was still wet when I stepped out of the bathroom, and I didn't bother drying it, instead letting it air dry in its natural wavy form. I slipped into a pair of cotton shorts—maybe just to tease Knox more—and put on a loose T-shirt without a bra. Then I added some mascara and lip gloss, finalizing my effortless look that in reality took... about an hour to do.

I wondered how Knox and my kids were doing. This house was big, but surely the tour couldn't last an hour. I cast a glance at the sun setting over the grounds and sending orange hues throughout the room before going to find them. This place really was beautiful.

I could hear them all talking, playing out in the living room. I had just barely rounded the corner, seeing Knox sitting in front of the couch, Jackson standing between his legs while Knox held his hands to give him support.

Emily was on her knees beside Knox, making funny faces at Jackson.

They were so happy, laughing, playing.

They couldn't see me, so I leaned up against the wall, taking it in, my heart feeling so full it could burst.

And then I heard Jackson say, "Dada."

My heart stopped. I couldn't have heard him right.

Knox and Emily gave each other a surprised look. Then Knox said, "What did you say, Jax?"

"Dada."

Clear as a bell. From my baby's mouth.

Liquid emotion burned my eyes as I watched Knox's softening expression. He looked at my baby with nothing but love in his eyes. "Oh, buddy, I'm not your dada. Can you say mama?"

"Dada," Jackson said again.

Emily leaned her cheek against Knox's shoulder. "I wish you could be our dad."

I pressed my hand against my chest, fighting a sob.

"Oh, honey." He pressed his cheek against the top of her head, his expression full of emotion. "I can't be your dad; no one will take his place. But I'm here for you no matter what, okay?"

Jackson toddled forward, putting his forehead on Knox's chest.

"You want in on this too, huh?" Knox asked, hugging him and then pulling Emily into the hug as well. His eyes slid closed as he squeezed them tight.

It felt wrong to watch the moment, and I could barely stand still with the pain of my past telling me to run. After taking a deep breath and gathering myself, I walked into the living room. "Hey, I'm out of the shower."

They all glanced up at me, an unreadable expression on Knox's face. Emily jumped up, barreling toward me like a train without breaks. "Jackson said his first word!"

I gave a faltering smile, rubbing her back, and looked at Knox as I said, "I heard."

Silent communication passed between us, expressing all the things we couldn't say out loud. My heart was in knots, but I put on a brave face like I'd been doing for so long now and said, "Can you all give me a tour of the house?"

ABOUT AN HOUR LATER, Ford came home with takeout, and we all ate around his table, talking and enjoying the food. Emily had a million questions for him about the game, and Ford finally said, "You're either going to be a coach or a reporter one day. I'm calling it."

We all chuckled, and it was nice to hear the warm sound that passed Knox's lips. He sat across the table from me, holding Jackson in his lap, and didn't seem to mind when Jackson grabbed food off his plate. Jackson had refused to be held by anyone but Knox, and I had to admit, I was panicking inside, a torrent of worry under the smooth surface I tried to portray.

I knew Knox promised to be there for him. And I had to trust he'd follow through on this word or stop this from going any further.

With a yawn, Ford got up from the table, saying, "I'm gonna hit the hay, but *mi casa es su casa*. If you need anything, Knox knows where to find it. And don't worry about the dishes. Housekeeping will be by in the morning.”

Knox got up, giving Ford a one-armed hug while holding Jackson in the other arm. “Thanks for having us, brother.”

“Any time.” Ford looked at me. “I mean that. Little Miss Emily can keep me sharp for interviews.”

I smiled at my daughter, who didn’t have a shy bone in her body. “Thank you, truly. It’s been one of the best days ever.”

Emily nodded quickly. “Thank you!”

Jackson said, “Dada!” He’d been saying it all night, proud to use his own voice.

Ford smiled at us all. “Night.”

When Ford walked out of the room, I said, “We should all get to bed too.” Emily started arguing, but I shook my head at her. “It’s been a long day. Let’s go get in our jammies, and I can tell you a bedtime story.”

She perked up. “Can Knox tell me one?”

I glanced over to Knox.

“I’d love to,” he said. “If it’s okay with your mama.”

I wrapped my arms around my chest like I could hold my aching pieces together. “That’s fine with me.”

“And then you can sing me that song,” Emily said. “It was pretty.”

The expression on Knox’s face told me it meant a lot more to him than that. I squeezed his hand, and we went to put the kids in bed.

We ended up, all in pajamas, curled in a cushy king bed while Knox told a story about a little prince and princess who saved the world from danger and lived happily ever after. And then he sang “Red River Valley,” the sweet, heartfelt way he sang it bringing unshed tears to my eyes.

As my children's eyes slid closed, I silently wished that life could be as simple as the story Knox told. That what I had thought would be my happily ever after with Seth was only the turmoil leading me to the true happiness we all wanted. But if life had taught me anything, it was that men left. And it hurt even more worrying that Knox would be one of them.

31

KNOX

I COULD TELL Larkin was tense since Jackson said his first word.

She tried to put on a brave face, but I could see it in the slight hunch of her shoulders, like she was attempting to make herself small enough to avoid being hurt. I could see it in the pinch around her eyes, the small crease in her forehead. I could hear it through the emotionless facade of her voice, like if she pretended not to hurt, those conflicting feelings might just go away.

But if I knew one thing, it was that pain didn't just evaporate over time. It needed an outlet. A release.

Once the children's slow breathing filled the room, I looked over at her and whispered, "Follow me."

She nodded, slowly creeping out of bed as I had and then rested Jackson in the crib Ford kept for family visitors. Once he was settled in, I linked my fingers with Larkin's, giving her a reassuring squeeze.

I wasn't running away from the messy parts of a relationship. When I was younger, running away had only ever gotten me in trouble. In my job, running away could get me killed. And with Larkin, running away could cost me everything I've been wanting for longer than I wanted to admit.

We tiptoed through the house, and I opened the grand sliding door leading to the backyard with the glittering blue pool. She set the baby monitor on one of the pool chairs and then joined me standing beside the water. The night air was warm against my skin as I slid out of my shirt and then began taking off my pants.

"What are you doing?" she asked, gazing around the empty yard, back through the big sliding doors to the dimly lit living room.

I quirked an eyebrow at her. "Swimming with you. Naked if you want." I winked.

"What if someone sees you?" she asked.

"Your monitor has a motion detector, so it'll warn us if the kids stir, and Ford knows not to come out here."

"How?" she asked, but my smile told her all she needed to know. She smiled, but then her expression sobered. "But I... I..." She glanced at the pool with worry filling her eyes, illuminated in streaks of blue light.

I didn't want her to be upset. "You know how to swim, right?" I asked. We hadn't covered that yet—maybe it had been wrong of me to assume.

"It's not that," she said. "I—" She looked down, fiddled with her fingers.

"What is it?" I asked, stepping closer in nothing but my boxer shorts. I ran my hands over her arms, seeing goosebumps there. "He keeps the pool heated. It won't be cold."

She let out a sigh. "I'm not twenty anymore."

My eyebrows drew together. "That's one of the things I like about you."

She let out a humorless chuckle and then looked away. "I've had two children, and Seth... He said one of the reasons he cheated was because he didn't like the way my body changed."

Red hot rage flared through me, and I sucked in a breath. He had *not* said that to her. To this beautiful, strong, compassionate woman in front of me. The woman who selflessly carried his children and then cared for them all on her own. How could he be so far off base?

"Look at me," I said.

Her eyes met mine, worried, vulnerable.

I reached for her shirt, slowly sliding it up her skin.

Her breath hitched as I pulled it up.

"You can tell me to stop," I said, not an ounce of humor or play in my voice. If she wanted me to, I'd step back, wait until she was ready.

She stayed silent.

The thin cotton followed the path of my hands, revealing her stomach, soft with scores of stretchmarks catching the poolside lights. Then her breasts. Full, hanging heavy with the same marks lining her stomach, thinner this time, like silver pieces of thread.

And then I pulled the shirt over her head, wavy brown hair falling through the opening and then settling around her bare shoulders.

I took her in, making sure she saw me looking at her, not shying away. Not for a second.

Then I reached for her cotton shorts, hooking my thumbs through the waistband and tugging them down over her full hips. The dimples and spider veins on her legs caught the shadow and light, contrasting her pale skin.

Her breath faltered as the fabric reached the ground, and she stepped out, leaving her clothes in a pile. I stood facing her, and she tried to wrap her arms around herself again, but this time I took her hands in mine.

I held them both in one hand and cupped the side of her face with the other, angling her chin so she was looking in my eyes, seeing me with each word I spoke.

"Larkin." My voice was clear, firm. "Can I tell you what I see when I look at you?"

Her eyes were glassy with unshed emotion as she nodded.

I bit my lip and nodded in return, then moved my lips to her forehead, kissing her softly. "I see a smart woman who knows what needs to be done and acts on that knowing."

I moved my lips to hers, kissing her just because I wanted to.

Then I lowered my mouth to her shoulder, bare skin heating under my mouth. "I see shoulders that carry more than they should ever have to." I moved my lips to her chest, the spot right over her heart. "I see so much more love than I knew a person could hold."

Her hand caressed the back of my head.

My lips traveled to her breast, and I teased her hard nipple into my mouth. A soft gasp escaped her lips.

Then I moved to her stomach, kissing the lines I could tell she worried so much about. "I see proof that you brought two of my favorite people into the world."

I heard her breath shudder, and when I looked up to

her, the emotion spilled from her eyes. I rose to wipe her tears, not wanting her to cry. "Larkin, I—"

She covered my mouth with her hand. "Thank you. For letting me see myself through your eyes." She removed her hands and pressed to her tiptoes, kissing me.

But this time, there wasn't a jumbo screen with thousands of people watching. There wasn't a fresh fight with her ex looming over our heads. No children nearby to make me hold back. Hardly any clothes separating the softness of her skin from the heat of mine.

I tilted my head, deepening this kiss, and swept my arms around her to pull her even closer. She whimpered against my mouth, sending a bolt of heat straight to my cock. I wanted her, all of her.

I broke my lips apart from hers to kiss her jaw, to scrape my teeth across her neck.

"Knox," she gasped.

Fuck me. I wanted to hear her say my name like that until she was breathless and begging. My cock was hard, pressing into her side with all the desperation I felt coursing through me.

"What if someone comes outside?" she asked, tangling her fingers through my hair like even she didn't want to hear her question.

The odds were slim, I knew, but I didn't want her worried for our first time. I scooped her in my arms, relishing the way my muscles worked against her full figure.

"Knox!" she yelped.

"I've got you," I said to her, making the shock turn to heat in her eyes. Forget working out for defined abs or to be prepared for duty—it felt like I'd been training every day of my life for this moment. To make her feel weight-less, safe in my arms.

She held on to my neck as I took her to the pool steps and carried her into the heated water, where she became truly weightless in my embrace. The water and lights swirled around us, casting shadows on the natural stone pool floor rough underfoot. The smell of salt water and Larkin's perfume hit my senses, and I thought I'd never smelled anything better. Anything hotter.

She swam out from my arms and dipped her head under the surface. As she came up, water spilled over her features, down to her bare chest, her nipples just cresting the surface. Fuck, I wanted to taste the salt water on every inch of her.

She blinked her beautiful eyes open, a ghost of a smile on her lips.

She was letting go. My girl was letting go. For me.

I guided her to the wall of the pool, the edge reaching her shoulders. "Enough privacy?" I asked her salaciously.

She nodded, biting her bottom lip.

I dipped my head to her breast, sucking one nipple while teasing the other between my thumb and finger. She moaned softly, nails dragging across my wet shoulders in a way that only made me want to please her more.

I found her sensitive nub and swirled two fingers across it.

"Fffuck," she moaned.

"Mmm," I hummed against her tits, making her cry out more. I loved how easily she reacted to me, like she was waiting for this moment long before we reached the pool.

I hurried the circles, building the pressure, and her

head fell back, resting on the pool's edge, wet hair falling over her back, her shoulders, as her chest arched for me.

"That's my girl," I said, coming up from her tits, and then I took a breath and brought myself underwater.

Her body stilled for a moment before my tongue found her clit. I held on to her thighs and darted my tongue against her sensitive spot, tasting the best combination of salt and her. My cock was hard, straining against my boxers I'd neglected to take off. The ache drove me on, sliding fingers inside her in time to feel her walls tightening.

My lungs ached for air but not as much as I ached for her.

Her fingers gripped my hair and pulled me up above the water. I opened my eyes to see her frenzied look before she drew me to her lips, kissing me with a passion I'd never felt before. This wasn't simple desire—it was a *need*—as much for her as it was for me.

She broke apart from my lips and said the sexiest line I'd ever heard: "If I'm coming, it's going to be on your cock."

32

LARKIN

I'D NEVER BEEN this woman—the one who had sex in public or swam naked or let my need for a man take over my previously logical thoughts.

But I'd never been with Knox before either.

He drew it all out of me—the emotions, the excitement, the *need*.

I needed him like a wilting flower thirsted for water. I was surviving before, but now I knew what it felt like to be in *bloom*.

He caught my bottom lip between his teeth and tugged. "I don't have a condom with me."

"I'm on the pill," I said, not sure I could hold back even if I wasn't. "Are you clean?"

"I'm clean," he confirmed.

"I need you," I gasped, my voice desperate in a way I never thought I could be for a man.

He kissed my lips, long and tantalizingly slow. "I'm not holding back," he said.

I nodded, understanding what he meant. Because

even though we'd only known each other a short while, I could feel myself starting to let go and give in to him. No matter how much I wanted to fight it. No matter how irresponsible it seemed or how soon it was after the divorce. It wasn't logical. It was a sense deep inside that Knox was special, different than anyone I knew.

He hooked one of my legs over his arm and guided his cock to my entrance. His tip was hard, full, stretching against my opening.

"Knox," I cried, already on the verge of tears from the emotional overwhelm.

"I know, baby," he whispered, easing in, inch by inch, until I was full.

Full of his cock.

Full of love.

Full of emotions.

Full of *him*.

Overwhelmed by it all, I ground my hips against him as tears slid down my cheeks, desperate for more, to ease the ache building within me.

"God, that's it," he said, voice tight, like it took all of him not to be rough with me, to let me guide the pace.

But I didn't want that. I wanted him to let go, freefall with me and catch me on the way down.

"Give it to me," I begged. "Give me everything."

He kissed my lips, hard. And then his hips wound back, and he pumped into me, water splashing over my chest, the pool edge biting into my back.

"Hold on," he ordered, a darkness, a heat in his eyes, burning with abandon.

I put my arms to the side, bracing myself against the pool edge as he pounded into me. The pleasure, the pain, it all blended with each stroke of his hips, with each lap of the water spilling over my chest, my arms.

"Knox," I begged, I gasped, the only thing I was capable of uttering while he consumed every one of my senses.

Sparks ignited in my chest, and I dropped my head back, losing myself in it all.

"Look at me," he ordered. "Eyes on me." I rolled my head up, seeing the desire in his eyes. "You need to see exactly what you do to me." He pumped into me. "How you make me lose all control." He pounded again. "How I've been able to think of nothing but you since I saw those blue eyes looking up at me."

And I saw it all, felt it in every stroke. I thought I was just a plus-size single mom, discarded by her ex. But to this man, I was everything and more.

He was working his way past my every defense, and I didn't know how to keep myself safe, or even if I wanted to if I had to choose between safety and this. "Knox," I wept, cradling his face in my hands.

"Larkin." He dropped his forehead against mine, my name a prayer, a plea, a song on his lips as he shuddered into me, releasing all he had inside me.

I cried out his name, unable to stop myself, to stop the orgasm that wracked through my body until it was all I could do to hold on to him and let the waves fade. I gasped for breath and rested on him, my body limp with the force of it all.

I held on to him, knowing my chances at guarding my heart... were gone.

33

LARKIN

I TIPTOED into Knox's room early in the morning while the light was still pale outside and the house was quiet with sleep. His breath was soft and slow, one arm over his head, the other under the covers, rising and falling with his chest.

I set the monitor on the nightstand, so I'd know if the kids woke up. Lifting the covers up, I curled into Knox's strong chest. His arms tightened around me, and his lips pressed a sleepy kiss to my forehead. I opened my eyes to look at him, the strong planes of his face, the small ridge in the middle of his nose. His long eyelashes forming a fringe along his closed eyes.

"You're staring," he mumbled, holding me tighter.

My lips lifted, and I reached up, brushing my hand over a faint scar on his cheek. "I had to come in here and make sure this is real."

His eyes drifted open, and he took me in, the room soaked in pale, early morning sunlight. "It's not."

My eyebrows drew together. "What?"

He gave me a crooked smile. "I'm just kidding." He kissed me softly. "It's better than real—pretty sure I'm living a dream."

To hear someone, Knox, talking about me like that made my heart melt. I kissed him again, just wanting to feel closer to him. His grip on me tightened, and he shifted his hips, his length hard against me. And now that I knew what it felt like to have him inside me, my body instantly reacted, wanting more.

I brought my hand down, sliding it over his hard stomach and then feeling him through his sweatpants.

He moaned quietly. "Don't tease me, baby."

"Who said I was teasing?" I replied, slipping my hand under his waistband to feel his bare erection. I ran my thumb over his tip, feeling the bead of moisture forming there.

"Fuck me," he muttered, leaning closer, nipping the shell of my ear.

I wanted to drive him just as crazy as he made me. "Feel how wet I am for you."

He reached his hand between my thick thighs, running his fingers along my slit. "Larkin." He drew one finger inside me, then two.

I clenched against his hand, making him moan. "Who's the tease now?" I replied.

"I'm ready for you," he replied.

Feeling bold, feeling like I could make love to him all day and night, I moved under the blankets, shedding my shorts, and straddled him.

"Good thing I locked the door," he said, his heated gaze on me. Usually, I was self-conscious in this position, but Knox left no room for me to doubt how he felt about me.

"Now give me that pussy," he ordered, holding his cock for me. I angled my hips until he was at my entrance, stretching my tender sex like he had the night before. I let out a quiet moan.

"Fuck," he breathed as I lowered myself all the way down and ground against him. "Take your shirt off. I want to see you."

He held on to my hips while I lifted my shirt over my head, letting my loose and wild waves fall around my shoulders.

"God, you're hot," he said. "I can't get enough of you." He gripped my hips in his large hands, guiding me over him, up and down in a steady rhythm that drove me wild. I held on to his strong shoulders, riding him until we were both breathless.

Moving a hand from my hip, he slipped his thumb to my clit, rubbing tantalizing circles to the beat of our bodies meeting until I could hardly hold myself up anymore.

"I'm coming," I breathed before the first wave could crash over me.

"Come with me," he said. "Come with me."

I held his gaze, like I knew he liked, and fell apart with him. I rode every wave until I couldn't anymore and fell to his chest, skin on skin.

He brushed my hair away from my sweaty face and kissed my forehead. "You did so good, baby."

My heart swelled at the praise. I loved how he never let me doubt myself. "That was amazing," I whispered, my hand splayed on his chest.

He smiled against my forehead. "Want to shower with me before the kids wake up?"

"How you could think about moving right now, I have no idea." I laughed tiredly.

He chuckled with me. "Maybe because I've already started my day in the best possible way."

JUST WHEN I thought the day couldn't get better, Ford had breakfast delivered, and it was honestly some of the best food I'd eaten. Then I got to watch two big Madigan men playing with my children, making them laugh and giggle. And there were the secret smiles Knox sent my way that made me feel like the most special person in the world, just to be bathed in his unique brand of sunshine.

After spending the day hanging out on the grounds at Ford's place, swimming in the pool, and stealing kisses with Knox when I got the chance, we drove back to Cottonwood Falls. Emily chose the music the entire way home, and it felt like one of those days where you were riding on a cloud.

Even though I could have spent the night with Knox all over again, we parted ways in the driveway so I could get the kids ready for bed and he could get ready for work.

Once my kids were in bed, I called my sister. I had *so* much to tell her.

"It's five in the morning," she mumbled as she answered.

"I HAD SEX WITH KNOX!" I cried from the safety of my bedroom with the door firmly shut. It was like being young all over again, telling my big sister I got my first valentine from a boy in my class when Mom was cooking so she couldn't hear.

"Well, that woke me up." She let out a scratchy laugh. "Give me a sec."

I heard a shuffling of bedding on the other end of the line, then a splash of water followed by the sound of a door opening and closing. "Tell me everything."

I grinned, lying back in bed, and told her all that had happened since we last talked, from the fight with Seth to the game and then the night we shared in the pool. "It's been like a fairy tale," I said.

"Oh no, it's better than a fairy tale," she replied. "No one has sex in those."

I laughed.

"But I can't believe Seth said that shit to you. I mean, I always thought he had some narcissistic tendencies, but it's like he went off the deep end."

"I know." I frowned. "I hope he settles down and comes around."

"Me too. He would flip if he knew Jackson called Knox "dada." How did he feel about that, by the way?" she asked. "A lot of guys would run the other direction."

"He told the kids that he couldn't replace their dad and that he would be there for them no matter what. And then you know what we did after."

She giggled happily despite the early hour. "I can't wait to meet this guy. Please tell me he'll come to Thanksgiving with you guys. I'll get him a ticket too."

"Oh my gosh, that sounds amazing." My brain was already going wild, fantasizing about a romantic trip to Paris with Knox, drinking wine in the park while the sun set behind the Eiffel Tower as its sparkly lights came on. "But it's probably a bit too soon to be making those kinds of plans."

"You dated Seth for two years before you got married and look how that turned out. Time is relative when it comes to love," she said.

"Paris is wearing off on you," I observed, wishing for the good old days when I had a phone cord to twirl around my fingers.

"Or maybe it's this new guy," she said.

My eyes bugged out. "What?" Taylee didn't fall for guys. She enjoyed them while it lasted.

"I'm at his place right now. Sitting on the very pretty balcony with a view of the Eiffel Tower."

"Your life is a fairy tale," I said. And just before she could protest, I added, "With a whole lotta sex."

"Amen," she teased. "Now get some sleep. Sounds like you didn't get too much last night."

I laughed and said, "Goodnight. I love you."

"I love you too."

I WOKE up in the morning to a text from Knox.

Knox: Good morning, beautiful.

I smiled at the screen, still fully in that hazy glow of new love. And I tried to let myself enjoy it without worrying that the other shoe would drop, that he was like the other men I'd known in my life.

Because deep down, I *knew* he was different, and I couldn't let my fear or my history take him away from me, or my children.

Larkin: Good morning, handsome.

I bit my lip, imagining him lying in his bed across the way, thinking of me right when he woke up and sending me a message just to make my day even a little bit better.

Knox: Care for a latte?

This man came straight from my dreams and into real life.

Larkin: Like I care for air.

Knox: You're funny.

Larkin: One of my finer traits.

Knox: Half an hour work?

Larkin: Perfect. See you soon.

Since the kids were still sleeping, I hurried out of bed, getting myself ready for the day, quickly doing my hair and makeup and then slipping on a clean pair of scrubs. When I checked the time, I still had ten minutes until he was due to be over. A glance in the kids' room showed them still resting, so I went to the kitchen to prepare their breakfast.

I'd already cracked three eggs when my phone vibrated on the counter, spinning in small circles. I hurried to rinse the eggs off my hands and answered it without checking the caller ID. "Hello?"

"Larkin." It was Nancy.

I raised my eyebrows as I cracked the eggs. "Hey, everything okay?" I hoped she wasn't sick. It wouldn't be good for me to miss another day of work this early in the job.

"Actually." She let out a sigh. "Honey, I'm sorry, but I can't watch the kids anymore."

I nearly dropped the egg. Instead, I set it down and braced myself on the counter. "What?" I'd moved to town specifically so I could have their help. What would I do in a new town with no support for my kids and a measly budget for daycare? "Did you get a job or something?"

"No, but Seth just left my house this morning. He was gutted after your fight, and the things you said to him? They were completely uncalled for. And then for you to go flaunting your new relationship on a jumbotron at a televised game?" Her voice shook. "I love my grandbabies, but you've clearly made your bed with Knox Madigan, and now you need to lie in it."

My jaw dropped. I'd let myself get swept away for a moment at the game, and even in Dallas, the small-town rumors came back to haunt me. But there was more to her statement than just the kiss. "What did Seth tell you I said? Because I can promise you the things he said to me—"

"I don't want to hear it. Because while you were at the NFL game in Dallas, he was at my house, barely able to get out of bed. Said he came to see his children and you wouldn't let him. That is unacceptable, Larkin."

Now I stared at the phone in shock, anger flooding my blood stream until my head felt hot. But the logical part of me fought for attention. I couldn't give in to my emotions, couldn't let Seth control my children's childcare and my success at work. "Nancy, surely we can come to an agreement. The kids love being at your place, and I *really* need the childcare."

"You need to apologize to my Seth." I opened my mouth to argue. But then the other shoe fell. "And you need to break things off with Knox Madigan so you and Seth can have another chance. My grandbabies don't deserve to grow up in a broken home when their parents could work on it."

If I was mad before, it had nothing on the anger raging through me now. The hypocrisy of it all made me want to scream—Seth had cheated on me, left our family for another woman, and made no efforts to see the kids until he got jealous of me dating someone new. "Your son cheated on me. Not the other way around."

"He's not the one asking me to babysit for free."

I raised my eyebrows, angry tears already starting to fall. "They're his kids too, Nancy. You're going to let your grandchildren, his children, suffer because you don't like what *I'm* doing?"

"Tell yourself what you want to make me the bad guy, Larkin. It doesn't feel right to support the decisions you're making. My decision is final."

34

KNOX

I SHIFTED my to-go cup to my other hand and knocked on Larkin's door. I may have just been bringing her coffee, but with all the jitters going through my system, it felt more like picking up a date for prom, hoping she liked the corsage Bora, the florist, said would match her dress the best.

But when Larkin opened the door, she had tears rolling down her cheeks.

My heart instantly fell. "What's wrong?" I asked. What had changed between our texts this morning and now?

She was shaking as she fell into my arms. I carefully held the coffee, trying not to spill it on her while hugging her back as best as I could. Her voice trembled as she began telling me about an awful call with her mother-in-law.

I set my coffee down and guided her to the couch so we could sit while she filled in the details. Every word she spoke made me hate Seth even more. I'd tried to keep my feelings neutral, for the children's sake. But this? It was lower than I thought a person could go.

He was a coward. Worse than a coward. Because he was willing to let his children suffer just to get back at Larkin. And for Nancy to go along with it and enable his terrible behavior? Now we knew where Seth got his shitty streak.

"I don't know what I'm going to do," she whispered into my chest. "I'm going to miss work. I can't pay much for childcare as it is, and if I can't go to work, I can't even pay for this house. Just when I thought I was finally getting my life together." She broke down into sobs, her whole body shaking with the force of them.

I held her on the couch, wanting to punch Seth, wanting to talk sense into his parents, wanting to take all the worries off this woman who held so much weight on her shoulders and didn't have the support she deserved.

As her breathing evened, I promised, "We're going to figure this out."

She looked up at me. "We? I'm surprised you're not running away from this mess."

I tilted my head down, pressing my forehead against hers. All her makeup was in streaks down her face or staining my shirt, her eyes were red and puffy, and yet I still thought she was the most beautiful woman in the world.

"I told you," I said, "I'm showing you how a man should treat you. And believe me, a man doesn't run when things get hard."

She broke down in a fresh wave of tears, holding on to me like I was the only thing keeping her upright. She didn't know her own strength.

"Look at me," I said. And she did, eyes red and puffy. I put my hands on either side of her face, using my thumbs to wipe away her tears.

"I don't want to leave you," she admitted, fresh tears streaming in the black mascara tracks down her cheeks.

I kissed her lips. "Like I'd let you go when it took so long to find you."

"But how is it going to work?" she asked, looking up at me. "I need childcare."

"Give me a day," I said. "Give me a day to figure it out. I have today off for picking up that shift on Saturday —I'll watch the kids while you're at work."

"Are you sure?" she asked. "I feel like you've already done too much."

Larkin amazed me. She was going through all this and still thinking about me, not wanting to take advantage of me. "You're so used to being strong for everyone else. When are you going to let someone be strong for you?"

She searched my eyes with hers, and she was about to answer when Emily came down the hallway, dragging her blanket with her, her hair a mess atop her head.

"Hi, Mommy. Hi, Knox."

Larkin quickly wiped her face and went to pick up her daughter. "Are you okay to spend the day with Knox today?"

Emily grinned. "More pranks."

Larkin let out a tearful laugh and set Emily on the couch. "I'm going to apply some fresh makeup. Will you listen for Jackson, Knox?"

I nodded. "Of course."

While Larkin went back to the bathroom, I looked at

Emily with a smile. I hadn't been planning to spend the whole day with her and Jackson, but honestly, the day off looming in front of me without Larkin and her family made me realize how empty my life had felt before. "What do you usually do first thing in the morning?" I asked Emily.

She looked up like she was thinking. "I get dressed, Mama does my hair and brushes my teeth, and then we eat breakfast."

"Perfect. Why don't you get dressed and I'll start cooking."

"Good idea." She nodded and hopped up from the couch, leaving her pink fuzzy blanket on the cushion. As she flounced away, I had to wonder—how could anyone want to miss out on this?

And then an even worse thought came to mind: if I couldn't help Larkin find a solution, I could be missing out on this too.

35

LARKIN

I KNEW Knox said he would help me figure out childcare, but they were my children, my responsibility. I didn't have much downtime at work, but during my bathroom break that morning, I got on the phone and called the three childcare centers in town.

Two of them didn't have any openings, and the one that did was way out of my price range. The cost would have eaten up eighty percent of my earnings, and that didn't include the diapers and meals I'd have to pack for both children. Maybe I could swing it once Emily started school in the fall, but it would be really tight even then, and that didn't cover the hours from three to five either.

I was feeling hopeless as I sat down at my desk to chart the morning medications for each of the clients. It took all I had to smile when Bernice approached my desk.

"Hi, Larkin." She sat in the open chair across from me. "I wanted to check in on you. See how it's going."

With my job? "Great. I love it here." A lump formed in my throat, and I swallowed it down.

"That's great news," Bernice said. "You've been here a little while now, and I like asking all our employees a few questions once they get a feel for the culture. Do you have a sec?"

"Sure," I said. It would be a welcome break from all the stewing I'd been doing this morning.

She crossed her legs and laced her fingers around one knee. "What are some changes you think we could make to improve the residents' quality of life here?"

I blinked. At my last job, the retirement home director was far more concerned with paperwork and selling rooms to new clients than she ever was with her employees' opinions. "You're asking me?"

She smiled. "Of course. Unless you're hiding the real Larkin under your desk."

I chuckled, pleasantly surprised by the joke. "Actually, there has been one thing."

"What's that?" she asked.

I leaned my elbows on the desk. "I started doing yoga after having Jackson, and I've seen how good it's been for my physical strength and for my stress. I think it would be great to add some yoga, even chair yoga, to the activities schedule."

Bernice raised her eyebrows like my suggestion surprised her.

"Bad idea?" I asked nervously.

"Not that. Most people just want better chairs for the break room, things like that."

I chuckled. "I mean, that would be nice too."

She smiled at me, like she was seeing through me. "I know you love being a nurse, but I won't be able to work here forever. With your heart, I could see you doing a great job as a leader here."

My eyes stung at the compliment. At someone seeing my good qualities instead of looking for the negative, like Seth and his parents. Was there some kind of magic about Cottonwood Falls that led me to Knox and now this? "That means a lot, Bernice."

"Oh, honey," she said, reaching out and patting my hand. "I call it like I see it, you know that."

I smiled and nodded. "I do. Thank you."

"Let me think on the yoga and I'll get back to you, okay?"

"Sounds great."

She left my office, and I had to wonder how I could feel so many different emotions in the span of a few hours. But now a sense of desperation was covering it all. It felt like I could have a real future here in Cottonwood Falls, not just a stopover while I was recovering from the divorce. But how could I have a real future here when the choice was stay with the man I was falling for or support myself and my children?

My phone vibrated on my desk, and I half hoped it was one of the more affordable childcare centers calling to let me know a spot had miraculously opened for both of my children.

Instead, it was a new text message.

Liv: Are we still on for lunch?

"Shit," I muttered. I'd completely forgotten we'd set a lunch date for when I came back from Dallas. There was so much going on in my personal life, I wanted to cancel and sulk by myself in the break room, brainstorm new ideas, but Liv knew so much more about Cottonwood Falls than I did—maybe she could help me come up with a solution.

But first I needed to text Knox and see if they needed me over my break.

Larkin: Hey, everything good there? Do you need me to come home and help at lunch?

After a few minutes, I got a text. A picture of Emily on a horse.

"Oh my gosh," I whispered to myself as I zoomed in on the picture. Emily was smiling so big up there. She was having the time of her life. How could I let Seth and Nancy take this away from her?

Larkin: That's amazing!!! How did you make that happen?!

Knox: Took the kids out to my dad's!

He sent me another picture of him holding Jackson, a red barn in the background. At this point, my heart was a puddle.

Larkin: Have I mentioned you're the best?

That I'm falling in love with you? I didn't add that last part, but it was more than true.

My feelings were coming so fast, so strong, but Knox was so different from any man I'd known. Liv had been right to hope there'd be something between us.

I changed my messages to the thread with Liv and texted her back.

Larkin: I'll be there.

But then I flipped my phone over so I could focus on these charts until it was time for my lunch break.

I was walking to Woody's Diner when my phone rang

with a call from Knox. Hoping everything was okay, I answered and said, "How's it going? No broken bones? No one bucked off a horse?"

"We're great, more than great," he said.

I stopped on the sidewalk, the late summer heat already making sweat bead on my forehead. I couldn't dare to hope. "What is it?"

I heard the wind blow past his speakers and Jackson babbling away in the background. It was like since that first word came, he wanted to make all the noise he could. And then Knox said, "I found a solution."

"Knox..." I covered my mouth. "You didn't."

"Liv was a nanny before she married my brother. She said she would love to keep Jackson and Emily until Emily starts school in the fall. Then she'll watch Jackson during the day and pick up Emily from school." I could hear the confidence in his voice, the joy he had in helping me, in being strong for me.

Through the incredulity, I was about to thank him, tell him he was incredible when he added, "And on the days Liv can't watch them or pick them up, my friends Henrietta and Tyler Griffen will watch the kids. They're thinking of starting a family of their own soon, so it will be great for them to be around kids more often. And then for backup sitters, Rhett and Maggie Griffen offered to step up, but fair warning, Rhett has a potty mouth, so Em might come home with a colorful vocabulary."

I let out a tearful chuckle.

"And in a pinch, our friends Camryn and Cooper will babysit. Since they already have a one-year-old, I think they'd be extra good with Jackson. My dad is great with kids too as a backup, even though he's getting older—there may be some more TV time there. Between the lot of us, we have you and these precious babes covered."

Tears fell down my cheeks now, and I pressed at the corners of my eyes, unable to believe what he'd accomplished in less than half a day when I thought my world was falling apart. Just when I felt like my back was against a wall, he showed me I could lean on him. But it couldn't be that simple.

"I can't pay Liv the going rate for a nanny," I admitted. "I can't even afford half of that."

"We worked out a deal. You pay what you feel comfortable with, and I have the rest covered."

My mouth gaped open. He wanted to pay for my children's childcare? That couldn't be right. "Knox, I couldn't ask you to…"

"No money is changing hands," he assured me. "You'll see."

I raised my eyebrows. "Wait. What? It's nothing illegal, right?"

He laughed. "No, but it should be."

I shook my head in pure disbelief and continued walking along the sidewalk. "How did you do this all in a morning?" I asked. "I tried and failed with three different daycares. This feels too good to be true."

"It's Cottonwood Falls," he said. "We take care of our own. And, Larkin, you better believe you're one of us."

We ended our call, and I reached the restaurant, seeing a table full of my new friends through the window and was almost overcome with emotion again. These beautiful women had stepped up to be there for me, not much more than a stranger. And they loved Knox enough to care for me by default.

Part of me worried that they would cast me off if things didn't end well with Knox, but deep down, I knew there was a magic about this place. Seth may have been a bad seed, but it seemed like he was an apple that fell far away from the Cottonwood tree.

I made my way inside the restaurant, relishing the cool blast of air and the sound of friendly conversation that hit my ears. And when I got back to the table, I gave them each a big hug.

As we sat down, Liv said, "Tell me all about your babies. I'm so excited to start babysitting them!"

Henrietta nodded with a friendly smile, and even Della, Maggie, and Camryn leaned in like they were truly interested in hearing about my kids.

I smiled, getting to talk about my favorite people with my new friends.

Liv and I made plans for me to drop the kids off at her place the next morning, and then I had to ask...

"What's the deal Knox made with you?"

A wicked grin formed on her lips. "Come over for supper tonight and find out."

AFTER WORK, I met Knox at my house. He came to the bedroom with me while Emily watched an episode of *PAW Patrol* and Jackson played in his playpen. And when I told him that the kids and I were going to Liv and Fletcher's place to see what kind of deal he worked out, his jaw dropped.

There was even some color in his cheeks as he said, "You don't have to do that, do you?"

My hands stalled at the hem of my scrub shirt. "Knox Madigan, are you *blushing?*" An incredulous smile touched my lips.

"No." He fought a smile that came back right away. "Not at all."

I had to chuckle at him and went to hug him. I kissed his lips, savoring the feeling of kissing someone I knew had my back one hundred percent. "You're not going to tell me what this arrangement is?"

He smirked down at me, blue eyes impossible to look away from. "Sounds like you're finding out anyway. You'll have to handle the suspense."

"Is that so?" I arched an eyebrow. "I can think of a way or two to work the truth out of you." I winked.

He closed his eyes like I was already testing his willpower.

I stepped back from his arms, slipping my shirt over-head. "Good thing for you I like surprises."

"You do?" he asked, unabashedly checking me out. I would need to get used to that, not turning away from him when I was changing just because my ex didn't like my body.

I nodded and pulled on a tank top. Then I changed out of my scrub pants, saying, "Don't you love the antici-pation of knowing something good is coming?"

He leaned back on my bed, tilting his head to the side. "You think it's going to be good?"

With my shorts on, I walked to him, straddling him on the bed. "Anything that makes you blush like that is good to me."

A teasing look played on his face before he flipped me over on the bed and kissed me breathless, almost making me forget I had something to look forward to outside of this magical, heart-pounding moment.

"TURN ON THE MOWER!" Liv yelled. "Yank that chain!"

I shook my head at her. It was one thing to stand in my brother's front yard wearing nothing but cowboy boots, pink heart boxers, and a cowboy hat. It was another thing entirely to have my brother, sister-in-law, and the woman I'd fallen for as an audience. Thankfully, the kids were too busy swinging and playing in the back-yard to be bothered by this fiasco.

Larkin's face was pure joy as she wolf-whistled. "Get it, baby!"

Well, if Larkin wanted a show, I'd give her a show. I'd embarrass myself a thousand different ways to make her smile like that.

I pointed my ass their direction, bent over nice and slow, and made a show of pulling the lawn mower chain.

"Ow ow!" Liv yelled.

Fletcher guffawed.

And Larkin's tinkling laugh hit my ears. God, anything to make her laugh.

I shook my ass and then theatrically pulled a second time, my arm muscles and abs flexing with each movement.

Larkin laughed even harder, gasping for air.

My smile had to be just as big as hers. With my back to them, I schooled my expression, then I finally pulled the cord so the mower roared to life. I slowly snapped back up, rolling my hips in a sexy dance move on the way.

Fletcher yelled, "You chose the wrong profession!"

"Cop, stripper, what's the difference?" I tossed back. I turned up the throttle on the mower, then clamped the starting bar together. The self-propelled mower started moving, and I strutted along with it, moving my hips side to side, playfully adjusting my cowboy hat.

And then someone drove by. And slowed down.

And reversed.

Oh dear Lord. If one of the other cops happened to be out here...

But when I looked over, I didn't see another cop. Rhett Griffen had pulled alongside the road and had his phone camera pointed right at me.

My jaw dropped, and I turned to Liv. "You put him up to this!"

Tears were streaming down her face she was so amused, and Larkin was bent over the fence like she couldn't stand up straight with how hard she was laughing.

And then all hell broke loose when the door to the truck opened, and that damn pig he and Fletcher pranked me with the year before came running toward me.

I let go of the mower and said, "You've got to be shitting me."

The sound of laughter blended with the squeals of the pig. Even Graham, Maya's dog, was barking happily in the background.

"Better get the pig!" Rhett yelled. "Wouldn't want him getting lost!"

"My flowers!" Liv shrieked as the pig darted straight toward her pretty landscaping. "Get him, Knox!"

"Oh, now it's my job, not Rhett's," I muttered, tossing the cowboy hat on the ground. But I couldn't let Liv's flowers get destroyed either. This meant business.

I started slowly after the pig, trying not to scare it into the bed of petunias and trample it further while he rooted around with his flat pink nose.

The animal was so distracted by Liv's flowers, it hardly noticed me creeping up. I lunged for it, wrapping my arms around its pot belly, but it squealed and slipped out of my arms, almost like it was covered in...

I turned back to Rhett. "YOU *GREASED* IT?!"

His face was red from laughing so hard as he pointed to my brother. "It was Fletch's idea." Liv and Larkin were holding each other up, in stitches.

"I hate you, all of you," I said, turning to see where the pig had gone. He was prancing and snorting in the new natural stone fountain Liv and Fletch had installed up front. Figuring I had a little time, I jogged up to the fence where they were all hooting and hollering.

Larkin was breathless as I drew near. I leaned in, whispering in her ear, "I'm punishing you for this later."

Her spine stiffened, and she met my eyes. I gave her a teasing grin before pulling my T-shirt off the fence and sneaking back toward the pig. He was happier than a... pig in mud, splashing around in the water.

So happy that he didn't notice me launch forward with my shirt and wrap it around him. I picked it up by the pot belly, holding the snorting, squealing thing in my arms like a trophy. "Gotcha!"

The traitors watching me burst out in applause. If I had a free hand, I'd give them all the finger. Instead, I marched the pig to Rhett's truck, muttering, "We have got to stop meeting this way, Porky."

He stilled like he sensed defeat.

Then I put the pig and the shirt in Rhett's arms. "Go on, get."

"Worth the fifty bucks," he muttered.

I smirked. "Worth the revenge that's coming your way?"

Rhett tossed his head back and laughed.

Pretty sure at this rate we were going to make the teens who owned this potbellied pig filthy stinking rich.

As Rhett drove away, I turned to face the people watching at the fence, and I couldn't help but feel triumphant as I put my cowboy hat back on and finished mowing the rest of the yard.

Because later, I'd get to punish Larkin for being a bad, bad girl.

I couldn't fucking wait.

37

LARKIN

"I HAVEN'T LAUGHED that hard in months," I said to Knox on the ride back to town. The headlights illuminated gravel roads and dark ditches as he drove us in my minivan. And while I liked him driving his truck, there was something just as sexy about him feeling so at home in my car too, especially with his hand resting on my thigh.

He rolled his eyes, but there was a smile on his lips.

Emily asked, "What was so funny, Mama?"

Remembering the sight of him dancing in his pink boxers, I said, "Knox was being silly earlier while you kids were playing in the sandbox."

"Knox is *always* silly," she replied, like I was just stating the obvious.

Knox glanced over his shoulder at her, sitting in her car seat. "Always?" he said.

I looked over my shoulder to see her face scrunching up thoughtfully. "Sometimes you're really nice too. Like when I'm sad, you always make me feel better."

My heart completely melted as Knox smiled back at her in the mirror. "I'm here for you, Em."

She nodded and then changed the subject. "Can I have a popsicle at home?"

"No," I said. "It's already getting late, and we need to get you to bed." Not just because I was excited for what would happen once the kids were asleep. I had another full day of work tomorrow, and I wanted to get the kids to Liv's house early so I could help them settle in, even though they seemed plenty at home this evening.

Once we got back to my place, Knox said he was going back home to get ready for bed and that I could text him once the kids were down. My thighs clenched just thinking about it.

After he left, the kids and I went through our usual bedtime routine. I gave them a bath together, then brushed their teeth and set out their pajamas for after I applied their lotion. Jackson was getting so big he was almost ready for 2T clothing, even though he was just fourteen months now.

That familiar tinge of worry hit my gut, wondering when he would finally take his first steps independently instead of crawling and pulling himself up on couches and the like. His pediatrician said if he was pulling himself up on things, we really didn't need to worry for another couple of months. That still didn't stop my mama's heart from worrying.

But I reminded myself he'd already said "dada," even though I'd been concerned about his speech too.

As I slid lotion over his skin, I asked, "Can you say Em?"

His lips moved as he went, "Emmmm, Emmmm."

Emily jumped up and down. "HE SAID MY NAME!"

I grinned over at her, loving how excited she was for her brother's progress.

"That was great, Jacks," I said to him, then squeezed him to my chest. "You are getting so good with your words!"

"Emm, Emmm," he hummed.

Emily came beside us, putting her hand over her chest. "That's me. I'm Em!"

"Emm. Emm."

I smiled at them both and continued putting on lotion then their PJs. "We're all ready for bed, time for a bedtime story! Do you want to pick one?" I asked Emily.

She nodded, walking dutifully to the stack of books on a closet shelf and picked her favorite as Jackson babbled to himself. Tomorrow I would ask Liv to practice his words with him. Maybe he was just slow to talking and had plenty to say now that he'd found his voice. I guessed in some ways, Jackson and I were both finding our voices, learning to stand on our own two feet.

I climbed into Emily's twin-sized bed, gathering both children in my arms, and read them the story, making all the voices, pouring all the love I could into every word. And when their eyes slowly drifted closed, I tucked them in under the covers.

My heart raced as I gently shut the door behind me and went to my room. I didn't have much in the way of sexy lingerie, but I found my one set, a red lacy bra and a matching thong with a bow tie in the back.

Once it was on, I got my phone off my dresser. I

unlocked the screen and sent a text I never would have before I met Knox.

Larkin: I'm naked in my bed.

38

KNOX

I SET a clean dish in the sink and looked at my phone, lying faceup on the counter.

Larkin: I'm naked in my bed.

"Fuck," I hissed, my cock already tightening for her. I'd had to work on the dishes to keep my hands busy, even though my mind was thinking of all the things I wanted to do to her.

Larkin and I had already had needy sex, sweet sex, and now I wanted to play with her. Tease her until she begged for a release. And then *I* would be the one to give it to her. My name would be the one on her lips.

I grabbed a bag that was hanging by the door, and then I walked outside, going to her house. Even though we weren't more than twenty feet away, it could have been a mile. My hardening cock rubbed against my jeans, and all I could think about was her soft pussy, how it would feel to slide inside of her, feel her shudder around me.

I didn't bother knocking on her door, knowing that my girl was lying in her bed, ready for me. I hope she was touching herself, getting herself warmed up for my thick cock.

I tiptoed through the dark living room and then reached her bedroom door, closed. My hand gripped the handle, hard, and I twisted it, biting my lip because I was so damn ready to see her.

Instead of lying on her back facing me, she was on her hands and knees, her ass in the air with the bow tied like she was a damn present for me. "Fuck," I muttered.

She twisted her head so that her long brown hair fell over her shoulder and glanced back at me. "I'm sorry I was a bad girl earlier."

My lips twitched into a sultry smile. I loved this side of Larkin—she was hot and playful and fun and everything I wanted to experience with her. I loved the sight of her, loved that she was already feeling more confident around me.

I dropped my bag on the floor by her bed, and metal chinked inside. Then I walked to her, rubbed my hand over her ass, and slapped, hard enough to leave a light red mark, but not so hard as to really hurt her.

"Fuck me," she hissed.

I grinned at her, tugging off my T-shirt. "You liked that?"

She looked at me, heat in her eyes, and said, "I deserved it, didn't I?"

Damn. She really was perfect.

I reached for the button on my jeans, freeing my cock from the unforgiving fabric, and her eyes drifted to where it strained against my underwear. I pulled them down too, watching her. She flipped her hair over the opposite shoulder and gazed up at me with pouty lips, asking, "What are you going to do to me, Officer Madigan?"

I bent for the bag I brought over and drew out a pair of handcuffs. "Hands behind your back, ma'am."

I could see her shudder with excitement, and when she shifted to lie on the bed facedown with her hands behind her, I noticed the wet spot in her silky red underwear. She was just as ready for me as I was for her. But part of being a bad girl meant you had to wait.

I took one cuff and secured it around her wrist, relishing the feel of her skin underneath mine. Then I took the other end of the cuff and hooked it to her other wrist. Now she lay on her front, arms pinned behind her, ass looking juicy as fuck.

"These underwear need to come off," I said. I untied the bow and unwrapped her like the present she was. I tossed the material to the side, then I hovered over her back, running my tongue over her ass, biting small marks up her back till I reached her shoulders, her neck, the shell of her ear.

Her hands reached for me, and a low chuckle passed my lips. "You can touch me when I say you can."

She let out a moan and shifted her hips.

"You want some relief?" I asked.

Her hair fell over her face as she shifted and gasped, "Please."

I reached around her waist, drawing her hips up so that I had perfect access to her pussy, and I ate her from behind until she was wetter than ever before and whimpering, begging me for release.

But just as I could feel the muscles of her ass tighten, I

drew away. I picked up my shirt off the floor to wipe my face and said, "Not yet."

She groaned, and my cock was so hard I could feel the skin tight around its length. I wanted a release too, but not before I teased her, not until she was begging for me. I reached for the keys for my cuffs and unhooked them.

She rolled over, face red, hair askew, hands over her head. When I noticed faint red lines along her wrists, I drew them to my lips, kissing the tender spots. Then I pinned her hands above her head, her tits lolling to the side as she lay on her back.

Her stomach was so soft, ridged with stretch marks. I kissed a path down until I reached her swollen clit and sucked.

She let out a whimper. "Knox."

She wasn't begging. Yet.

I darted my tongue over her clit again, and again, until the only thing she could say was a gasping, "Please."

Feeling her body tense beneath me, I said, "On your hands and knees."

As if there wasn't an ounce of resistance left in her body, she rolled over, doing exactly as I ordered. I loved her ass in this position, the curve of her hips. And I was so fucking glad that I didn't have to wear a condom because I wanted to feel every ounce of her heat.

With one hand on her hip, I guided my cock to her entrance, pressing the swollen head and slowly sheathing myself inside of her. She moaned as I did, adjusting to my size, adjusting to the sheer pleasure we both felt at being this close together.

And when she adjusted, I drew back, burying myself

in her again, loving the way her ass rippled as I slammed against it.

I gripped her flesh, hanging on to handfuls as I gave it to her over and over again until we were both nearing the edge.

"I'm close," she gasped.

"Come with me," I told her. "I want to feel this with you."

Her back tightened underneath my hands, and I could feel the wave starting to come inside her.

I wanted to see her, so I fisted my hand in her hair, making her look back at me. She let out a strangled sound, and it tipped me over the edge. I spilled all I had inside of her and continued pumping until each of her waves faded.

When we finished, I carefully pulled out, spent. I reached for my T-shirt again, using it to wipe myself up and then cleaning her up as well. And then we lay on the bed, completely exhausted, facing each other. Her cheeks were flushed with her orgasm, her hair wild, but there was a soft smile on her lips.

"I didn't know punishments were supposed to feel so good," she said in a teasing voice.

"Baby, everything with you feels good."

She smiled over at me and reached for my hand. Her fingers easily slipped through mine. "I love having you here," she said.

"Me too," I whispered. I wished I could stay over, wished I could spend every second just getting to know her, but I wanted to respect her boundaries too, not take this too fast. So I said, "I can lie with you until you fall asleep."

With a squeeze of her hand, she whispered, "I'd love that."

I shifted in the bed until she had her back to me and curled my body around her curves, feeling like this was just one of many ways we fit perfectly together. I tucked my arm around her soft waist and brushed back her hair with my other hand, kissing the top of her head.

She let out a contented sigh, and it did something to my heart. Made it swell until I felt like I could burst.

I'd never felt like this before, so complete, just lying next to another person. And as Larkin's breathing slowed and she drifted to sleep in my arms, I prayed like hell that I'd be the last person she ever went to bed with.

39

LARKIN

WHEN I WOKE up in the morning, Knox was out of my bed but in my phone inbox.

Knox: Do you know how hard it was to leave your bed last night? I missed you the second I walked away.

My heart fluttered at the text, and I shifted my covers up to my chin. I always left the windows open at night to let in the cooler air. I loved this time of the morning. When the kids were still sleeping and the house was quiet. It felt like I had the whole world to myself. And now, I could share it with Knox.

My fingers tapped over the screen as I sent him a response.

Larkin: Think you can handle it another night? ;)

I bit my bottom lip, smiling like a lovestruck fool at my phone as the three dots appeared at the bottom of the screen.

Knox: Wouldn't miss it for anything.

So Knox and I continued our routine throughout the next several weeks. We both went to work, the kids had a great time staying at Liv's house, from going swimming to playing in the backyard. Every day Emily had something fun to tell me about her time with the Madigans. And then at night, he came over and showed me every way he could make me come. Once we finished, I'd fall asleep in his arms, and he'd leave the house before the children could find him in my bed in the morning.

I'd complain about the loss of sleep, but I'd never slept better than I had lying in Knox's arms. It was like we were in our own little bubble. Everyone in town knew we were seeing each other, thanks to the Dallas Diamonds game, but that was as far as it went.

Until Knox asked me to go on a date, just the two of us, on Friday night. I told him yes, if I could find a sitter, but of course he told me Tyler and Henrietta were already excited to watch the kids at their place. And some of the seniors who lived at their schoolhouse-turned-apartment building were eager to see the children as well.

But on Friday night, I still didn't know where we were going because, of course, Knox wanted it to be a surprise. So I put on a simple cotton dress and sandals while Knox watched the children in the living room.

Once I was ready, we drove to The Hen House. Knox said to the kids, "Are you excited to spend some time with some new friends tonight?"

Emily said, "I know Hen. We hang out with her somctimes with Liv. Yesterday, we picked tomatoes from their garden, and the ladies there showed us how to make fried green tomatoes!"

I squeezed Knox's hand. I hadn't gotten around to telling him that bit because last night, my mouth had been otherwise occupied.

"That's my favorite," Knox said. "Did you like them?"

Jackson babbled while Emily said, "Yes, especially with ranch."

"That's my girl," I said with a laugh. Anything tasted better with a little ranch dressing on it.

Knox ran his thumb over the back of my hand, asking Emily, "What do you think you'll do tonight?"

"Mama packed board games, so maybe that?"

I smiled back at her. "Which one is your favorite?"

"Maybe Chutes and Ladders... or Candyland... or Connect Four, or..."

"You like them all, huh?" Knox teased.

Emily said, "Yeah." And we were already at The Hen House, so we got out, walking toward the cute brick building. I held Jackson on my hip, and I watched as Emily reached for Knox's hand, holding it on the way up the stairs.

My heart did its balancing act, walking on the tightrope between happiness that I was with a man my daughter loved and utter terror that he'd someday break all our hearts. But I knew Knox, I reminded myself. He was a good man. He wouldn't do that to us. He couldn't.

We reached the door and knocked, and pretty soon, Tyler and Henrietta were letting us inside. I stared at the grand entrance and the lobby area. They had it all set up with a giant projector screen, a cute old-timey popcorn machine, and big inflatable cushions. Some of the residents were sitting in folding chairs or milling about. And there was even a little ball pit in the corner for the kids to play in.

I went to hug Henrietta. "Oh my gosh, this looks amazing!"

She grinned at me and then gave Jackson a little wave. "We do a community activity every Friday and decided to make this week a family movie night! We're watching *Shrek*."

"Oh my gosh, I love that one," I told her.

Jackson cooed like he agreed. He still hadn't added more than "dada" and "Em" to his vocabulary, but I swore he was getting more expressive by the day.

She held her hands out to Jackson, "Can I hold you, sweetie?"

He wasn't so sure at first, but he let her hold him, and soon she had him giggling by making silly faces at him. It warmed my heart to see my new friend be so sweet with my baby. With Jackson happy with Hen, I looked over to see Tyler Griffen, a guy around the same height as Knox with tattoos up and down both his arms and dark brown hair, showing Emily the popcorn machine while Knox watched. He plucked a piece of popcorn out and tossed it in the air before catching it in his mouth. Then he let Emily try. It bounced off her forehead, making all of them laugh. I smiled at the sight.

Was this what it felt like to live around family? To have more than just you loving your children, adding to your life?

I knew Tyler wasn't technically related to Knox, but they grew up together as neighbors and felt as close as brothers.

Knox turned to me and walked my way. "I think we lost the kids to the party," he said.

I smiled at the way he talked about my children.

"What?" he asked.

I reached for his hand, lacing my fingers through his.

"I just love the way you talk about my children. It means a lot to see you so sweet with them."

He dipped his head to kiss my temple. "They're part you," he said as if that was all the explanation he needed. "Ready to go?"

"Let me say goodbye to the kids, and we can head out." I went and told them goodbye, although it seemed like they hardly noticed I was there at all, and then Knox and I walked out to his truck. He went to my side, reaching for the handle. He looked so amazing in tan pants and a button-down shirt with the sleeves rolled, showing the tattoos on his forearms.

"Knox Madigan, are you holding the door open for me?" I asked, smiling at him.

His gaze heated as he pulled the door open. "Of course I am. But only so I can make out with you when you get in."

I giggled, all breathy and filled with butterflies. He made me feel so young. So whole.

He held my hand as I got into the vehicle, and once I was buckled up, he held true to his promise, kissing me right there in the parking lot until I forgot anyone inside could see us and could only remember the way his lips felt on mine.

When he broke our embrace, I asked, "Are you sure you don't want to go back to your place and have sex without worrying about being quiet?"

He closed his eyes like it took all his willpower to remember we had a date. "There will be time for that. On another date."

My heart skipped a beat. I loved when he so casually

dropped little hints at the future like that—like he wanted to keep taking me out—like it was a given.

He squeezed my thigh with his large hand and then carefully shut the door and walked around to his side of the truck.

Once he got in, I said, "Now will you tell me where we're going?"

He glanced my way, a crooked grin on his lips. "Somewhere I think you'll love."

40

KNOX

I COULDN'T HELP LOOKING over at Larkin as we drove down the winding country road and approached the Minnicks Ranch with a bright yellow sign that said GOAT YOGA in bold black letters with a thick arrow pointing left.

Her mouth fell open in the cutest way as she did a double take between the sign and me. "You're kidding," she gasped, slapping my thigh. "You're kidding me!"

I grinned at her. "Goat yoga and then a farm-to-table dinner. What do you think?"

She let out a squeal, a giddy sound I'd never heard from her before, and it made me feel so damn light my seatbelt was the only thing that kept me from floating away. I chuckled and said, "I'm taking that as a win."

"Of course it's a win, but..." Her face fell. "I can't do yoga in a dress."

"I packed us both workout clothes. Didn't want to spoil the surprise."

She ran her hand over my thigh, making warmth

spread through my body. "You are amazing, Knox Madigan."

I covered her hand with mine, squeezing it. "You remember that day I texted you, and I asked you what you loved?"

Her expression turned serious, and she nodded. I glanced at the road ahead of me, parking in the grass parking lot before a pretty outdoor area surrounded by twinkle lights. It wasn't dark out yet, but twilight was coming.

With the vehicle stopped, I looked over at her, drawing her hand to my lips and kissing her knuckles. "I think you're so busy taking care of everyone else, you don't notice."

"Notice what?" she asked, blue eyes dark in the dimming light.

"The things that make you light up." I held her hand on my lap, looking into my favorite feature of hers—those pretty blue eyes that were so expressive they told me everything I needed to know. "Your children... your work... creating new things with your Cricut machine.... and yoga. And then there is a certain twinkle when you're about to—"

She lightly smacked my hand. "You're trouble."

I laughed, loving that we could banter. I wanted a mix of that in my relationship—playfulness and realness alike.

"But you're right," she said. "I love this idea. Thank you for taking me here."

I nodded. "Ready to go?"

She smiled so big, her eyes got squinty as she nodded. "Yes!"

I drew her in, kissing her cheek, then we got out of the

truck, and I reached into my toolbox in the back, getting the gym bag I sneakily packed for her last night after she went to bed. She instantly opened it, peeking through the contents.

"What, are you checking on me?" I asked, feigning indignation.

She rolled her eyes at me. "I've made the mistake of asking a man to help me pack before."

I tried not to be bothered by the reminder of all the experiences she got to have with another man. We'd create memories of our own. "Not Knox Madigan," I countered.

"True," she replied. She held up a thin black band. "You even got me a hair tie? Thanks, babe." She lifted to her tiptoes to kiss my cheek.

And even though I loved the newness of everything happening between us, I had to admit I loved how easily she called me babe, how customary it seemed to have those lips on my cheek.

"Any time." I settled my hand low on her waist, right above the swell of her delicious ass, and walked with her toward the outdoor area where they held the goat yoga within a fenced-in wooden area. There was a woman at a folding table near the entrance, checking in couples.

We fell into line, and I read off our names.

"Gotcha," she said, marking us off the list with a flourish. "Bathrooms are in the shop. We're starting in ten minutes."

"Thanks," Larkin said sweetly, and then we turned back toward the metal shop building, weaving past the wrought iron tables set up outside for the dinner we'd have after yoga. "Gosh, it is so pretty here. I never thought myself a country girl, but the longer I spend in Cottonwood Falls, the more I think how nice it would be to have my own little place in the country where I can watch the kids play barefoot outside, explore, really get their hands dirty. Somewhere I could see forever."

I rubbed my hand over her back. "There has to be a front porch then, so you could sit and take in that view. And a porch swing."

She looked up at me, her blue eyes full of admiration. "As long as there's room enough on the porch swing for two."

We reached the shop building, and she pushed through the door like she hadn't just made me the happiest I'd ever been with just a few words. Once inside, we went into the bathroom, changing into our workout clothes. I wished I could have spent more time admiring her body without clothes on, but damn...

"Have I mentioned how I know there's a God?" I asked her.

She gave me a curious look as she worked her hair into a ponytail. "I don't think so?"

"It's those pants," I replied.

She huffed out a laugh, letting her hands and ponytail fall. "You're ridiculous."

"Do a spin," I told her, guiding her shoulders so I could look at her juicy ass. "Should get on my knees and worship dat ass."

"Oh my gosh!" She laughed and gave me a shove, but I reached for her hands, taking her with me. I backed up to the blank restroom wall, and she stood chest to chest with me, looking up at me.

"You are sexy as hell, Larkin," I told her, not a hint of a joke in my voice. "I'm so lucky to be here with you."

Her eyes searched mine, looking for the truth, and when she found it, she pressed a kiss to my lips. Before I could get carried away, she pulled back and said, "Now let's go see those goats!"

41

LARKIN

WE STEPPED into the pen with about fifteen other people just in time for the class to start.

When I was with Seth, I would have been nervous to be around so many attractive women in fitted clothing. He had a wandering eye, and I just wrote it off as being a man thing. But Knox never let his eyes stray to another woman.

He held my hand, making me feel like the only girl in the world as we set out our mats and chatted while waiting for the event to begin.

A pretty lady wearing bright pink tights and a matching pink sports bra stepped to the front of the yoga pen and began speaking. "Welcome to goat yoga at Minnicks Ranch!"

Everyone there began clapping, especially me. This was so special and new, and I couldn't wait to share it with Knox. Couldn't wait to tell the kids about it!

"Don't worry about taking pictures because my assistant will be walking around with her camera taking pictures of everyone. She'll edit and send them out while you're enjoying dinner."

A younger girl, maybe still in high school, with a camera held around her neck with a pretty strap gave us a wave.

The instructor, who said her name was Penny, talked us through what to expect and what to do if a goat went rogue or did something we didn't like. "Just start shaking, like this." She shimmied her shoulders, making her full breasts wiggle.

I looked to Knox, fully expecting him to be gawking at her. Instead, he was grinning at me, shimmying his shoulders. "Come on, Larkin. Shimmy."

I let out a relieved, happy laugh and shook my shoulders.

"You're a natural," he said, smiling back at me.

I smiled then redirected my attention to the teacher. She said, "We're going to start in a comfortable seated position, taking easy breaths in and out, while we let in the goats."

Goat braying filled the air as they got closer, and I craned my neck to see them through the fence as an older man in jeans and a T-shirt herded the goats to the yoga pen. Then the gate opened, and at least ten tiny goats came rushing into the place, prancing about.

Forget steady breathing, everyone just sitting, hoping a goat would run by. A tiny black and white one pranced over, and Knox reached out, rubbing it between the ears.

"Jealous!" I said. "I want to pet it."

He easily picked it up, the animal looking even smaller in his hands, and held it between us.

I rubbed its belly, and it flopped over like a dog. Laughter burst through me, and Knox chuckled with me. Our gaze met, and we were all smiles.

"This was such a great idea," I said to him.

Penny, the instructor, spoke up to draw everyone's attention back to her. "Now let's get on our hands and knees to do a few cat cows."

We followed her instructions, and I had to laugh when Knox got to the cow position and let out a moo.

I usually took yoga so seriously, just moving through the poses and trying to steady my mind. He brought *fun* to it as well.

We went through a warmup flow, following Penny's instructions as goats pranced around us and climbed over us. And I was thinking I had to bring goat yoga to the retirement home, until Knox was in a tabletop position, on his hands and knees, and a goat jumped onto his back.

The photographer came by, snapping photos of Knox while he held still to help it stay in place.

And as the shutter sounded, the goat let loose a sound of its own.

Yellow liquid splattered down from the goat, staining his shirt, and he let out a strangled cry, shimmying his body like he'd been electrocuted so the goat would stop. But it took its sweet time, finishing the job before jumping off and prancing elsewhere.

Knox stayed frozen in tabletop position, staring at me in abject horror as the liquid kept spreading.

And I burst out laughing.

"Larkin!" he said. "There's pee all over me and all you can do is laugh!?"

I laughed even harder, gasping for breath. The problem? I wasn't as young as I once was. Two pregnancies had done a number on me.

"Oh no!" I cried, squeezing my legs together. I so could not pee my pants on my first date alone with Knox. "Oh no!"

"Now you're getting it!" he cried. "I can't take off my shirt! I'll get pee on my head!"

"Stop!" I cried, laughing even harder.

"It peed on me!" he yelled.

"Oh shit," I said, covering myself as I peed my own damn pants.

"What?" he said.

Now my expression matched Knox's while I widened my eyes and yelled at the instructor. "Penny? Tell me you have a shower somewhere."

♏︎

THEY ONLY HAD one shower stall, and there wasn't room for much in here other than a shower and a small bench to keep your things. And I was *mortified* as I took off my pee-soaked yoga pants. Knox had the decency to turn the other way and took off his shorts and underwear.

Without speaking to him and wishing I could just disappear down the shower drain, I turned on the water. Knox came over, wrapping his arms around me from behind. His skin was warm, chest firm against my back.

"Are you sure you want to touch me?" I only half joked.

"Hey, some guys are into golden showers."

Anytime now, floor. Please, swallow me up.

When I didn't laugh, he twisted me in his arms and

hugged me. "Babe, do you know how many people have peed their pants from laughing too hard around me?"

I looked up at him. *This had to be a joke.*

He lifted his gaze toward the sky, racking his memory. "The first time was when some out-of-town cousins came to visit. She was seven years old and peed her pants out by the barn."

I let out a chuckle. "So, a child."

"I'm not done. There was my first girlfriend, when I was sixteen. There may have been some alcohol involved. Then another girlfriend at twenty-one. Fletcher at twenty-four—"

"Wait, I need to hear that story," I said.

"Fletcher would kill me," he deadpanned. He reached for the water, and satisfied it was warm, he shuffled both of us under the stream, still hugging me. The water splashed up from the spot where it hit our shoulders as he continued the list all the way up until tonight. "You make lucky number twelve."

"I hate you," I said.

He dipped his head down, kissing my cheek, my neck. "Is that so?" he hummed.

Fuck. "You're not supposed to be turning me on right now. I'm embarrassed." Still, my traitorous hands went to the back of his neck, nails scratching at his scalp.

He dipped his head farther, drawing a nipple into his mouth and sucking until heat pooled at my core.

"Knox, we're in public..."

"Door's locked," he said before teasing my other nipple.

I held on to him, legs feeling weak as hot water blasted over our bodies, adding to the slickness. His cock was hard, pressing against me. I reached down, taking it in my fist. This man had a way of distracting me, of making me lose all control. And after being the one in charge for so long, I loved that he could give this gift of wild abandon to me.

"Baby," he moaned softly against my chest.

"I want you," I told him.

"Back up." He guided me until my back was against the shower wall, the stream of water completely forgotten now. Then he hooked his hands around both my knees, lifting me off the ground. Seth had never been strong enough for this, especially after I gained weight. But Knox? He made it seem easy as he guided his cock into me, filling and stretching me until I had to bite down on his shoulder to keep from crying out.

"That's it," he said, slowly pumping into me.

"God, your cock feels so good," I said to him.

"Give me your eyes," he ordered. "I want you to look at me when you speak with that dirty mouth."

I did as he asked—would do anything he asked of me—and held his face in my hands, watching his expression, the subtle flex of his muscles as he fucked me, eyes on me like I was the hottest woman in the world.

"You look so good when you're getting fucked by me," he said, eyes full of heat.

"I can't get enough of you," I said, wishing he could somehow get deeper. Wishing I could put words to this overflowing feeling in my chest. And then it hit me. "I love you." The words spilled out of me before I could even think of holding them back. Before logic could tell me it was too soon to be thinking things like that, let alone saying them. But it was Knox. What we had existed outside of societal norms.

It was more than a relationship. What we had was... everything.

He paused, inside of me, his eyes full of emotion. "Do you mean that?" His voice was rough... vulnerable.

Fear piqued within me. What if he didn't feel the same way?

But I was tired of being afraid, tired of being less than myself to please a man. So I nodded, cradling his face in my hands. "I know it's early, but I love you, Knox."

He brought our lips together, kissing me as he ground his hips into me, filling me, bringing out even more emotions within me.

"I love you," he said. He pulled back so I could see his face, read the truth in his eyes. "I love you so damn much, Larkin."

"Oh, Knox," I whispered, tears already falling down my cheeks. "I love you."

"I love you," he said, picking up pace, pounding inside of me until I could think or feel nothing outside of him and his love for me. "I love you."

"Baby, I'm close," I said.

"Eyes on me as you come," he said. "All of you is mine."

I nodded, determined to give him everything he wanted. And I came around his cock so hard I saw stars in my eyes. But most of all, I saw him coming with me, shaking with the force of it all.

When all the waves had passed, he slowly lowered me and held me until I found my feet. "Knox," I whispered, looking up at him. This was all so overwhelming, so new.

"I know, baby," he said, drawing me into the shower stream. He ran his hands through my hair, making sure it was soaked to my scalp and then used the products attached to the wall to wash my hair with so much tenderness and care, I melted even more right there.

I loved that Knox cared for my kids. But it was even better knowing he could love and care for me too. It was dangerous to hope, to dream—I knew that from experience—but I could imagine us on that front porch together, watching the sunset well into the future, even after the kids were grown and busy living their own lives.

I just hoped that nothing would come along to bring my dreams crashing and burning to the ground.

42

KNOX

LARKIN and I walked to the outdoor dining area where all the other couples were already sitting, my arm around her shoulder, her arm around my waist, her wet hair tickling my arm. All of her makeup may have been washed off and her hair unstyled, but she'd never looked more beautiful to me than she did right then under the twinkle lights.

There were a few eyes on us as we went to the table with a place card that had our names on it in swirly letters. "Looks like this is us," I said.

We parted from our embrace, and I helped her into an open chair.

"Such a gentleman," she said with a wink.

I had to chuckle as I sat across from her. I moved my foot under the table so my leg could brush with hers.

I'd never felt this way before, and just when I thought everything was perfect with her, it got even better.

Hearing her say those words? It meant the world to me. It meant the world to my teenage self who thought he was unlovable and irrevocably damaged. It meant the world to my current self who worried that Larkin would keep her walls up indefinitely, never fully giving herself to me.

But she loved me.

She loved me.

Penny came over, now changed out of her pink yoga outfit and into a pair of jeans and a buttoned black shirt, carrying two carafes. "Here is your tea and water, and we'll be bringing you the first course soon. Goat cheese crudités. The dip is to die for."

"Thank you," Larkin said.

"We also have conversation cards right here." She pointed to what looked like a regular card deck in the seasonings and napkin holder. "They are questions for you based on the stage of your relationship. We've had some couples coming long enough that they get to move up from new relationship to married!" She gave us a wink and then left us to it.

Before Penny walked away, she reached for the tea and poured us both a glass while I reached for the cards that said New Relationship on the outside of the pack. I'd wondered why they wanted to know the state of my relationship while booking the class. "Wanna try these?" I asked Larkin.

"Sure," she replied and took a sip of her iced tea.

I got the cards out, and since they had the look and feel of playing cards, I shuffled them a few times before drawing one from the top. "What is your love language?"

Larkin smiled gently. "Words of affirmation. You?"

"Physical touch." I winked.

She laughed.

"And quality time," I added. "I just like being with you. Doesn't have to be anything special."

"I can do that," she said with a smile. Then she drew a card off the top of the deck. "Where do you see us spending holidays?"

"We usually do holidays at my dad's place," I said. "But if you wanted to do something together, I'm all for that."

She bit her bottom lip. "Actually, I'm planning to do Thanksgiving in Paris with my sister. And she offered for you to come along."

My jaw dropped. "You're kidding."

Larkin shook her head. "You can say no if you want."

"Why would I say no to Paris with my girlfriend?"

Her lips parted.

"What?" I asked.

"You said girlfriend." Her cheeks heated like she was almost embarrassed to bring it up.

"Shit. Was I supposed to ask?"

Her laugh made me buoyant. "I don't know. It's been a long time since I dated."

"Well, I don't care what I call you as long as I can call you mine."

She reached under the table, squeezing my knee. "I'll be your girlfriend, Knox Madigan."

Now I was grinning like a fool as I reached for the next card. "Tell me something I don't know about you yet."

Penny came back with a platter of vegetables and sliced bread and a few ramekins of different goat cheese dips. We both tried some, and they were just as good as Jenny had promised.

"Something I don't know about you?" I prompted Larkin again. I wanted to know everything about her.

She twisted her lips to the side as she thought. The votive candle on the table cast a flickering glow on her skin. "I passed out in the ER when I was doing my nursing school clinicals."

"What?" I asked, surprised by her answer.

"I don't do well with trauma wounds," she said. "That's one of the reasons I've always worked in residential settings."

"Fletcher is the same way," I told her. "He worked in the children's ER for a while, and it really took a toll on him."

Her face was full of empathy. "Oh, I bet that would be really hard... So what about you?"

I thought of all the things I'd told her, and one I hadn't. "I'm a jealous man."

Her smile turned playful. "Is that so?"

I nodded, leaning forward and holding her hand under the table. "I want to buy you new lingerie so I know I'm the only man you've ever worn them for."

A flame sparked in her eyes. "I'm up for any chance to turn you on."

Damn, I needed to cool it, or I'd be hiding a semi under the table. "Okay, next question before I get carried away."

She drew a card from the deck and frowned slightly before clearing her expression. "How many children do you want to have?"

"I already know two perfect children," I said, nudging her leg.

Her expression eased.

"I'd love to have a big family," I admitted. "Our house was never quiet, and I always have someone to count on, no matter what... What about you?"

But she didn't get to answer because Penny came back with the main course. Free-range chicken breast, home-grown mashed potatoes, and gravy made with milk from cows on the Minnicks Ranch. There was even a side of fried okra that came from their garden.

We ate and chatted, enjoyed each other, until it was time to go pick up the kids from Henrietta and Tyler's. I could tell Larkin was tired—she scooted to the middle seat and leaned on my shoulder as I drove us home, the radio playing softly.

The kids were half asleep when we picked them up, and it was easy to help them settle in at Larkin's place. Once they were down, I followed her to her bedroom to tell her goodnight.

But she looked up at me with wide eyes and said, "Will you stay the night?"

I couldn't believe she was asking. Sure, we went on vacation together, and I came over for short bits of time while the kids were asleep, but something about being here when they woke up felt like a big step for us. Even bigger than saying I love you and calling her my girl-friend. "Are you sure?"

She closed the distance between us, kissing me softly on the lips. "I would love to wake up next to you."

I smiled at her and said, "Let me go get my pajamas and a change of clothes so I don't scare the kids in the morning." I couldn't wait to wake up next to her, to make breakfast for her and the kids... I just didn't know how wrong it would go when we woke up.

43

LARKIN

I CHANGED into pajamas while Knox was gone to his house getting his things. And when he came back, we slept under my covers, him in buffalo plaid pants and a black shirt, me in a matching pajama set I got on sale at Walmart. And even though this was a simple life, we didn't have a fancy home like Ford, and I wasn't with my first husband, this life felt rich to me. Knowing my children were sleeping happily and that when they woke up, they would be loved and cared for.

I fell asleep with Knox's arms curled around me and only woke up when Jackson cried out in the night. I went to his room, holding and rocking him until he fell back asleep and I could settle him in his bed. But since it was only half an hour away from the time I usually wake up for the day, I couldn't exactly go back to sleep.

I slipped into bed, lying in Knox's arms, and was in that blissful place between being awake and sleeping when his phone vibrated on the nightstand.

I wondered who could be texting him so early but

wrote it off as he tightened his strong arms around me. This had to be my favorite place to be.

But then his phone went off again, and again.

"Are you going to get that?" I asked him.

"Just mute it for me," he mumbled into the back of my neck. Sleepy Knox had to be the cutest. I reached for his phone to silence it but found it was already muted. "You have to turn off the vibration in your settings," I told him.

"How do you do that?" he asked, eyes still closed, long eyelashes pressed together.

I kissed the tip of his nose. "I can do it for you. I just need your password to unlock your phone."

He muttered off a string of numbers that I tapped in. But then another text message came across the screen.

Garth: Found this pic of them at Minnicks.

A photo came through, a screenshot of something posted to the Minnicks Ranch Facebook page. Knox and I were sitting at a table together, holding hands on the tabletop and looking into each other's eyes. We looked like we were in love. I smiled at the photo, making a mental note to ask Knox how to access the rest of the photos when he woke up. But then another message came through.

Dennis: Looks like Knox has a thing for the single mom. Think she put out last night?

Garth: Damn, now we know why he was so defensive with me.

Dennis: You sure you wanna raise Seth's kids? What if they turn out like him?

Trent: Yeah, Knox, can't you find someone who

doesn't have so much baggage? I mean, there are still some single girls in town. What about Della?

My heart sank as the messages slid over the screen. And I knew I shouldn't have done it—after all, curiosity killed the cat—but I tapped through to the prior messages, going back to see what they were referencing about Knox being so defensive. Surely he wouldn't be okay with his friends talking about my kids and me like this.

But then I saw the text that they had sent back and forth the first time. Messages with pictures from the first night I went out with Liv and the girls. My stomach turned at the things they said about me. And then I felt like I could throw up when I realized that Knox had said nothing to defend me.

Along with the nausea, my heart sank. Felt like it was breaking.

Beside me, Knox still lay there, peaceful in my house. My children, the ones his friends were insulting, sleeping in the next room.

Suddenly his arms around me felt like heavy weights starving me of oxygen.

Knox opened his eyes, asking me, "Did you figure it out?"

I slid out from his arms, handing his phone to him. "I think you should read these messages. Your *friends* want to talk to you." My voice shook with anger, with embarrassment. If he let his friends speak to him like this, how did he think about me under his perfect, charming exterior?

His eyes snapped open as he went to the texts, reading them, and his face fell. "Larkin, did you read these?"

I got out of the bed, pacing the floor, and whispered,

"I didn't mean to at first. They were just coming over the screen. Is this really how your friends feel about me?" I couldn't bring myself to ask him if this was how he felt about me too. I cannot believe just last night I was so happy that I was dreaming about what the future held for us. Now I wondered if a future with me felt like settling to him.

He sat up on the bed, facing me, and dumped his phone face down on the tousled sheets. "Larkin, they're just being shitheads."

I shook my head, tears already building in my eyes. This was not how I wanted to wake up this morning. "You sure as heck didn't say anything back the last time they commented."

He got out of bed, taking my hands in his. "I didn't text them back because I went and talked to him. That's why Garth apologized in the first place and said I was defensive."

I wanted to believe him, but Seth had worked things around in his favor so many times that I didn't know what to believe. "I mean, they're right." My voice shook. "Why not Della? Why not someone who doesn't have so much 'baggage?'"

He got a fierce look in his eyes and said, "Don't you ever call Emily and Jackson baggage."

An uncomfortable, guilty feeling swirled in my gut because he was right. My children weren't baggage. They were blessings. But just because they were my blessings, didn't mean that they needed to be his. I stepped back, putting space between us. "What if your friends are right? What if you wanted to start fresh with someone? You said yourself you wanted to get me new lingerie in case I'd worn mine for another man. What about children that I made having sex with someone else? Could you ever look at them without seeing him?"

A furrow formed between his eyebrows. "Larkin, when I look at your children, I see all the best parts of you and all the pieces that are uniquely them. They're their own people."

I drew my arms around myself, feeling so ashamed, feeling stupid for letting this relationship move so quickly. "And what about kids? You said last night you wanted a big family. What if I don't want to have any more? What if I have too much trauma from Jackson's pregnancy and don't want to go through that again? Will you be okay with my children being the only ones we have?" I knew it was too soon to ask him something like this, but now a million thoughts were spinning in my mind, and I couldn't move forward with him without knowing his answers.

"Why are you borrowing trouble?" he asked, a furrow in his brow. "Everything has been going great between you and me."

I shook my head at him. This wasn't borrowing trouble; it was being practical. "I'm a single mom, Knox. I don't have the privilege of just living my life day by day. I have two children who are counting on me to make good choices for them, and I know you said you would be there for them always, but what about me? I fell for you, I *love* you, and I don't want you to resent me because of my family. I don't want you to end up hating me because I don't want to put myself through another pregnancy. I don't want you to feel like you missed out on anything in life, because you deserve so much. And I hate to think that every time you go out with your friends that some part of them thinks the life you have with me isn't good enough for you..." Then an entirely new fear came to mind, and I had to sit on the bed to stomach it. "Is that how your family feels about us too?"

"Larkin, stop," he said with all the authority he had spoken to me with on that very first day we met. He knelt in front of me, taking my hands in his. "I don't give a shit what anyone else thinks about my life. I don't want to create a life that looks good to other people. I want to create a life that feels good to me." He brushed his fingers over my cheeks, and I could only imagine how I looked, my hair a mess, my eyes still drooping from sleep, worry creasing every line on my face. But he spoke to me like I was beautiful, saying, "Being with you feels good to *me* right now. That's all that matters."

I shook my head sadly, realizing how different our lives were, our priorities were. Because while Knox could choose what was best for him in the moment, I would always have to choose what was best for my children now and in the future. "Actually, it's not all that matters to me. I need to know that if we continue this, you would be okay with just me and my kids. Five years from now. Ten years from now. Twenty years down the road. Because I don't want to fall in love and get broken up with and go through this heartbreak again. I don't know if I could survive it and be the best mom to my kids."

It felt foolish to say it out loud, that I couldn't survive a breakup with Knox, considering what I had gone through in my life, but I knew deep in my heart it was true. Knox was a once-in-a-lifetime kind of man. And while I didn't want a chance of another man leaving them, I couldn't risk them feeling like a burden like all of Knox's friends thought they were.

Knox cast me an incredulous glance. "You think I haven't thought about our future?" he asked softly. "You think that first day you came over I didn't imagine what it would be like to kiss you? Do you think that night I babysat I didn't wonder what it would be like to care for your children as my own? Do you think that first morning I woke with you coming into my bed I didn't imagine what it would be like to wake up with you every damn morning for the rest of my life?"

I looked him in the eyes, as if I could remember every bit of color in them, as if I could permanently trace the edges of his lips into my mind. "I need you to think about what I said, Knox. Take time to really think about if this is the life you want. And whatever your decision is..." My voice broke as tears threatened to fall. "Whatever your decision is, I promise I'll understand."

He looked like he wanted to say more, but I held up my hand to stop him. If he argued any more, I didn't know if I could stand strong. This request wasn't just for me and my kids. It was for him too. Knox was like a diamond shining against mud. He deserved everything he wanted and more. And I never wanted to be the person who held him back from the life of his dreams, even if it wasn't with me.

So I said, "I need you to go, before the kids wake up. We'll talk soon, okay?"

He nodded sadly, then gave me a slow kiss on the lips before walking out the door. And I hoped that he would come back knowing exactly what it meant to be with me.

44

KNOX

NO WALK of shame compared to slipping out of Larkin's house and skulking down the sidewalk with a heaviness in the pit of my stomach. One moment I was on top of the world and now it was all slipping away from me. I understood why she was scared, and I *hated* that she'd seen those messages. Hated even more the lowlifes that sent them. Couldn't believe I'd ever called them my friends.

I held my phone in one hand, my bag in the other, wondering why the fuck those guys had to be like that.

I guessed I'd kept them in my phone thinking they were harmless—they could say crappy things, but I didn't have to wallow in the filth with them. Now, it was different because their behavior was hurting the woman I loved and messing with my life. A life I thought I'd begun building with Larkin.

I walked inside my house, dropped the bag on a chair at my kitchen table, and got out my phone to text them back.

Knox: I don't want to be a part of this group chat anymore.

Messages started coming through, telling me they were just kidding, saying that they didn't mean it and would back off. But I didn't care.

Knox: It was one thing to insult a single mom, another altogether to insult my woman. Fuck off.

I blocked every one of their numbers and then tossed my phone onto the table, going about getting breakfast ready even though the thought of eating made me sick. It kept my hands busy while I thought about how to fix this mess. I needed someone to help me understand what the fuck I was doing and how to show Larkin that I understood what I was getting into.

As my eggs were frying in the pan, I got out my phone and called Fletcher. He hadn't married a single mom, but he had been dating Liv as a single dad, and he had put up a fight against love just like Larkin was doing now.

In a short phone call, we'd agreed to meet at the clinic for lunch so we could eat and talk without the prying eyes and ears of everyone in Woody's Diner. I wished we could have met sooner though. I didn't know how I could focus on work with thoughts of losing Larkin on my mind.

And to make the situation even worse, it was one of those mornings when every damn song that came on the radio was one about breaking up. I switched from channel to channel, getting everything from "Achy Breaky Heart" by Billy Ray Cyrus to "Since I Don't Have You" by Guns 'n' Roses.

With a grunt, I turned off the radio and patrolled the town for the first half of my shift. I wanted to text Larkin, call her and fix this. But I knew I needed to give her space to sort through her feelings. And maybe it was good for me to figure out my own as well.

Not that we Madigan men were great at getting to the heart of things. Hell, everyone knew Dad had a thing for Agatha at the diner, and he was still pushing that "just friends" BS on us.

Finally, noon hit, and I parked in the lot in front of the old house-turned-doctor's-office with the Madigan Medical sign out front. Just my car, Fletcher's truck, and his nurse Brenda's car were in the lot.

As I got out of the car, the front door of the practice opened. Brenda walked outside, pink weights strapped around her wrists and ankles. She'd worked for Fletcher for the last couple years, and I'd always seen her walking around town at lunchtime, even before Fletcher came back.

"Do you ever take a day off?" I asked her.

She grinned at me, still moving her feet and arms like she was warming up, and said, "The day I take a day off is the day you need to send me to a hospital."

I grinned as best I could with a broken heart. "Good to know."

"Have a good lunch with your brother," she said, breezing by me on the sidewalk as I walked toward the entrance.

My heart beat fast as I approached the building, desperation building in my chest. I needed advice, and I hoped that he could give me an answer that would fix this situation with Larkin. Just the night before things had been going so well, but now it felt like the future I imagined with her was slipping through my fingers.

I went through the front door, bells ringing as it

opened, and Fletcher called, "Lock the door and meet me in the kitchen."

I shut the door and locked the deadbolt like he asked. It was like being a kid again, yelling at each other across the house. After the door was locked, I walked back to the kitchen area, seeing him setting out a steaming casserole on the table along with a mixed salad.

"This is way better than the ham and cheese I packed myself," I muttered.

He laughed, saying, "Liv told me if I didn't finish the leftovers, she'd have my head. So we both get to enjoy them."

I smiled, wondering how Liv was doing with the kids today. I bet Emily was in seventh heaven, getting to spend all day with her idol, Maya, and Jackson was surely having fun playing with Leah outside.

Fletcher began dishing a plate for himself, and then he cast me a curious look. "So what's going on? Usually it's you, me, and Hayes meeting at the diner. His birthday is coming up... Are we planning a surprise party for him?"

"You know Hayes hates surprises," I said. "It's Larkin."

Fletcher's eyebrows drew together. "What's happening? Liv showed me that post online of you two at the Minnicks Ranch. She wants us to do a double date there next time."

I cut my fork through the lasagna, the cheese melted and pulled. It really did smell good, but I was so upset I had a hard time bringing a bite to my mouth. "Well, last night, I stayed over at Larkin's, and the group chat with those guys went off. They saw that post too and had lots to say about it."

Fletcher winced. "Do I need to ask what they said?"

I shook my head. "It was just about as bad as you could imagine. And Larkin saw it."

Fletcher finished chewing his bite and swallowed before saying, "Was she going through your phone? That's a red flag, Knox."

"No, it wasn't like that. My phone was going off, and it kept vibrating, so I asked her to turn the vibrating off because I didn't know how to do that, and then of course the messages kept going over the screen. And I think she did go back and see some of the older messages, but I mean, can you blame her? They were talking about her."

Fletcher let out a sigh. "I guess you're right. So what happened after she read them?"

I ran my sweaty hands over my pants, like that would somehow ease the aching in my chest. But I had no idea what else to do. "She told me that I needed to think about what it meant to be with a single mom, that I needed to make sure I was okay being with a woman who had kids with another man and who might not ever want to have kids with me."

The weight of those words hung between us, and Fletcher's dark eyes took me in. He had our mother's eyes, but I had our dad's. I was always a little jealous of him, and maybe a little mad too, because every time I looked at him, I thought of her.

Then Fletcher said, "Larkin has a good point. Have you really thought about what it means to be with a single mom? Dating a parent isn't like dating someone who's single and has no kids in the picture. The kids come first. And once those kids get attached to you, it's not fair for them to lose someone all over again."

Now he really did sound like Larkin, and that's exactly why I needed to talk to him. But I was upset too because I already knew these things. I knew that those kids needed someone to stay in their life. "Why does everyone act like just because I don't have a kid that I don't understand how important they are?"

"I know you care." Fletcher wiped the corners of his mouth and set the paper napkin on the table. "It's hard to understand what it's like to have a child and know that you are their person. Everything they need, their whole life and future rests on your shoulders."

I sat back in my chair because... he was right. I'd never understand that because no matter how much I loved and would be there for her kids, I'd never be their dad. They'd always have their mom and dad to count on.

Fletch leaned forward, his elbows resting on the table. "Are you sure you're okay with never having children of your own?"

Of my own... I shook my head. "I'd love a big family, but honestly, I don't give a fuck if I pass my genes on to someone else."

Fletcher arched an eyebrow. "What does that mean?"

I leveled a look at him because after all we'd been through, I knew I could be honest with him. "Tell me that you're not worried that someday Maya or Leah will get cancer like our mom did. Tell me you're not worried that you'll get it someday and have to leave your kids like Mom left us."

Fletcher's expression cracked, showing just how close my words hit home. "I'm scared of it every damn day," he admitted, his voice barely a whisper. He blinked quickly then met my gaze. "But you also know that life can be over before you know it. I'm not regretting a moment of life with my little girls, no matter what hard things life throws our way. No matter how dark it feels like the world can get, they're the bright spot in every day." He pinned his gaze on me. "If Larkin and those kids were the only family you got... would you be okay with it?"

I chewed the inside of my cheek as I thought it over. I thought I knew my answer, but everyone I spoke to seemed to doubt me.

Fletcher patted my forearm, saying, "It's a lot for a new relationship—to think about the future when you're still figuring out the present. Liv and I were lucky, because we were friends for a long time, even before Maya was in the picture. For Larkin and you, it's all pretty new. There's no shame in taking time to figure it all out."

"That's the problem. I know. I decided, Fletch. How can I show her that I'm not going to walk away? That I'm okay with the life I'm choosing now?"

"You might know, Knox, but she needs to see you solid in your choice. Take time to think, like she asked you to. I know you always look out for everyone else, but you need to include yourself in that list too. Make damn sure that this is what *you* want, because it's one thing to walk away from a grown adult, another to leave a child."

45

LARKIN

"THANKS FOR SENDING those school supplies for Emily," I told my sister on a voice call over my lunch break. It was a cooler day, and I wasn't very hungry, so I decided to walk around the neighborhood and give her a call.

It was noon here, and nearly seven o'clock there. I could hear the sounds of a streetside café in the background along with the hum of vehicles. "Of course," Taylee said over the noise. "I can't believe she's going to kindergarten next week."

"Me neither. It's like I blinked and my little six-pound, two-ounce baby isn't a baby anymore."

She smiled, and I could hear her take a drink—probably of her favorite red wine. "Good thing you have a hot cop to distract you."

I paused, my heart aching as I walked along the sidewalk. "About that..."

"What's going on?" she asked.

I filled her in on everything that had happened with

our date, saying I love you, and then the things that I had found on his phone.

"What a bunch of pieces of shit," she spat, and then she let out a string of curse words in French. "Please tell me Knox was not texting them back and talking about you that way."

My leg brushed against a dandelion tuft as I walked, and I picked it, thinking that my children would really love it. I hoped they were having a good day at Liv's place with summer coming to a close. "He wasn't texting them back, and he told me that he confronted them about it earlier in person. I just get worried with the way that Seth was. You know he could twist things to make himself the hero or the victim, never the villain."

"I mean, I agree you need to pay attention to the red flags up front, especially since this is the best that it gets in a relationship, right? The early part, when you're still being extra nice and extra sweet and he hasn't seen you poop with the door open yet?"

"Seth never saw me poop with the door open. I'm half convinced he didn't know I pooped at all," I replied.

She giggled on the phone, and then she waited while a loud engine passed by. "So what did you tell Knox about the texts?"

"I told him he needed to think about what it meant to be with a single mom and that we couldn't move forward unless he knew what he really wanted."

"How did he take it?"

The haunted look in his blue eyes sent pain straight to my stomach. "He told me he would think about it."

She hesitated for a moment.

"Say it," I told her. Taylee always had an opinion and, more often than not, advice to go along with it.

"Are you sure you're not pushing him away because you're afraid?"

"Something snapped in me, seeing his friends talk about my kids like that."

"And what if he says his friends are right, that he doesn't want to be with a single mom?"

Just the thought of it made me want to disintegrate into the sidewalk, but I spun the dandelion stem around in my fingers, wishing love was just as simple as "he loves me, he loves me not." But Tay was right. I had been the one to push him away; I knew that. "If he already knew, he won't be upset by me asking him to think it over. And if he didn't know before... now I'll know he really wants to be here."

"And if he doesn't?"

The words hung in my mind, impossible to ignore. "I'll find a way," I said. There was no other option.

After a beat, my sister said, "Have I told you how brave you are?"

That stopped me in my tracks on the sidewalk. I was in a residential part of town, standing in front of a house with pretty landscaping out front. A woman came rushing by, walking quickly with pink weights on her wrists and ankles.

She gave me a quick wave and a wink before continuing on her way.

"What do you mean?" I finally said to my sister. Me? Brave? I felt like the biggest coward on the planet, running away from a man who just the night before said he loved me.

Her tone was pure as she said, "A lot of women wouldn't have had the courage to leave Seth like you did. They would have stayed with a man who was sleeping around on them because they were afraid of starting from scratch. But you left with those two babies, and you made a life on your own, even if it wasn't as nice of a house as the first one you had, even if it wasn't what felt comfortable. You moved to a whole new town and made friends and fell in love and stood your ground when Seth's parents were trying to force you down a path you didn't want. I think it's amazing, and I really, truly am proud of you."

My eyes were stinging, and despite my best efforts, a spot darkened on the cement as a tear dripped down my chin. "Thank you," I managed, continuing down the sidewalk before someone came outside and told me to move along.

"Of course." She paused for a moment. "If Knox comes back to you, we'll know he's a man worth his salt. And if he doesn't, I know that you'll be just fine. You have me, you have your friends, and you have your kids. And most importantly, you have yourself. You've got everything you need to build an incredible life wherever you go."

I sniffed, wiping at tears. Rumors would probably be all over town with people speculating about why I was walking around sobbing in the middle of the day. Through sniffles, I said, "One of these days, I'm going to be the strong one and it won't always be me crying on the phone when you call."

"We can take turns," she said.

I smiled. "I'm so grateful I have you as a sister."

"Same here."

We hung up, and I continued walking around town before getting back to work. I was in the midst of the afternoon pill rounds when Bernice found me in the hallway. "Great news, Larkin!" she said.

I looked at her curiously. "What's going on?"

"Our activities director is excited about your yoga idea! I'm going to have her set a meeting with you so you can plan out the pilot program." She leaned in closer, whispering, "This will look great on your application in a couple years when I retire and the board is looking for a new director."

My mouth fell open. "You mean it?"

She nodded and gave me a quick hug. "So glad to have you on the team."

As she walked away, I reminded myself that my sister was right. Regardless of what happened with Knox, I had what it took to make a really good life. I just couldn't help wishing that he would be in it as more than a neighbor.

46

LARKIN

AFTER WORK, I drove on the dirt roads out of town to Liv and Fletcher's pretty white farmhouse. It was gorgeous with wide windows facing the countryside and a sprawling green lawn. The fenced-in backyard had a trampoline and a swing set and plenty of space to play.

When I pulled into the driveway behind Liv's truck, I got out and breathed the fresh country air. I wondered if Knox and I would ever have a little farmhouse of our own, like we talked about on our date.

His laugh was enough to brighten even the darkest days. And the way he stood up for me to Seth, I'd never felt so protected and cared for. I wanted to run to him, hold on to him forever, but I knew it wasn't fair to him either. He'd never been married, never had children. Before we took our relationship any further, I needed to know he was all in and that a future with me was really what he wanted.

I tried to clear my mind of all the angst I was feeling as I walked to the door and knocked. Through the front glass, I could see the older three kids playing in a blanket fort in the living room. Maya was crawling on her hands and knees into the fort with Emily and Leah riding on her back like a horse.

The sight brought a smile to my lips. They were having so much fun.

Liv approached holding Jackson on her hip, a bib around his neck. She swung the door open, saying, "Hey, girl, hey!"

I grinned at her, and Jackson reach his hands out, saying, "Mama!"

My mouth fell open as I reached for him. "What did you say?"

"Mama! Mama!"

Tears formed in my eyes as I held him close, his soft cheek brushing against mine. "Did you help him with that?" I asked Liv.

She grinned, nodding. "Em and Maya helped too. Come in. I made enough supper for everyone."

I carried Jackson into her home, and Emily ran up to me, wrapping her arms around my waist. "Hi, Mommy!"

I grinned down, hugging her back with my free arm. "Did you have a good day?"

She nodded so quickly her pigtails bounced. "We did practice for school!"

Maya said, "You'll love school. Grammy D teaches there, and it's the best."

With a smile, Liv said, "Okay, girls, go wash your hands. Maya, help Em and Leah, please."

I smiled, going to join her at the island, where she had grilled cheeses cooking on a griddle and what looked like green beans heating in the microwave. "Has anyone told you that you're Supermom?" I asked her.

She batted the spatula at me. "You came in at a good time. You missed the bath I had to give Jackson because Emily decided it would be fun to paint hearts on him with mud."

Jackson said, "Emm, Emm."

I let out a laugh, the image forming easily in my mind. "Have I said how thankful I am for all of this?" I asked her.

She tilted her head with a smile. "I'm happy to help. Your kids are the sweetest, really."

I smiled, bouncing Jackson on my hip. He was playing with my ponytail, running his fingers through the strands.

"How are things with Knox?" she asked. "Fletch said they had lunch together today."

I frowned, and her lips parted.

"Oh no, did something happen?"

I bit my lip, worried if I told her that our relationship might not work out, I'd lose babysitting too. "We're… taking a pause right now. He didn't do anything wrong. I just…" I took a breath and turned to check that Emily couldn't hear, but the girls were all yelling their ABCs as they washed their hands in the bathroom. "I wanted to make sure he had time to think about what it meant to date a single mom before things got any more serious."

Her eyes filled with compassion. But before she could say anything, I continued, "I know you're babysitting partly as a favor to him, but if I need to pay more, I can find a way if you give me some time to catch up. The down payment on my place and all the fees to turn on utilities and getting things for the house really wiped me out, but I'm slowly building my way back up."

Liv turned off the griddle and walked around the counter, putting a hand on my shoulder. "Babe, hear me out, okay?"

I nodded, my heart beating quickly.

Her brown eyes held mine as she said, "What happens between adults doesn't affect how we treat the kids. Promise. No matter what happens with Knox, Fletch and I here for these babies, okay?"

I nearly let out a sob. It was exactly the kind of support I'd been hoping to get from Seth's parents, but somehow, I'd found my own dream family in this tiny little town.

And maybe, a small voice said, *maybe Knox was just like Liv and Fletcher.*

Maybe he was telling the truth when he said those people in his phone had no bearing on how he or his family thought about my children and me. I really wished my hopeful heart would be right.

47

KNOX

FLETCHER WAS RIGHT; this wasn't a decision like any I had ever made before—I needed to give it honest thought. So when I got off work, I didn't drive home, where I'd be right next door to Larkin. Instead, I drove out to the country to spend some time with Dad.

I asked him all the questions I might never have an answer to on my own, like what it felt like to see your baby born. What it was like to watch one grow. I asked him why he didn't remarry after losing Mom and heard every single worry he had as a single dad with five kids.

And when we were done talking and eating dinner, I went back to my place and spent the night alone, wondering what it might feel like to go to bed every night without Larkin by my side. Without the crackle of the monitor or the soft tune of the sound machine coming from the other room.

And it felt fucking terrible.

But I tried to imagine too what it would be like to know a baby was on the way. To watch my child grow in my wife's stomach and see her give birth and support her through it. To hold a child who looked like the best parts of me and my girl. Admittedly, that sounded nice too.

Not nearly as nice as what I'd miss out on if I stayed away from Larkin. I knew that on day one of the pause Larkin and I were taking.

But I did my best to continue thinking it through. For what seemed like the longest week of my adult life, I gave her space. I went to work. I hung out with my family. I came home. I tried not to focus on the people I loved just a house away.

I left a little toy snake on their front porch to prank Emily and found a plastic pile of poop on my own the next morning.

By Friday, I'd about hit my wits end with the whole damn distance thing. But I knew there was one person left I had to see. The one I'd been dreading most, if I was being honest.

So when I got off work Friday night, I didn't go straight home or hang out with Hayes at his garage. Instead, I took a dirt road to the cemetery outside of town.

The path was more than familiar, although I didn't traverse it as often as I used to. Still, it was practically muscle memory, following the dirt roads, parking along the path, and getting out to find my mother's grave.

The cemetery was empty, my truck the only one there. And I walked over the short green buffalo grass making it swish underfoot with every step until I reached my mother's headstone. I remembered it had taken months after her death for it to be ready, but now the granite stood out amongst a sea of memorial pillars, her name etched forever into its surface.

Maya Madigan
   Beloved wife and mother.
   "Lead with love."

THERE WERE several items around the stone. Bright yellow silk sunflowers. A ceramic bowl Maya made in art class, colored in orange and red. A small rock turtle I'd gotten for her one year on vacation. And a few other items my brothers and dad had left behind.

I knew we all came out here when we needed her most and sometimes just because. Even though we knew her soul wasn't here, it was a spot dedicated just to her and her memory.

But being here also made me remember that mad version of me. The one angry at God for taking my mom away when I wasn't yet grown. The one scarred by images of my mother, wasting away in her bed at home, hair gone, eyelashes fallen away, bruises on her pale, papery skin from blood draws and medications that never did what the doctors promised they would.

I balled my fists at my sides and then released a breath, letting the evening breeze wash over me. I wasn't that mad little kid anymore.

Heaving another sigh, I settled onto the ground before her headstone, careful not to sit on the spot above her casket. "I know my brothers always say they feel you here, but, Ma, I gotta be honest. I don't feel comfortable with a bunch of other ghosts listening in."

I imagined her laugh. She had the best laugh. Loud and carefree, and it always crinkled her eyes at the corners, like she felt her happiness with her whole body. Nostalgia washed over me.

I wished Mom could meet Larkin and her kids. Mom was so good with children, and not just her five little boys. She was the kind of person they were drawn to, kind of like Liv. Even now, I could feel her presence drawing me in, holding me close. So I started talking, hoping somehow she could hear me.

"I'm dating this girl, and I know that's the kind of thing you probably hear more from Hayes." My lips tipped because Ma and I both knew "dating" was the nice way to describe it. "It's been hard for me to meet someone I click with here in Cottonwood Falls. And if I'm being honest, I was kind of thinking I'd be single forever, like Dad's determined to be. But then I met Larkin..." Another breeze swept by, rustling the grass.

"She has two kids, and she's worried about me being happy with that, feeling like I missed out if I don't have biological children. But I've only ever felt like I was missing out before I met her. My life's never been more full."

I looked at her stone, those words staring back at me.

Lead with love.

Mom used to say that all the time. She wanted our hearts to be the guide—she said they'd never steer us wrong. When I'd get mad at my brothers, she'd ask me, "What would love do?" and that was always meant to be my next step. I could just picture her now, asking me the same question.

I laughed softly to myself. This whole week, I'd been wracking my brain for what to do, but I already knew what was in my heart.

I just needed to let it take the lead.

And it was pointing right back at Cottonwood Falls.

48

LARKIN

WHEN I GOT BACK from picking up the kids, I couldn't believe my eyes.

Knox Madigan was sitting on my front porch steps, two bouquets of flowers in his hands.

My heart leapt at the sight of him, hoping beyond all hope that the flowers weren't for consolation.

"KNOX IS HERE!" Emily yelled in the back seat. "But we don't have our prank stuff ready!" she lamented. She'd been planning to leave fake spiders on his door handles next.

I smiled at her excitement. I knew she'd been missing him just like I had. A few pranks here and there weren't enough—not anymore. "I'm sure there will be time to prank him soon," I said. The circumstances of the prank, however, were still up in the air.

Knox and I looked at each other through the windshield, and his lips lifted slightly. It was like a peace offering of sorts. But I still couldn't quite tell what it

meant. I couldn't read people as well as he did. So I got
out of the car, letting Emily out first.

She ran up to him, jumping into his arms. My heart
was in so many knots I had to look away as I went around
the minivan to take Jackson out of his seat. As soon as I
had him in my arms and he saw Knox, he yelled,
"DADA! DADA!"

There went my efforts at not crying. My eyes stung
with unshed tears, and I blinked quickly to hold them
back. How would we survive if his answer was no?

Knox smiled at Jackson, and my heart bounced all
over the place, a ball in a painful pinball machine. He
squirmed and wiggled and fought in my arms.

"Fine," I said to Jackson. "I'll hold your hand, and
you can walk." I set him down, reaching for both of his
hands, and he stood, feet dancing over the concrete like
he wanted to take off. "MAMA!" He screamed, fighting
at my hands.

"Okay, okay," I said, letting go of one of his hands.
"Is that better?"

But he yelled at me again.

"You want to walk?" I asked him.

He nodded and screeched at me again.

So I carefully removed my hand from his and put my
hands behind him, ready to catch him if he fell.

But he didn't fall.

He walked the next five steps like he'd been walking
his whole life just to fall into Knox's strong hands.

"You're walking!" Knox said, his face and voice full of
love.

"No, that was the first time!" Emily cheered.

When Knox looked to me for confirmation, tears were rolling down my cheeks. "Those were his first steps."

Knox kissed the top of Jackson's head. "I'm so proud of you, buddy." Then he looked at me, his lips spread into a gentle smile. "Why the hell would I want to miss out on a life like this?" He opened his arm to me, and there was no more fight left in me, no more wall around my heart as I fell into his embrace.

Emily announced, "I'm going to get my spi—toys."

I chuckled at her announcement. "Go ahead." I handed her the keys, and she fiddled with them until she turned the lock.

"Do I need to know what that was about?" Knox asked, adjusting Jackson on his knee and letting me sit on the steps between his legs.

I shook my head, taking his free hand in mine. "I missed you," I whispered, lips trembling. Now that we were together, I could feel how hard it had been to be apart.

He cradled me with one arm, holding my son with the other. "I missed you too, baby," he whispered back. He met my eyes. "I want you to know I choose you, Larkin. I choose you and this family. And you can wonder all you want if you need to, but I'm sure, baby. I'm sure. And I'll show up every day to show you just how sure I am."

And as I met his blue eyes, full of emotions, I knew he was telling the truth. It didn't matter what anyone thought of us, because we had each other, and we had his family, and we had my children, who were looking up at him with all the adoration I felt in my heart.

"Thank you," I told him.

He looked at me. "For what?"

"For helping Jackson find his voice—and for helping both of us find our feet. And for showing me what it feels like to truly have a home."

He leaned in, giving me a kiss that may have been short but held so much emotion I had to smile against his lips.

I'd never been happier. Because finally. *Finally*. I knew I was with a man who saw love as something real.

49

KNOX
TWO MONTHS LATER

I WAS at Larkin's place rolling a ball across the floor with the kids while she made supper when her phone rang. I watched from the living room as her expression pinched at the name on the screen.

"Who is it?" I asked.

She glanced at me, saying, "Ancy-nay."

I chuckled at her use of Pig Latin. "Ice-nay."

Emily gave me a weird look over the big inflatable bouncy ball. "The ice is in the freezer, Knox."

She'd only been in kindergarten for a short while, but she'd already grown up so much and was speaking in longer sentences. That sass would always be there, though, just like her mama. She rolled the ball over to me.

Larkin brought her phone to her ear, offering a tentative, "Hello?" Leaning back against the counter, she had her arm over her chest. "I see."

Oof. "I see" was never a good thing in mom speak.

"So, you refused to watch them and now you want to visit them?" she asked.

I hid a wince as I rolled the ball back to Jackson. I didn't want them to glom on to Larkin while she tried to have a conversation because they sensed something wrong from me.

"Of course I'll let you see them," Larkin said. Her voice was firm as she added, "However, it will be at my house. You're all welcome to come over for supper this weekend."

Now my eyebrows rose, but I kept my gaze down on the blue and white marbled bouncy ball rolling my way. *You're all welcome?* I wondered to myself, *Did that mean what I thought it meant?*

"One moment," she said, then she waved me over while holding the phone to her chest. "Can you be here for dinner Sunday after the game?" she whispered. "The andparents-gray and eth-Say want to come over for dinner."

Concern knit my brows together. "Are you sure you want them all here?" I whispered back. "We could do it at my place."

"We?" she asked, a small smile playing along her lips.

"You know it's you and me, babe."

She gave me a thankful half-smile, then drew the phone back to her ear. "Knox will be here. It will be a great chance for everyone to bond." She went back around the corner, and I could hear the spatula over the pan as she stirred dinner.

"You two play," I said to Em and Jackson, then went to Larkin, hugging her from behind and dropping a kiss on the cheek opposite her phone.

"Yes, he will be here. This is my home," she said.

Damn straight. I was proud of her for standing up for herself. She'd walked on eggshells with them before, not wanting to lose her childcare. But now that she was covered, she had no reason to accept less respect than she deserved.

"Great. We'll see you Sunday at seven." She hung up and leaned back into my chest.

It was the best feeling, having her lean on me. Then she turned, wrapping her arms around my neck and placing a kiss on my lips. "Have I mentioned how incredible you are?" she asked.

I nuzzled my nose against her. "Never hurts to hear it."

Her lips tilted into a smile. "You. Are amazing, Knox Madigan." She kissed me again for a moment before a little voice interrupted, saying, "What are you doing?" We broke apart, seeing Emily staring at us. "Were you kissing *forever*?" she asked exasperatedly.

Larkin said, "Not forever. I have to breathe sometime."

I laughed at her quick response and then said to Emily, "Looks like dinner's almost ready. Let's go wash up."

She walked with me, and I scooped Jackson in my arms, even though he was officially in the phase where he hated being held. He didn't fight me too much as we walked to the bathroom and I helped him onto the counter to wash hands.

And in true Larkin fashion, I came up with a song on the spot while the three of us cleaned up.

Because I'm washing.

Wash your hands if you feel
Like a kid who's extra clean!
Wash your hands if you feel
Like germy germs are the worst.
Wash your hands if you know
That cleanliness is the truth.
Wash along if you feel like
You're ready for some food.
Because we're washing.
Because we're washing.

The kids giggled at my silly lyrics, and I saw us all in the bathroom mirror, thinking to myself that this is what I loved. These kids, this woman, this home... this *family*. It didn't matter how it came to be because I knew what it was now: *mine*.

50

LARKIN

I KNEW I shouldn't be nervous, but as I pulled the lasagna out of the oven, I could feel my heart bouncing around my chest with adrenaline. My in-laws and my ex were coming over to dinner tonight. At my place. With my boyfriend.

I'd spent all day cleaning and finishing up last-minute decorations, but the house was still small, still dated, still sparse. Nancy and Jerald hadn't been over here before, and Seth had only been the one time for a brief moment before storming away. I hoped today could be more peaceful for all of us.

PAW Patrol played on the TV, and it was just the kids and me at home while I waited for Knox to get back from a Dallas Diamonds watch party with his family. It was looking like Ford's team was going to be playing in the championship game this year. Gray had invited me and the kids over to watch, but I wanted to get ready for today instead.

Then the thought occurred to me. What if Seth and his parents didn't show up? It wouldn't be the first time they'd flaked on me, but I'd been so stressed about dinner I hadn't even considered the possibility.

I picked up my phone, dialing Nancy's cell number, and held it to my ear.

After a few rings, she answered. "Hi, Larkin, we're on our way out the door now."

"We're?" I asked, just to make sure.

"All three of us are coming," she confirmed.

I put on a falsely cheery voice. "Great! Dinner will be ready when you get here."

We hung up, and then I took a deep breath because I had to tell the kids their dad and grandparents were visiting. Even though I'd been worked up, I'd learned a long time ago not to get the kids excited for something I couldn't control.

"Emily, I need to pause the TV," I warned, stepping into the living room and using the remote to still the screen. Chase's puppy dog face froze in place, the picture of authority and confidence. Sometimes I wished I had some of his chutzpah.

"Mom," Emily whined, and Jackson copied her, saying, "Mama. Mama!"

I smiled at him, picking him up and squeezing him. Something about baby cuddles made everything better. Even if he was over a year and a half old, he would always be my baby.

"So I have a surprise for you."

Emily perked up. "Presents?"

"Your dad and grandma and grandpa are visiting!"

Emily screamed, jumping up and down while Jackson said, "Da da da da."

I nodded. "Knox will be here too. Are you excited?"

Emily did half a handstand on the couch, kicking her feet into the air. She was getting dysregulated, and I couldn't say I blamed her one bit. I sat on the couch, letting Jackson back on the ground. He crawled over to his toys, and I asked, "Emily, are you nervous?"

Her eyes darted all over the place as she danced next to me.

"Baby, get in my house," I said. I made my hands like a roof over my eyes, and she did the same, coming closer until all she could see was me. "I know it's been a long time since we've seen them, but they love you," I said.

"Okay," she whispered.

"If you need any space at all, you can go to your room to read. Want to come up with a code word?"

"Yes," she said softly.

"What should it be?"

She looked thoughtful, her eyes turning toward our hands. "What about Marshall?"

I smiled. "That's a great code word. So, when you say Marshall, I'll know you're going to your room to read, and you can come back out when you're ready. Okay?"

"Okay."

I pulled my hand down and gave her a squeeze. "You can watch until they get here."

"Okay."

She bundled up on the couch, and I watched her for a second before picking up Jackson to put him in his play pen. He yelled at me every time I tried to set him down, so I brought him to the kitchen with me. I set him on the floor with a plastic bowl and a couple spoons to play with. Of course, he immediately started banging the "instrument." He was a natural at making noise.

Then I picked up my phone and called Knox while getting the plates out. They were plastic—the cheapest I could get at the store, but as I looked at them, I realized I was proud of my discount dishware.

I'd gone from being a stay-at-home mom for six years to making a whole life for myself here. Who cared if I had to start out with plastic dishes? No one who mattered.

Knox's voice came over the phone as I set the plates on the table. "Hey, babe."

My heart fluttered. Would I ever get over him calling me that? "Hey. Do you know when you'll get here?"

"Funny you should mention that." The door opened then, and I grinned at him, still holding his phone. "Hey," he said warmly.

"Hey," I replied, slowly lowering my phone. "I'm so glad you're here."

Jackson yelled, "Dada!" He pushed himself up on the bowl, bottom going up first and then tottered to Knox. "Dada!"

"Say Knox," Knox prompted. "Na na."

"Dada!" Jackson insisted, arms outstretched for Knox.

Knox picked him up, and I worried my hands. If Seth heard Jackson calling Knox "dada," I wasn't sure how he'd react. But Knox came over to me, kissing the top of my head.

As if reading my thoughts, he said, "It's on Seth to control his reaction, not you."

My heart slowed, instantly comforted by his words. "Thank you."

"Of course." He went to the living room to play with Emily while I finished up, and soon, Emily shouted, "THAT'S THEM!"

I braced myself for the first dinner as one big... happy-ish family.

51

KNOX

EMILY RAN TO THE DOOR, throwing it open, and we all stood awkwardly, watching the three march up the sidewalk, Seth in between his parents. They looked up at us, Nancy smiling at her granddaughter, Jerald looking supremely uncomfortable, and Seth staring down at the ground like one misstep would cause him to trip and fall.

There were a million things I wanted to say to Seth. I wanted to tell him how to treat a woman, how he should be tending to his kids instead of the few phone calls he'd managed to make in the last couple months. I wanted to tell him all that he lost and... selfishly, I wanted to thank him for what his foolishness had allowed me to gain.

And even though Jackson usually got all squirmy with new people, he held on to my arm tightly like no one could entice him to let go.

"I've got you," I whispered against his short brown hair. "I've got you."

After what felt like hours, the three reached the front door, and Emily swung it open for them. "Daddy?" I hated the way she said it like a question, like she didn't know if he would leave right away. It seemed like we were all holding our breath to see how he would respond.

But he put a smile on for her and hugged her tight. "I've missed you, Em," he said.

"I missed you too!" she cried, looking so happy my heart almost broke for her.

He picked her up and walked with her through the door, and then Nancy and Jerald followed him in. Nancy looked at Jackson as if I wasn't holding him at all and said, "Come here, baby."

Jackson seemed nervous at first, but I said, "It's okay, sweetie. Want to see your grandma?"

He seemed to ease up, like he could remember who she was, and went to his grandma, holding on to her but looking around. "Mama?" he said.

Everyone quieted. And it struck me: none of them had spoken to Larkin to know that Jackson had taken his first steps or said his first words.

"I'm here," Larkin said, carefully watching to the side.

"He's doing a lot more than talking now," I said to Nancy, trying to break the ice. "Set him down."

Several emotions flickered across her face so quickly a regular person may not catch it. Regret. Shame. Sadness. Wonder. She set him down, like I asked, and her hand covered her mouth as Jackson proudly walked to his mom and put his arms up to be picked up.

She scooped him into her arms, grinning at him, and then looked around to see how everyone would react. Jerald was the first to break the silence, smiling and clapping his hands together. "Great job, Jacks!"

Nancy followed suit, clapping, and Seth said, "Great job, son!"

Jackson smiled toothily, loving being the center of attention.

Then I said, "Dinner smells great, Lark. Should we eat?"

"Yes, of course," she said as if being snapped out of a trance. "Everyone take a seat."

It was one thing for us and all our emotions to be crowded into her small living room, and another for the six of us to be surrounding her used dining room table, the leaf inserted and folding chairs added to make room for everyone. I'd offered to host everyone at my place, but she was determined to have it here, to make a statement that this was her home.

As dinner began, everyone seemed to laser focus on the motions we could control. Passing the lasagna around, then the salad bowl, then the garlic bread. Then making sure everyone had the drinks they wanted.

Emily didn't leave her dad's lap, but Jackson was hesitant to go anywhere but mine, Larkin's or Nancy's laps. Larkin eventually buckled him into his highchair so we could all eat without him playing musical chairs between us. For a moment, there was only the sound of scraping silverware.

I met Larkin's eyes, and I noticed the panic there. Enough time with her had taught me that she didn't like the silence in uncomfortable situations. Couldn't predict what was coming next if she didn't have a conversation to follow. So I stepped in. I wanted to show them that blending a family could be done successfully. Fletcher and his ex had struggled at first, but once they all found their footing, things were good. For Maya especially, who had a mom and a dad and two stepparents who cared for her.

"Seth, how's work going in the city?" I asked. "You're still in sales, right?"

Everyone's head swiveled to him, and he finished chewing. "Right. Work is good. Been putting in a lot of hours with the launch of some new imaging equipment."

Emily looked at me, explaining, "Daddy always works a lot. That's why we spend so much time with Mommy."

No one would meet her eyes except for Larkin, who said, "That's right. I used to watch you all the time. Why don't you tell Daddy and Grandma and Grandpa about Liv's house? You're having so much fun there after school."

Emily launched into an explanation of how much she loved her new babysitter, and I noticed Nancy shifting uncomfortably in her seat. Finally, Seth said, "That's great, honey." I could hear the strain in his voice, but I had to applaud him for trying. It was more than he'd done in months.

Nancy whispered, "Oh my, look at Jackson."

We all turned to look at him, fighting to keep his eyes open, lasagna sauce all over his cheeks. We held back laughter as Larkin got up to wipe him down with a wet rag so the acid from the tomatoes wouldn't burn his skin. But soon enough, he was drowsing again.

"Wish I could do that," Larkin commented.

Jerald said, "Wait another twenty years and you will."

Nancy chuckled. "As long as the golf channel is on."

It was a moment. A small one. But it was enough to break the ice.

Things seemed to ease up a bit after that. We talked

about Emily's school, and Jerald even asked me about my work and how my family was doing. I started to think this situation might never be truly comfortable, but maybe we could make it work. And judging by how happily Emily was staring up at her dad, I really wanted it to.

52

LARKIN

AFTER WE FINISHED EATING, I carried Jackson back to his bed while everyone else hung out in the living room. Emily loved being surrounded by her dad and grandparents, all the adults doting on her like they used to before Jackson was born and she had to share the spotlight.

I laid him down in his crib, watching him turn and lie on his side, pudgy little hands pillowed under his cheeks. Through the closed bedroom door, I could hear everyone laughing, probably at something Emily had done.

There was a sense of peace washing through me. We hadn't arrived where I'd like to be yet, but we were on our way.

I thought back to when Seth admitted he had been cheating on me through my pregnancy with Jackson and continued to after he was born.

It had seemed like my life was over. I had no idea how I would make it work with two children and such a big gap in my employment and no real support system around. I wished I could go back and scoop that broken woman up in my arms and tell her she was stronger than she thought. That somehow, it would all work out, and even if it didn't, she was strong enough, brave enough, to handle it one step at a time.

I smiled down at Jackson. He'd grown so much since then too, finding his voice and even his steps.

"Goodnight, baby," I whispered. I turned on the sound machine to peaceful music then turned and left him in the bedroom.

My eyes adjusted back to the bright light in the living room, and I saw Knox sitting on a folding chair while Nancy and Jerald sat on the couch watching Emily and Seth play a game on the floor. When I came out, they all looked up at me for a moment before watching Seth and Em again.

I walked over to Knox, standing by him and putting a hand on his shoulder. He reached up, holding my hand. It felt right, to be here with him, to have him in my corner.

Seth finished the game, and Nancy took a turn, getting onto the floor with Emily, a pillow under her.

Seth came over to Knox and me, asking, "Is it okay if I speak with you outside, Larkin?"

Remembering the last time Seth and I spoke outside, I stiffened.

Knox squeezed my hand, and it was the reminder I needed that he was there for me if I needed him, that I could handle this.

"Sure," I said, turning and leading the way outside. This time of year, it was starting to get chilly at night, so I wrapped my cardigan tightly around me as Seth stepped down the porch and then onto the sidewalk. He awkwardly scratched the back of his neck.

"Emily was happy to see you," I said, breaking the silence.

His expression was tortured as he said, "Jackson hardly recognized me."

My heart hurt for him, just for a moment, because he was in a mess of his own making. "It's hard to know someone you hardly see."

He looked down at the sidewalk again. "Guess I deserved that."

I folded my arms across my chest, waiting for him to explain what we had to talk about.

Finally, he said, "I was wondering if I could start taking my visits every other weekend? I feel bad about the dad I've been, and I know I need to do better. They're growing up... without me."

Fear squeezed my chest. Seth had hardly ever watched the kids by himself when we were married, and now it had been months. That didn't sound good for the kids or my anxiety. But I also knew he was legally entitled to his visits. Divorce fucking sucked.

"Is there a chance you could do the visits at your parents' for a little while? Save them the driving back and forth?" I asked. It would make me feel better if Seth had some backup and the kids were closer to home.

Home. That's what Cottonwood Falls was for me now.

Seth nodded. "It would be nice to have some help with them too. Mom said Jackson's still waking up at night?"

"He was when she was watching him, but he's been sleeping through the night for months now," I said, relieved I could sleep through the night too. That first year it took him to find his rhythm had been exhausting.

He nodded. "So next weekend we can do the visit?"

"Sure," I said. A chilly breeze blew my hair over my face, and I tucked it back behind my ears.

We stood silently for a moment.

"So Knox." He nodded toward the house.

My protective defenses came up, especially after Seth had insulted him last time. Knox had been there for me and the kids in a way Seth had never been. "What about him?"

"He's the one you want?"

My lips lifted into a smile of their own accord. I glanced back toward my house, and through the front window, I saw him helping Nancy back up and then dancing with Emily in the living room. It wasn't wholly accurate to say Knox was the man I wanted.

It made it seem like I was picking out a handbag from a department store shelf. But I didn't need him either. I knew I had what it took to stand on my own two feet. And yes, I loved Knox, but one thing I learned from my failed marriage with Seth was that a relationship took more than love.

So I settled for the truest words I knew. "He's the one I choose."

53

LARKIN

THANKSGIVING

"TAYLEE!" I yelled, running to my sister and hugging her as soon as she opened the door to her fancy Parisian apartment. My arms were tight around her, and there was no chance I was letting her go. Every bit of me relaxed, nearly succumbing to tears at how good it felt to be with my sister again. I'd missed her so much, and I was so damn glad to finally see her again.

She stroked my hair like she did when we were kids. "It's so good to see you," she said, her voice full of warmth. When we pulled back, I noticed moisture shining in her eyes as well. We were all that was left of our family, and now we were together.

Grinning through the tears, she kissed both my cheeks and then said, "Let me see those babies!" She got on her knees, seeing Emily and Jackson walking toward her cautiously, as Knox followed them into the flat.

"Hi, Aunt Tay," Emily said.

Taylee gave her a squeeze, then letting Emily go, said, "Is that Jackson? He is so big!"

Emily nodded. "He just turned two."

"Good thing I have presents for both of you." She held out her hands, and Jackson walked to her like he instinctively knew Taylee was our people.

Taylee kissed his cheek and then stood up. "I need to meet this man!" I noticed a subtle French lilt to her voice, like she'd been spending so much time with Claude that his accent was wearing off on her.

Knox sent her a warm grin, extending his hand. "Knox Madigan. Nice to meet you."

She batted away his hand. "We're in France! We hug, we kiss." She drew him in, kissing his cheeks. "It's so nice to finally meet you in person." She sent me a wink. "Video chats did not do you justice."

Knox glanced my way, saying, "I like her already."

I laughed, already knowing they would get along famously.

Emily broke up the meeting, saying, "Where's my present?"

"Let me show you." Taylee took Jackson's hand and guided him and Emily back to her living room with a view of the Seine. And with the kids occupied for the moment, Knox had a little sliver of peace. I leaned into his arms. "Can you believe we're in Paris?" I asked, looking up at him.

He shook his head. "I've never been out of the states before. This is amazing."

I lifted myself onto my toes so I could kiss his freshly shaven cheek. "I can't wait to share it all with you."

Hugging me tighter to his side, he said, "Same here. I mean, a French lunch, the Arc de Triomphe and the Eiffel Tower later tonight? Makes for an amazing day."

I nodded. "We've got a week here. I want to make the most of it."

He kissed my temple. "I want to make the most of every minute with you."

54

KNOX

TAYLEE AND HER BOYFRIEND, Claude, took the kids for a walk around the stream near the Eiffel Tower while Larkin and I sat on a blanket with personal-sized bottles of wine and looked up at the structure. The sun had set over the horizon, and now the sky was a mix of pastel blue and purple. It was cool in late November, so both of us wore thick sweaters and coats.

Then, the lights came on, shimmering across its surface.

Larkin's face was full of wonder as she smiled up at the structure. "It's so pretty."

It may have been, but I couldn't take my eyes off of her. She was so damn beautiful, those lights twinkling in her eyes.

That was one thing I loved about her. No matter what she'd been through, no matter what people said to try and bring her down, she found the light, the good in the world. I loved seeing it through her eyes.

I always wanted to see it through her eyes.

And I knew I couldn't wait anymore. So I reached into my pocket, taking out the blue velvet box that had been waiting for the perfect moment. Then I got onto one knee in front of her. She glanced at me and did a double take, setting down her little bottle of wine and covering her mouth. "Knox," she whispered.

"Larkin." I pulled the lid back, revealing a diamond ring with one center stone and two surrounding it. One for her and two for her children, because I knew this wasn't just about her and me. Not even close. "The first day I met you, I knew you were something special, even though you were pissed at me for pulling you over."

She giggled, and I loved the sound.

"The first time we hung out, I could see how well you fit into my family, just a day in."

She smiled, like she could picture Maya and Emily playing together in the sandbox, the way Jackson had let me hold him, feeling comfortable in my arms. The way the girls had giggled with that prank.

"The first time you went out with a man who wasn't me, I knew I couldn't let it happen again. Knew you couldn't be anyone's but mine."

She brought her hand from her mouth to her heart, eyes shining with more than just the reflection of the lights.

"Back in August, you asked me to think about the kind of life I wanted, and all I could think about was the kind of life we could build together." I reached for her hand, holding it. "I pictured a life with two perfect children waking up every day knowing how much we love and care about them. I pictured a life where we go to bed together every night and where you're the first person I see when I wake up. I picture a life where our neighbors, our families, know we're always in their corner, no matter what. And I picture a life that I know my mom would be proud of, with you and Emily and Jackson by my side."

My voice broke, and I blinked back liquid heat. "I got this ring with three stones so you could always look at it and know, without a doubt, what I want. I want that life with you more than anything, Larkin. I wanted to know if you do too."

She got to her knees in front of me and gently kissed my lips. "I thought that divorce would be the worst thing that ever happened to me, to my children. But moving to Cottonwood Falls... meeting you..." Her voice cracked, and she wiped a tear from her eyes. "I don't regret a thing about my past because that's what it took to be here with you. Of course I'll marry you, Knox Madigan."

At those words, the ones my heart had been longing to hear, I scooped her into my arms and kissed her, right there under the Eiffel Tower.

This was the best day of my life.

But I knew, with Larkin and her children, it would only get better from here.

EPILOGUE
FORD MADIGAN

I STOOD off to the side of Knox and Larkin's wedding reception, watching all the kids dance and pop bubbles from the bubble machine by the DJ. Emily and Jackson might have been new to the crew, but they fit right in, and all us Madigans adored them like they were blood.

Dad's pool of grandkids was growing, and he liked to remind me that I was next in line. I'd just laughed. I had a championship season to worry about. A relationship could come after I retired—with a few heavy rings on my hand.

But I was happy for Knox. Since everyone was dancing, he and Larkin sat together at the bridal party table, lost in their own little world. She was gorgeous in a long, cream-colored dress, and the way my brother looked at her, I knew this was it. They were end game.

I'd known, when I met her that first day at Knox's barbecue, that she was something special. And I was glad for Knox that he'd found his happily ever after. Whether he wanted to admit it or not, I knew he got lonely here in Cottonwood Falls.

It wasn't like that in Dallas. There was no way to be lonely when you were the leading quarterback in a professional football league. No, I was constantly surrounded by teammates, girls who wanted to get with a pro, and in the off-season, my family. That was enough for me.

Luckily, I'd signed onto the team in Dallas, giving me a chance to get back home on the rare day off. But my mind was on this season. We had a real chance at winning the whole thing, and after this wedding, I'd get back to training, to the next game.

I'd have to be more focused than ever to lead my team to a victory.

Nothing could distract me from that goal.

I'd been the first professional football player from Cottonwood Falls, and now I'd be the first one to earn a ring. I wanted to show everyone in this small town what was possible when you put your mind to it and didn't let anything take your eyes off the prize.

A pig ran squealing past me.

But first, to make sure this damn pig didn't ruin the reception.

WANT to find out where Larkin and Knox are in the future? Check out Welcome Home, the free bonus story of them moving into their new home!

Be sure to read Ford's story in Hello Quarterback!

Get the free bonus story today!

Get your copy of Hello Quarterback today!

AUTHOR'S NOTE

You might not know this about me, but I'm a very futuristic person. Sometimes I get so wrapped up in dreams of the future (and sometimes worry) that I forget what's happening right now. It's like my brain has all these little highways, saying, "If this happens, then this will happen next." In an instant, I can work out all these possible paths and outcomes. Have you ever had that happen?

I could just imagine how it felt for Larkin to get the news that her husband was cheating on her. Her mind must have come to a million different possibilities for the choices she had in front of her. What if she stayed with him and the infidelity continued? What if she stayed with him but couldn't find it in herself to forgive him? What if she left him and couldn't provide for herself and her children? What if she left him and found herself in an even worse relationship? What if she was alone for the rest of her life?

The thing about hard times is that we don't have the

option to ignore them, no matter how many negative outcomes our mind jumps to imagine. No matter how hopeless it seems, another day comes, and you have to choose. You can choose to run away from that hard time, knowing it will eventually catch up to you. Or you can choose to keep going and figure it out one day at a time.

We all know what Larkin chose. Larkin woke up every day, finding her way step by step. Job? Check. Childcare? Check. Home? Check. Dishes? Check. Food? Check.

Step by step, day by day, she put one foot in front of the other and when she looked up, saw the life she had created, she couldn't believe how far she had come.

That's the funny thing about futuristic brains. No matter how many outcomes you imagine, reality almost never turns out as planned.

She hadn't accounted for Knox to be her neighbor, for Liv to be her friend, for Bernice to give her the opportunity to truly make a difference at her job. But putting one foot in front of the other led her to incredible things.

I've been there before too, faced with something that seemed horrible in the moment.

In 2020, the world was reeling from the results of a pandemic. My husband was trying to grow his accounting business with just a little income at that time, and my job at a university was supporting us and our three young children. We had a little money saved up for disastrous moments, and I had hoped to start writing full time in the next six months or so, but I just wasn't there yet.

But then I got a call from my boss letting me know they were choosing to let me go. I felt so awful at being the one cut loose. Not just because of the money and uncertainty in the world, but at the heart of it all, getting fired made me feel disposable. I thought if I was so useful to the university, they wouldn't have been able to let me go. It made me question the work that I had done, if it was good enough. What my boss thought about me. I had to wonder what the conversations were like behind the scenes and how my name came up. How they spoke about me.

But I didn't have a choice other than to figure things out. Being a futuristic person, I examined a million different paths. Choosing another job that would require time away from my children who needed me at a crazy time in the world. Trying to piece together editing or writing gigs at the expense of my writing time. Asking my husband to get a full-time job, knee-capping his business and making me a stay at home mom. Or going full force into the unknown of being an author, knowing if I succeeded it could give me an income and the flexibility my family needed.

So I landed on two options: I could apply for jobs. Or I could make this writing thing work.

I buckled down, fighting for writing time with three children at home all day every day and a husband running his own business. And step by step, word by word, I worked to make my dreams come true. I was hopeful, but I knew success wasn't guaranteed.

What I looked at as a denigration on my job performance turned out to be the push out of the nest I needed to spread my wings and fly.

Now, in 2024, I've been full time as a writer for four years. I've had a full-time employee for a year and a half. I made it. The me who was looking to make just enough money to get by never could have pictured a writing business that looked like this. And I know I owe every bit of it to readers like you who supported me, and I'm so grateful for you every day.

I want to encourage you like so many of you have encouraged me on this path.

If you're in the middle of something right now, if your world has been rocked, I hope you know how powerful those little steps can be. Before you know it, you could look up and find yourself somewhere incredible, so long as you just keep going. I believe in you wholeheartedly. I hope you can find it in you to believe in yourself as well.

ACKNOWLEDGMENTS

Wow! I can't believe we're on book seven in the Hello Series!

It seems like yesterday I was writing my very first "spicy" romance novel. It's crazy what can happen when you put one word in front of the other and have some of the very best people in your corner.

Ty, thank you for being my partner, my friend, and a sounding board through every story.

Sally, thank you for being my bestie for the restie and the right-hand woman everyone wishes they could have! (But I'm so glad you're mine!) Your heart for readers and these stories makes all the difference.

Erin, thank you for coming alongside us and helping our readers get the very best care when they order from the kelsiehoss.com store! I know you're on to new and exciting things, and I'm so proud of you!

Mom. I love you. Thanks for reading these books and not judging me. (At least out loud haha)

Tricia, don't doubt yourself and your talents. I love working with you, seeing your comments in the docs, and knowing my story is in such caring hands. Thank you for sticking with me always!

Jordan, thank you for keeping an eye out for all the

small details that make a big difference in the story! I appreciate you and your enthusiasm for each project!

Najla and team at Qamber Designs, thank you for giving this story the cutest covers! I loved writing this book knowing what a pretty package it would be displayed in!

Luke and Allyson, thank you so much for narrating this story along with so many others in the Hello Series! I'm so glad to have found you both and to hear you bring the stories to life!

Dakota, thank you for editing my author's note so audiobook listeners can hear it in my voice! I love working on this with you!

Hoss's Mods, thank you for helping me keep the Hoss's Hussies' Facebook group a fun and safe place for readers of all kinds! Love partnering with you on this special place where we can talk books and body positivity!

Hoss's Hussies, I love each and every one of you! Seeing your enthusiasm for this series keeps me going on hard days and makes the good days even better!

And to you, sweet reader. Thank you for taking the time to get lost in these words. I hope you felt all the love inside these pages, and I can't wait to see you in the next story. <3

JOIN THE PARTY

Want to talk books with Kelsie and other readers? Join Hoss's Hussies today!

Join here: https://www.facebook.com/groups/hossshussies

ALSO BY KELSIE HOSS

The Hello Series

Hello Single Dad

Hello Fake Boyfriend

Hello Temptation

Hello Billionaire

Hello Doctor

Hello Heartbreaker

Hello Tease

Hello Quarterback

ABOUT THE AUTHOR

Kelsie Hoss writes sexy and heartfelt romantic comedies with plus size leads. Her favorite dessert is ice cream, her favorite food is chocolate chip pancakes, and... now she's hungry.

When she's not writing, you can find her enjoying one of the aforementioned treats, soaking up some sunshine like an emotional house plant, or loving on her three sweet boys.

Connect with Kelsie (and even grab some special merch) at kelsiehoss.com.

facebook.com/authorkelsiehoss

instagram.com/kelsiehoss